NO STRINGS ATTACHED

"Nothing to do with you, Maggie, but I'm not in the market for an affair."

"There's someone else?"

"No."

"I don't appeal to you, then?"

"I find you very appealing. I dream about you every night."

"You dream about me?" Maggie got that mushy feeling inside again. "Then, why . . . ?"

"I thought I made that clear. I am not in the market for a w-w-wi—"

"Wu-wu-wu? Oh, wife. But that's good. We have that in common, remember? I'm not ever going to marry, either."

"Of course you are."

"It is not a trick. I wouldn't trick you. I don't want a husband. And just to set the record straight, I did not say anything about a one-night stand." Maggie stood up fast, so fast she almost tipped the chair over. "Listen to me, Nick. I am not playing tricks. I'm doing the opposite. I'm telling you *exactly* what I want . . ."

BOOK YOUR PLACE ON OUR WEBSITE AND MAKE THE READING CONNECTION!

We've created a customized website just for our very special readers, where you can get the inside scoop on everything that's going on with Zebra, Pinnacle and Kensington books.

When you come online, you'll have the exciting opportunity to:

- View covers of upcoming books

- Read sample chapters

- Learn about our future publishing schedule (listed by publication month *and author*)

- Find out when your favorite authors will be visiting a city near you

- Search for and order backlist books from our online catalog

- Check out author bios and background information

- Send e-mail to your favorite authors

- Meet the Kensington staff online

- Join us in weekly chats with authors, readers and other guests

- Get writing guidelines

- AND MUCH MORE!

**Visit our website at
http://www.kensingtonbooks.com**

DREAMING OF YOU

Dixie Kane

ZEBRA BOOKS
Kensington Publishing Corp.
http://www.kensingtonbooks.com

This book is for Candace and Ben,
and for the sneezing ghost
at 1109 Royal Street.

PROLOGUE

Nicholas Gerard dragged himself through the door of the Manhattan offices of Renaissance, Incorporated. Collapsing into the chair next to the receptionist's desk, he croaked, "Any messages?"

Hildy Adams, Nick's secretary-receptionist and self-appointed surrogate mother—as if he needed another one—peered at him over the frames of her half glasses. "You're sick. Go home."

"I'm never sick." A hacking cough branded him a liar.

Hildy's left eyebrow shot up to her hairline. "Better yet, go to a doctor."

Shaking his head, Nick struggled to get his coughing under control. Once he could speak again, he said, "I hate doctors. About those messages?" He eyed the stack of pink message slips on Hildy's desk. "All business, I hope."

"You got it. The holiday season is over."

If his lungs had been working properly, Nick would have breathed a sigh of relief. Hildy was right. Barring death, divorce, or another marriage, Nick wouldn't hear from his parents, his assorted stepparents, or any of his various half- and step-siblings until next December. After five years, his so-called family had learned to obey his no-contact-except-in-emergencies-

or-at-Christmas rule. The exception for Christmas had
been a compromise. His relatives had argued for contact at *all* holidays, both religious and secular.

Nick had held his ground, and the family had reluctantly acceded to his demand. Some of them had
muttered insults, but he had expected that. Not one
of them had told him to take his money and go to
hell. A larger bunch of useless parasites would be
hard to find.

Even Hildy, the most sentimental woman in New
York City, agreed that Nick's family expected too little
from themselves and too much from him. They had
elected Nick patriarch, a position he had not sought
and did not want, the year he made his first million.
Nick had been twenty-three at the time.

At first, Nick had welcomed the attention given him
by his family. For a few months, Nick had felt as
though he belonged, that he had finally learned the
secret that opened the door to togetherness. His family had kept him on the outside looking in for years.

Ever since his parents had divorced and formed
new families, Nick had been the forgotten child. It
had taken his picture on the cover of *Forbes* for Nick
to be remembered by his immediate and not so immediate family members. Once his net worth had
become public, his mother and father and most of the
steps had begun calling to chat or dropping by his
office and inviting him to lunch, to birthday parties,
graduations, and Sunday dinners.

All that familial attention had been heartwarming,
and Nick's heart had basked in the warmth for a few
months—until Nick's head figured out what was
going on. The family's sudden interest in his well-
being had a cold, calculating rationale. The reasoning
ran along these lines: all problems can be solved by

money; Nick has money; therefore, Nick will solve all our problems.

Nick had taken the first giant step toward resigning the position of patriarch-cum-problem-solver five years ago. A few more years and Nick would rid himself of all contact with his family. He planned to retire somewhere far, far away. Alaska maybe, or a remote Pacific island.

Waving a hand under his nose to get his wandering attention, Hildy said, "You have three messages from that e-mail florist. They're desperate for your services."

Nick was a turnaround consultant, advising failing companies on how to succeed. He was very good at his job, so good that he could name his own price. Now. When he had started, his payment more often than not had been stock options in the companies he worked to save. Several of those once failing corporations now dominated the Nasdaq and the NYSE—making the stock, and Nick, worth millions.

"They should have gotten desperate sooner. All they can do now is sell their computer equipment and"—Nick sneezed violently—"and their customer list. Renaissance, Inc., is not in the business of selling used materials. Tell them to try E-Bay."

"And Corinne Ellis called. Your building hasn't sold yet."

"Why would it?" Nick grumbled. "According to Ms. Ellis, the tenants are intentionally sabotaging the sale. She wants to evict them."

Hildy sniffed. "At least she waited until after Christmas to come up with that plan. You don't believe her, do you? She may be the one responsible for the lack of interest in your building. Maybe you should get another realtor."

"Ellis Realty managed the building for years for my grandfather. And Corinne Ellis came highly recommended." Nick snatched a tissue from the box on Hildy's desk just in time to catch the fallout from another sneeze.

"Still . . . It might not be a bad idea for you to take a more personal interest in your property. And your tenants. That was a very sweet letter you got from one of them. Magnolia Mayfair was her name, wasn't it?" Hildy's attempt to project wide-eyed innocence failed miserably.

Nick knew that fake innocent look. Hildy was match making again. Not one of her better efforts—how could Hildy think she could interest him in a woman he would never meet? "I don't remember." Nick mumbled his second lie of the morning.

Remembering Ms. Mayfair's letter made Nick feel guilty, and Nick hated guilty feelings. Guilt was the only thing that kept him entangled and enmeshed with his much mended broken family. Anyone with sense would have ended *all* contact with them *ten* years ago. Nick had given up trying to figure out why he should be the one to feel guilty—some ingrained sense of familial duty was the best reason he had ever come up with.

Hildy clucked. "How could you forget a name like Magnolia? It's so southern and sweet."

"Ms. Mayfair is a sweet, southern idiot. Asking me not to sell the building because the tenants are like a family. Bull."

"She couldn't know how you feel about families. From the way she talked about the other tenants, you could tell she really cares for them. Poor girl. She must be an orphan. The tenants are probably the only family she's ever known." Hildy removed her glasses and blinked at him. "And you're going to evict them all."

"Is this where I twirl my mustache and laugh evilly?"

"You don't have a mustache, and if you try to laugh, you'll sound like a frog. But you are behaving like the wicked landlord in a melodrama. Why are you selling the building? You don't need the money."

"I don't need the aggravation, either. I may not need more money, but I don't like losing what I've got. That place is a money pit. The tenants are paying bargain rents, thanks to Grandfather Beaulieu, not nearly enough to pay the costs of maintaining the building. I had to get it treated for termites, remember? Plus, I've replaced most of the plumbing and all of the wiring, installed a new heating and cooling system, and had the place painted inside and out. Because the building is in an historic district, I couldn't even choose the paint colors. Anything I do to the damn building has to be approved by three levels of government, all competing to see which one can generate the most red tape."

Hildy stared at the ceiling. "I'm trying to picture you with color chips. Admit it, Nick. You didn't care what color they painted the building."

"That's not the point. The point is that it's *my* building. I ought to be able to paint the thing chartreuse with orange polka dots if I want to." Nick started to get up, but a sudden dizziness had him sinking back into the chair. "Why my grandfather left me the building, I'll never know. I only met him once."

Jerking her gaze from the ceiling to him, Hildy said, "You never told me that. When?"

"I was nine. Mother had just left Father, and she went to visit her father in New Orleans. She took me along." That was the last time Nick had spent any "quality" time with a parent. His mother had dropped Nick off at a boarding school in Connecticut on her way back to New York. Nick had lived at schools of one kind or another until he got his MBA.

Hildy's eyes lit up. "So, you've actually seen the building?"

"Once. Twenty-five years ago. Before Grandfather Beaulieu split it up into apartments."

Sighing dreamily, Hildy leaned back and stared into space. "Does it have those iron lace balconies like you see in pictures? Imagine owning a building on Royal Street, in the French Quarter of New Orleans." She sat up straight and looked him in the eye. "I don't see how you can give it up, especially since it's been in your family for generations."

"I have no problem giving up a building. I'd like to give up my whole damn family."

"You already have. You only allow them to contact you once a year."

"That small victory took years to accomplish. Maybe before I die, I'll manage to avoid them completely." Nick coughed again.

"You sound awful. I wish you would take some time off. If you didn't work all the time, you might have a social life. If you had a social life, you might have someone to take care of you when you're sick. I know you won't ask any of your mothers."

"You got that right." Nick knew exactly what his mother and any of the steps would say if he told them he needed a nurse. They would tell him to hire one.

"I would go home with you, but one of us needs to stay at the office." Hildy had that interfering innocent look on her face again. "What you need is a wife to tuck you up in bed and feed you chicken soup."

Nick shuddered. "Are you trying to make me feel

worse? The last thing I need is a w-w-wi—a mate. Marriage is the one family relationship completely within my power to avoid, and that's what I intend to do. Forever."

"All right, Mr. Go-It-Alone. But you need to rest and get over that cold. If you're not going to take on the e-florist, your schedule is clear for a few weeks."

"You may be right. I could use a little vacation."

Hildy's mouth dropped open. He had managed to surprise her. Nick rarely took Hildy's motherly advice—her business advice was another matter—and he never took vacations. But lately, he had been restless, unsettled. Nick felt as if he were waiting for something. Something he could not name.

Nick shook his head, then wished he hadn't. His vision blurred. Waiting for something? Something like for the next shoe to drop. His subconscious was probably anticipating the next family crisis. Or the return of the termites to his grandfather's building.

Snapping her mouth closed, Hildy reached for her stenographer's pad. "I'll make the reservations. Where are you going?"

"New Orleans. I'll kill two birds with the same trip. I'll rest, and while I'm resting, I'll put down the tenant revolt."

One

"The FOR SALE sign is not in the window. Again. What have you done with it this time?"

Magnolia Mayfair, proprietor of Mayfair's Masks, peeked through the mask she was modeling for a customer. She swallowed a groan. "Hello, Corinne. I changed the window display this morning. I guess I forgot to put the sign back."

"Uh huh." Spotting the Ellis Realty sign behind the counter, Corinne grabbed it and replaced it in the storefront window.

Surprisingly, the realtor did not launch into her usual diatribe on the sanctity of private property and the sacrosanct rights of property owners. Instead, Corinne planted herself next to the counter and waited.

Thankful her expression was hidden behind the mask, Maggie said, "I'll be with you in a minute, Corinne."

Turning her attention back to her customer, Maggie said, "I call this mask *Mercury.*" Adjusting the quilted silver mask, Maggie checked her appearance in the framed mirror on the counter. The mask fit her skull like a helmet, a helmet with silver wings sprouting from above her ears. Covering her face to the tip of her nose, the cloth mask left only her eyes and chin visible.

Maggie took off the mask and handed it to the attractive middle-aged woman. "Would you like to try it on?"

"No, thank you. That won't be necessary. The mask will make a perfect gift for my grandson. Billy is studying the Greek and Roman gods at the moment. I'll take it." Laying the mask on the counter, the woman rummaged around in her overstuffed purse and pulled out a folder of traveler's checks.

"Would you like for me to gift wrap it?" asked Maggie, aware that Corinne was tapping her foot in a time-is-money tempo.

"Yes, please."

Opening the armoire where she kept wrapping paper and ribbon, Maggie smiled at her customer. "This will only take a minute."

"While you're doing that, tell me where you found your outfit. I haven't seen a poodle skirt since I was in junior high school."

"Second Hand Ro's—I buy almost all my clothes there. Ro's shop is on Chartres—one block toward the river and three blocks toward Canal Street."

Corinne made a show of looking at her watch.

Expertly twisting pale green ribbon into a bow, Maggie finished the gift wrap and put the package into a shocking pink Mayfair Masks bag. She handed the bag to her customer. "Here you are. I hope your grandson enjoys the mask."

"I'm sure he will," said the woman, beaming. "You have the most unusual masks I've ever seen. Thank you, and thanks for the tip on the vintage clothes shop."

Corinne waited until the woman walked out the

door. "This is your busy time of year, I suppose. Christmas, Sugar Bowl, Super Bowl. Now Mardi Gras is just around the corner. Lots of tourists in town."

"Yes." After three years, Mayfair Masks was doing well enough that Maggie's accountant had cautiously predicted she would move into the black by year's end. But if she had to relocate. . . . Maggie decided not to go there, not with Corinne hovering about like some sleek scavenger about to feast on the corpse of Mayfair Masks.

Corinne held out a perfectly manicured hand. "I need the set of keys."

"Keys? To the building? Don't you have keys?" Maggie stalled.

"I did have a complete set. But the key to the second-floor apartment has gone missing again, and I need it."

Maggie busied herself straightening the stack of masks on the counter so she wouldn't have to meet Corinne's eyes. "I only have the keys to my apartment and the shop. I'm not sure who has the complete set. The professor or Shirley, maybe. I'll ask them. Later. I can't leave now. As you said, it is my busy season."

They hadn't expected the realtor to miss the key so soon. Jaye had lifted it from her handbag only a week ago, the last time Corinne had shown the building to a prospective buyer. The second-floor apartment was vacant, and Shirley had rigged some of her most startling effects in the unoccupied rooms. Maggie was almost positive they had finished concealing their latest spooky addition to the haunting theme, but she couldn't take a chance on Corinne stumbling across undeniable proof of the tenants' guerilla warfare. Jaye had taken Corinne's key so she couldn't appear unexpectedly and catch them in the act.

Maggie eyed Corinne, who was looking at her watch again. "Do you need the key right away? Are you showing the building today?"

"No. I need the key to let the cleaning service in, and I want to have a copy made for the new tenant."

"New tenant? Who would rent an apartment in a building that's for sale? Oh, my lordy me . . . Has the owner decided to take it off the market?" Maggie's heart beat faster at the thought.

Corinne smiled, showing her teeth. "You wish. Renaissance, Inc., has not taken the building off the market. The lease is short-term. With the usual clause about vacating the premises within thirty days if—that is, *when* the building sells. The new tenant is an author. He's writing a novel set in the French Quarter, and he wants to soak up atmosphere."

"Oh. I see. Well, I'll ask the others about the keys. When is the cleaning service coming?"

"I told them Wednesday—tomorrow. If neither of us can find a key before then, I'll have to call a locksmith." As she exited, Corinne added, "Nicholas—Mr. Gerard—is arriving late Thursday afternoon."

Maggie moved from behind the counter to the storefront window and watched Corinne walk briskly down Royal toward Canal Street. Ellis Real Estate had its plush offices in Canal Place, a high-rise building at the edge of the Quarter. Location, location, location, as Corinne actually said from time to time.

As soon as Corinne was out of sight, Maggie closed her shop, placing the BACK IN FIVE MINUTES sign in the door. She hurried across Royal Street to Oracles and Edibles and entered the tea shop.

Madame Fortunata—Shirley Wyclowsky to her friends—was just coming out of one of the three curtained cubicles where she and the other psychics read tarot cards, tea leaves, and palms. Shirley wore a purple silk robe patterned with gold fleur de lis. A gold turban covered most of her blatantly dyed red hair. A customer gushed praises for Madame's insight and foresight. "Fifty dollars, dawlin'," said Shirley, holding out a bejeweled hand.

To keep from wringing her hands, Maggie shoved them in the pockets of her fifties poodle skirt and waited for Shirley's customer to pay up and leave.

As soon as they were alone, Shirley scrunched her eyes closed and placed the fingers of her right hand on her forehead. "I sense a great excitement in you, sugar pie. Excitement and fear."

"You sense right, Shirley. We have to dismantle the ghost, and we have to do it fast."

Shirley's eyes popped open. "Why? We only just punched up the cold spot. Trust me, honey bunch, the cold spot is going to be even more effective now. Funny how people like the idea of owning a haunted building until they come up against something bone-chilling that they can't explain away."

"We'll have to move the ghost and the cold spot somewhere else—the attic, maybe?"

"No one spends enough time in the attic. Why do we have to do this, Maggie dawlin'?"

"Corinne just came by. The vacant apartment has been rented. She wanted the key. Do you know what Jaye did with it?"

"Rented the apartment?" Stuffing a stray strand of hair back under the turban, Shirley narrowed her eyes. "No one has lived in that apartment since Marcel died. Why would they rent it out now? With the building about to be sold out from under us?"

"It's a short-term lease to a writer. His name is Nicholas Gerard, and he arrives Thursday—day after tomorrow. Corinne needs to have keys made for him, and for the cleaning service she has coming tomorrow to clean the place."

"Gerard? I've never heard of him. What does he write?" Shirley had managed a used book store on Decatur Street after she reluctantly retired her ostrich plumes—she had worked as an exotic dancer before devoting herself to popular fiction. That was a few years and careers before she opened her tea and tarot shop on Royal Street.

"I don't know what he writes. Corinne said something about a novel set in the French Quarter. He wants to soak up atmosphere. Maybe Gerard writes under a pseudonym."

"I suppose that's possible. Why don't you check with that librarian friend of yours later? I sense this Gerard person is"—Shirley closed her eyes and rested her fingertips on her temples—"dangerous." She opened her eyes and lowered her voice to a conspiratorial whisper. "A spy, perhaps."

Maggie's hand went to the Peter Pan collar of her white cotton blouse. "A spy? Who would spy on us? Why would anyone spy on us?"

"That cold-hearted corporation that owns the building would, in a New York minute. Especially since catty Corinne is blaming us for scaring away potential buyers," said Shirley, all outraged innocence.

"They wouldn't send someone all the way from New York to spy on us," said Maggie. "Would they?"

"They might. After all, the building has been on the market for over eight months. Corinne has to be telling the owners that it would have sold by now but for the Formosan termites . . ."

"Aged sawdust artfully sprinkled about," said Maggie, modestly lowering her eyes. The termites had been her idea.

Shirley's blue eyes twinkled. "The dangerous electrical wiring . . ."

"Dangling wires sparking menacingly." Ed had rigged the fake wires. Maggie drew her brows together. Ed had never explained how a retired history professor knew so much about electrical stuff.

"The corroded plumbing . . ."

"Jaye's contribution. The rust-colored puddles of water around the toilets were especially effective, I thought."

"The ghost." Shirley smiled, showing her teeth.

"Especially the ghost. Your creation." Shirley had worked as a magician's assistant for a few years, another square in her checkered job history. Her expertise in all things spectral had been invaluable. The ghost moaned, it groaned, and, if prospective buyers stood in exactly the right spot, it chilled them to the bone.

Smile fading, Shirley said, "I really hate to dismantle our apparition—the ghost is the only thing the owner hasn't been able to repair out of existence. Are we sure it's necessary? Perhaps we could recruit the new tenant to our cause."

"I thought you sensed he was a spy."

"I sensed that Gerard was dangerous. The spy business was a guess. A bad guess, now that I think about it. A New York corporation isn't clever enough to send a spy." Shirley snapped her fingers. "I know why I went wrong. Gerard is a writer. Writers are critical observers of human nature. Observer, spy. Not a bad guess—uh, prediction—after all. In all the excitement, I got ahead of myself."

Maggie had to admire Shirley's ability to transform

her off-the-wall prognostication into an almost reasonable conclusion. "Spy or observer, the new tenant isn't going to care one way or the other whether the building sells. Corinne said he had a short-term lease. How long could it take to soak up atmosphere, anyway?"

"What do we know about this man? Other than his name and that he's a writer. Is he young? Old? Married? Divorced? More to the point, what color are his eyes?"

"I don't know. I didn't ask. What difference does that make?" Maggie knew very well why Shirley was interested in the new tenant's marital status and his eye color. She, Jaye, and the professor had decided Maggie needed a man in her life over a year ago, once they were sure her badly broken heart had finally mended.

Shirley's readings of Maggie's cards and tea leaves had begun to be filled with romantic predictions, until the day Corinne had put the for sale sign in the storefront window. Maggie's love life, or lack thereof, had been all but forgotten while the tenants plotted to save their building.

"It could make all the difference in the world," said Shirley, with a sly grin. "Well, do you know anything else about our mystery man? What does he write? Mystery? Science fiction? Did Corinne say?"

"No."

"Hmmm. If he's a writer, Gerard must have imagination. He might be able to come up with additions to our plan if we can convince him to help us. Let's see what else we can learn about this author."

"On the Internet? We could Google him."

Shirley's brightly painted lips curled. "No. Not from the Internet. From the cards. I'll use my special deck."

Taking a carved wooden box inlaid with silver from beneath the counter, Shirley ordered, "Follow me." She entered one of the curtained booths.

Maggie followed. When she was seated opposite Shirley, she said, "I don't really think we're going to learn anything useful from the cards."

"You wound me, Magnolia Mayfair. You should learn to trust the spirits to guide us."

"Sorry." The last thing Maggie wanted to do was hurt Shirley's feelings. When Maggie had arrived in New Orleans four years ago, Shirley had given her a job serving tea and pastries. Shirley had been looking for another tarot card reader at the time, but, according to Shirley, Maggie's psychic abilities were severely underdeveloped. By which she meant Maggie was a lousy liar. Shirley had hired her anyway, earning Maggie's lasting devotion.

As much as she loved Shirley, Maggie couldn't help being skeptical about Madame Fortunata's psychic abilities. The last time Shirley had read Maggie's cards, she had predicted that Maggie would meet a man who would sweep her off her feet. A very specific man, a man with coal black hair and silver eyes. That reading had taken place over eight months ago.

So far, Silver Eyes hadn't shown up.

Maggie was not holding her breath in girlish anticipation. She didn't need romance. Or love. Maggie had ruined herself for love. Of all the men in the world, her heart had chosen Robert Bennett to be her Mr. Right, and look how that had turned out. When it came to love, Maggie's heart was a big, fat flop.

Ever since she had forgiven her heart for making such a calamitous mistake, Maggie's life had become much more serene. She had her about-to-be successful business, she had her family, even if they were far away, and she had Shirley, Jaye, and Professor Ed. She felt good about the present and optimistic about the future. As for the past . . . It was past.

But lately, whether as a result of Shirley's and Jaye's nudges or her own neglected hormones, Maggie had begun to wonder about lust. It had recently occurred to her that she might not be ruined for lust. She had never given lust a chance.

Shirley finished shuffling the tarot cards. She divided the deck into three stacks. "Pick one," she ordered.

"Why me? This isn't my reading."

"Maggie. I can't do it. I'm the reader."

"Oh, all right." Maggie tapped the middle pile.

Shirley picked up the cards and laid them out. Maggie had had her cards read often enough that she could recognize the Celtic cross. Studying the cards, Shirley muttered, "What have we here?"

"Maybe we should do this some other time. I have to get back to my shop."

"This will only take a minute. A change is coming. Especially for you, sugar pie."

"Well, yes. Even I could have predicted that, Shirley. Someone will be living over my head. I'll hear footsteps on my ceiling. That reminds me. I need to make sure the trap door is bolted shut." A wrought-iron staircase in the corner of Maggie's bedroom spiraled up to one of the bedrooms of the second-floor apartment. Unused since the building had been partitioned into five flats, the staircase was blocked at the top by a wooden trap door.

Lines furrowed Shirley's brow as she continued to gaze at the cards. "Disaster threatens," she said, her tone matter-of-fact.

"Disaster has been threatening ever since Corinne

put that for sale sign in my store window last May," sighed Maggie.

The tenants referred to the day as Black Tuesday. It had started with Corinne and the for sale sign, and had ended with them pouring over their leases. Each lease had an identical clause which provided that if the building was sold, the leases could be terminated with thirty days notice to the tenants. "What does the new tenant have to do with that?"

"The new tenant may be the man you are destined to spend eternity with."

"Eternity? I don't think so, Shirley. He's only signed a short-term lease."

Ignoring Maggie's smart remark, Shirley tapped a red fingernail on another card. Her hand fluttered over the deck, but she did not lay down another card. Instead, she looked at the array she had before her. "There is something mysterious about this Gerard person. He has a secret."

"Don't we all?" Maggie muttered, beginning to be interested in spite of herself. "What kind of secret?"

"The cards do not reveal." Abruptly, Shirley picked up the cards and put them away. "Perhaps you are right. We should not trust this man until we know more about him. We will dismantle the ghost tonight."

"I'll tell Jaye and Eddie."

On Thursday, Maggie kept her shop open after her usual six o'clock closing time, waiting for the mysterious Mr. Gerard to arrive. She smiled. "Mysterious" only because she had not been able to find out anything about an author named Nicholas Gerard, not on the Internet and not from the New Orleans Public Library.

As she waited on a steady stream of customers, Maggie thought about the new tenant. Shirley's tarot cards had not been forthcoming. Maggie grinned. According to the cards, the mystery man might be her destiny, or he might be the precursor to disaster. Or both. If her past romance was anything to go by, definitely both.

Maggie had grown up believing that for every woman there was one special man. She had found hers when she was twenty. Robert Bennett had been everything Maggie had ever dreamed about—smart, funny, handsome, kind to animals and small children. She had fallen head over heels in love. Their storybook romance had progressed from first meeting to becoming engaged in a matter of weeks. Things had slowed down as soon as Robert put his ring on Maggie's finger.

She should have known something was wrong when Robert avoided setting a date for their wedding. But his reasons had always seemed so . . . well, reasonable.

They needed to graduate before marriage, Robert had said. Maggie's parents had agreed with him and told her how lucky she was to have found such a responsible young man. They graduated—Maggie got her bachelor's degree the same year Robert graduated from law school. She had thought they would get married then, but Robert insisted that he needed time to establish his practice.

After three years, Robert's firm promoted him from associate to junior partner. The promotion included a new, bigger office and the promise that he would not have to travel as much. After the move, Robert brought home several boxes filled with papers and other paraphernalia. He had told her he didn't want to clutter up his new space with old junk. After dropping the boxes on the dining room table, he had asked Maggie to act as hostess at a dinner party to celebrate his promotion. Maggie had agreed, her pulse pounding in anticipation, certain that the celebration would end with her and Robert agreeing on a definite date to meet at the altar.

On the day of the dinner party, Maggie had set to work with a smile on her face and hope in her heart. She had prepared Robert's favorite dishes; then she had gone to the dining room to set the table. The boxes Robert had brought from his old office were still there. In moving the boxes off the dining table, Maggie had dropped one. The box had split open and disgorged letters. Lots and lots of letters.

Love letters.

To Robert.

Unable to stop herself, Maggie had read all of the letters. Some of them had been embarrassingly explicit. All of them were postmarked after the date Robert had proposed to her.

When Robert had found her, she was sitting at the dining room table, with all of the letters arranged in stacks by sender. The letters had been written by *six* other women. Robert had mumbled something about wild oats. Maggie had told him the roast would be ready to come out of the oven in thirty minutes. Then she had handed him his ring and left.

The broken engagement had devastated her family. Appalled at being such a poor judge of character and embarrassed by the sheer number of other women, Maggie had been unable to bring herself to tell them about Robert's multiple betrayals. Her silence had

meant that her parents and sisters had not understood why she had given Robert his ring back.

Maggie had withdrawn from her family, unable to
face their disappointment. That had not been one of
her brighter moves. Her family loved her, and they
would have given her the comfort she had foolishly
avoided. At the time, she hadn't wanted their pity.

At least some good had come out of her self-induced
estrangement from her parents and sisters—she had
discovered where she belonged. A few months after she
ended her engagement, Maggie had taken a trip to
Mardi Gras. She had ended up staying in New Orleans,
and the healing had begun. Maggie's heart was whole
again, and she knew it would stay that way. After all, a
woman only got one chance at true love. Robert had
been her soul mate. She would not find another one.

Lately, it had occurred to her that love wasn't the
only glue that stuck women and men together. There
was also sex. Why it had taken her so long to recognize that fact was a mystery. Sex was everywhere—on
television, in films and books. Sex was one block over
at the gentlemen's clubs on Bourbon Street.

Why weren't there ladies' clubs? Closing her eyes,
Maggie imagined an almost naked-man doing a lap
dance for her. She was tucking a twenty in his G-string
when the bell over the shop door tinkled, and a couple entered. Maggie managed a welcoming smile.
"Feel free to browse," she told them, hoping that her
face was not as red as a Creole tomato.

The man picked up one of the masks. "Does this
lobster mask come in other colors?"

Maggie grinned at him. "It's supposed to be a crawfish. But the size does make it look more like a lobster,
doesn't it? Red is the only color I stock."

The man laid the crawfish mask on the pile on the

counter, and the couple continued browsing. Maggie's masks were displayed on the counter and in two antique armoires. Some of her masks were fitted onto mannequins dressed in Mardi Gras costumes; others were exhibited on wig holders.

As soon as the couple moved away from the counter, Maggie's thoughts returned to lust. Since there were no ladies' clubs, at least none that advertised, she let go of her lap dance fantasy. If she did decide to experiment with lust, how would she go about it? How did one go about arranging for casual sex? Without money changing hands, that is. Shirley and Jaye would gladly fix her up—they had offered to do just that on many occasions. Ed might even introduce her to one of his former students. But Maggie didn't want to involve them.

This was something she needed to do on her own.

Maggie glanced at her watch. A new man would enter her life in another few hours. It certainly would make things easier for her if Nicholas Gerard turned out to be thirtyish, single, and attractive. Nicholas met one important criteria for a brief affair. He wouldn't be around for long. Tapping her nails on the glass counter, Maggie wished she had asked Corinne more about him.

Assuming Nicholas turned out to be an eligible candidate for her experiment, would she find him attractive? It had been so long, Maggie wasn't sure what would be appealing in a man. Since her goal was only a very short relationship, she wouldn't have to know too much about him. Superficial sex wouldn't need any more than superficial attraction, would it?

Maggie felt her face grow hot again. She was fast becoming obsessed with sex. "Oh, my lordy me."

"Did you say something?" The couple was standing

in front of her, each wearing a mask. The woman wore Maggie's Tribute-to-Barbie mask, which featured long blond hair and rhinestone-trimmed sunglasses. Her companion had chosen the Gladiator mask.

"Nothing important." Grinning, Maggie took their money and rang up the purchase. When business was this good, why would she need a man? Her idle speculations about lust, coupled with the possibility of a new man in her life, sure had stirred up her hormones.

Maggie smiled wryly. It was time to get real. Some day she might be ready to try out her experiment with lust.

Someday. But not today.

At seven o'clock, an hour after her usual closing time, Maggie decided to call it a day. She locked the door, pulled the shade, and turned out the lights. Maggie exited her shop through a side door into the unheated passageway which led from Royal Street to the courtyard in the center of the building. All the apartments opened onto the courtyard.

Maggie shivered as she hurried down the cold passageway toward her door. The cashmere twin set she had found at Second Hand Ro's gave some, but not enough, protection from the damp cold. But the green color matched her eyes and went well with the tan corduroy pants she had bought at the same time.

Ed and Shirley nagged her to buy a coat, but Maggie refused. Maggie positively *hated* winter and the bulky clothes that went with it. Luckily for her, winter in New Orleans was a brief affair, often interrupted by balmy days. With a little judicious layering, she could do quite well without a heavy winter coat. It was only a few steps from the shop to her apartment—down the passageway, through the gate, and she was home.

The wrought-iron gate to the courtyard clanged shut behind Maggie, and Shirley poked her head out her front door. "Gerard never showed up?"

"No. I waited, but he must have been delayed. Or maybe he's not coming after all."

"Corinne should have let us know. We might have dismantled the ghost for no reason."

"If he doesn't show up tonight, I'll call her tomorrow and find out what happened to him." Maggie waved at Shirley, opened the French doors, and entered her apartment. Most of the first-floor front building was taken up by her shop, leaving room for a bedroom, bathroom, parlor, and a minuscule kitchen.

She had entered the parlor, although she could have gone directly to her bedroom, or to the bathroom, for that matter. Each room of her apartment, including the bathroom, had a French door opening onto the courtyard. The parlor boasted hardwood floors, exposed brick walls, and a fireplace on the wall opposite the entrance. The fireplace had been sealed and no longer worked, but Maggie had filled the cavity with potted plants and silk flowers. Pictures of her family crowded the mantel, sharing space with candles and other knickknacks.

After three years, the place had become more than an apartment. It was her home. She had furnished it gradually, scouring the used furniture stores on Magazine Street and the antique shops on Royal for each piece.

Maggie smiled as she looked at the cozy result. "I don't want to move from here. Ever."

She had made herself a nest, a haven, complete with a second family. Shirley, Jaye, and the professor had slowly filled the empty place in her heart. Maggie needed them, all of them, as much as she needed her family back home. Her smile broadened as she thought about her parents. They had visited New Orleans for the first time last Mardi Gras, and they had been enchanted with Maggie's adopted home. Once they had met Shirley, Jaye, and Ed, her mother and father had known Maggie was neither alone nor lonely any longer.

The building could not sell.

When Corinne had first put up the for sale sign, Maggie had written the absentee landlord, a corporation with headquarters in New York City, and begged them to reconsider. She had explained that Shirley had lived in the building for twenty years, the professor for twenty-three years, and Jaye for ten. The newest tenant at barely three years, Maggie had told the company that her fledgling mask shop was only now beginning to attract the locals as well as tourists, and that a move at this stage would mean the end of her business. She could not afford to start over. Maggie had also offered to discuss modest increases in the rents they paid.

The only response had been a curt, one-paragraph letter referring her "complaint" to the real estate agency that managed the building. To Corinne, in other words.

Corinne had offered to help them find new apartments. But she had admitted the chances of them finding four apartments and a commercial space in another French Quarter building were slim to none. She could sell them all condominiums, though, if they would consider moving to one of the renovated warehouses, across Canal Street and upriver from the Quarter. . . ?

They wouldn't. They couldn't afford the prices.

Maggie gave up rehashing the relocation problem and went to the kitchen. She took a container of frozen gumbo out of the freezer and put it in the microwave. As soon as it was heated, she poured the gumbo into a bowl. Shirley had given her the recipe after her first Thanksgiving in the building. Maggie had fixed the turkey for the tenants' holiday meal. The day after, she had asked, "What do I do with the leftover turkey?" And Shirley's matter-of-fact response had been, "You make your turkey gumbo, sweet pea." As a result of Shirley's lesson, Maggie's freezer was now well-stocked with gumbo made from her leftover Christmas turkey.

When she was finished with her meal, Maggie spent a few hours working on masks customers had ordered to match the costumes and gowns they would be wearing to the upcoming Mardi Gras parades and balls. Her workroom was a corner of her bedroom and consisted of a table for her sewing machine and open shelves stacked with materials, threads, and other adornments.

As Maggie worked she kept an ear cocked for the arrival of the new tenant.

Nicholas Gerard. Nice name. Hopefully, Mr. Gerard would be nice, too. With their homes about to be sold out from under them, the tenants did not need the aggravation of dealing with someone who did not fit in.

When the tiny stitches Maggie used to quilt her creations began to blur, she glanced at the clock on the wall. Almost midnight. She put down the mask, stretched, and walked to the French doors. Still no sign of the new tenant. She grinned. Anticipating the arrival of the new tenant had kept her awake way past her usual bedtime.

She should have called Corinne to verify Gerard's

arrival time. Maybe his plans had changed. At the
same time, Maggie could have tried to find out more
about him. Whether or not he was single, for instance.
Having an available male right upstairs might prove
interesting. Maggie's glance slid to the spiral staircase
next to her sewing machine. Convenient, too, if there
was even a spark of mutual attraction between them.

Oh, lord. She was so sleepy she was giddy. Day
dreaming about a man she had never met—for all she
knew, Nicholas Gerard could be fifty, bald and married—was a complete waste of time. Her sex-starved
hormones were making her crazy.

Even if Gerard turned out to be thirtyish, attractive and available. . . . Maggie grimaced.

She wouldn't have the slightest idea what to do with
him.

Two

Nick squinted at the brass numbers over the door. Eleven-thirteen. This was definitely the right place. He pushed the buzzer again. Nothing. The damn thing must be broken. It figured—everything that could go wrong with a building had gone wrong with this one.

Abandoning the buzzer, Nick pounded on the solid wooden door. The noise reverberated down the passageway in a most satisfactory way. He pounded harder. After several minutes of pounding, a faint light appeared at the end of the passageway. A woman hurried toward him, tying the sash of a robe as she approached. "Hush! Do you want to wake everyone in the building?"

"The damn buzzer doesn't"—Nick coughed and coughed—"work."

"Who are you?" asked the young woman, covering a yawn with her hand. She peered at him through the wrought-iron viewport in the door.

The glow from the quaint street light on the corner allowed Nick to see her clearly. Her shoulder-length hair was tousled, her eyes sleep-glazed. As Nick stared at her, her soft lips parted in another yawn. Not just her lips—she looked soft all over. Sexy, in an innocent, cuddly kind of way. She had obviously just gotten out of bed.

Bed. Nick had been yearning for a bed for the past six hours. It had not been a good day. His cold was worse, the trip had been a nightmare, and now a sleepy sex kitten was barring the door to what would probably be his last resting place.

"I'm Nick"—he sneezed loudly, three times in succession—"Gerard. I'm looking for apartment 2A. This is eleven-thirteen Royal Street, isn't it?"

"It is." She threw the bolt, opened the door, and motioned him into the passageway. "We were expecting you to arrive earlier, Mr. Gerard. Much earlier. Corinne left your keys at my shop."

"Yeah. She told me. Sorry about that." Nick walked past her, carrying his suitcase and his portable computer. "Plane was delayed—winter storm on the East Coast. Missed the connecting flight from Atlanta, and I had to wait for"—another fit of coughing overtook him—"the next one."

"My goodness. That cough sounds terrible. Have you seen a doctor?"

"Just a cold. I'm fine." He stopped at the wrought-iron gate at the end of the passageway. The gate opened into a large courtyard. The building provided three sides to the courtyard. A gnarled wisteria vine climbed the eight-foot stuccoed wall that completed the enclosure and separated his building from its neighbor. Nick remembered the wisteria vine, and the fountain that stood in the middle of the courtyard.

His guide stepped past him and pushed open the gate. "This gate isn't locked. It's the door to the street that keeps people out."

"Which way is the apartment?" Nick asked.

"Up those stairs," she said, pointing to a flight of

wooden stairs leading to the second floor. "I'm Maggie Mayfair, by the way. I live directly below you. There." She pointed to her apartment.

Nick glanced at the light spilling from her French doors. A stray beam hit his eyes, making him blink.

Maggie gasped.

He turned his head. "What?" he wheezed.

"Nothing. For a minute there, with the light in your eyes, your eyes looked . . . silver."

Nick snorted—it came out as a sneeze. "Gray. My eyes are gray."

"And your hair is what? Dark brown? It's hard to tell in this light."

"Yeah." Odd conversation they were having, Nick thought. But then, anyone who lived in the French Quarter was probably a little weird. "Brown. I have brown hair. What color is yours? It looks dark blond to me. In this light." Nick sneezed again, three times in rapid succession.

"Goodness. You sound awful. We'd better get you upstairs and out of this damp air." She started up the stairs. "My hair is light brown, Mr. Gerard."

"Call me Nick. What color are your eyes?" He followed her up the wooden staircase at an old man's measured pace. If his ears hadn't been stopped up, Nick was sure he would have heard his joints creak.

She glanced at him over her shoulder. "Green. My eyes are green."

Green. Cat eyes. An appropriate color for a sex kitten. Nick nodded his head, then immediately regretted it. Swallowing a moan, he said, "I saw the sign on the storefront. Mayfair Masks. Yours, I presume. Can you make a living selling masks?" Nick's interest in the varied ways people tried to make money surfaced, even though his throat was raw from coughing and his head felt as if it was about to explode.

"I don't just sell the masks. I design and make them, too. I will make a living at it soon, provided I don't have to move."

"Why would you move?"

"The building is for sale." She stopped in front of another pair of French doors. "Here we are."

From the brass numbers on the lintel, Nick guessed he was finally home. "2A. Is this it?"

"All yours." Maggie fished in her robe pocket and pulled out two keys. "Here. The smaller one is for the apartment door. The other one opens the Royal Street door."

Setting his suitcase and computer down, Nick took the keys from her and used the smaller one to unlock the door. He pushed the door open and entered the center hallway. "Christ. It's as cold in here as it is outside. I didn't expect it to be this cold in New Orleans."

Maggie followed him into the hall. "It's January. Even in New Orleans it gets cold in January. And we're only a few blocks from the river. The dampness makes the cold . . . colder." She shivered, pulling her robe closer around her. "I hate cold weather. The apartment is chilly because the central heat isn't turned on. The thermostat is right over there. The heating system is brand-new, and it works very well."

"It should," muttered Nick, remembering the bill. At Maggie's questioning look, he explained, "Based on the rent I'm being charged."

Maggie walked over to the thermostat and turned on the heat. "There. You'll be warm and toasty in no time. Which bedroom do you want to use? One overlooks the courtyard, and the other faces Royal Street.

That one might get a little noisy, especially at this time of year."

He gave her a blank stare. "Winter?"

"Mardi Gras. The parades and balls have already started."

"So soon? I thought Mardi Gras happened in February or March."

"It does. This year Fat Tuesday is on February twelfth, but the parades start in January. They don't parade through the Quarter anymore, of course, but a lot of the parade-goers come to the Quarter before and after the parades. It gets crowded. And noisy."

"I'll take the back bedroom, then."

"You can use the front bedroom for a study."

Nick rubbed his forehead. His thoughts were getting fuzzier and fuzzier. "Why would I need a study?"

"For your writing. Corinne said you were an author. Isn't that a computer you're carrying?"

"Writing. Oh. Yeah." He put the computer on the floor next to his suitcase. "I'll figure out where to set up my computer tomorrow." Rubbing his forehead, Nick coughed again. "Or the day after. Right now all I want to do is eat. And sleep."

"Follow me."

Nick followed and found himself wishing his new neighbor was wearing something a little more revealing. Maggie's hips had a seductive swing, even buried under pink chenille. If he had been feeling more like himself, Nick would have allowed his imagination to strip the heavy robe away. But his libido wasn't up to it, not in his condition.

Ms. Mayfair could have made it easier for him. Sex kittens ought to wear silk. Didn't she know that? He almost bumped into her when she stopped in the doorway to a bedroom.

"Oh, my lord," said Maggie.

"What's wrong?" Nick sniffed her hair. She smelled like gardenias, simultaneously sweet and sultry.

"No sheets or blankets." Taking a step back, her bottom ended up resting on his thighs. She looked at him over her shoulder, her eyes wide. "I didn't know you were so close."

Nick took a step back. "Sorry." He rubbed the end of his nose.

"I don't suppose you brought any bed linens with you?"

"You suppose right." Nick looked around the room. French doors opened onto the wooden balcony—he remembered his grandfather had called it a gallery— overlooking the courtyard. Wrought iron was reserved for the front balcony visible from the street.

The bedroom was furnished with a bed and an armoire. A small table next to the bed held a lamp. A faded Persian rug covered most of the floor. "What's that?" he asked, pointing.

"A trap door. It blocks off a staircase to the first floor."

"Why?"

"The staircase is in my bedroom. It's not used anymore."

"Never? Did you ever see that old Marilyn Monroe movie, *The Seven Year Itch*? Her apartment had a staircase like that." Marilyn, the ultimate sex kitten, had known to wear silk—or nothing at all. Nick's tired and hungry libido managed a vision of Maggie emerging nude from the stairwell.

Maggie gave him a stern look. "I saw the movie on TV. Tom Ewell's apartment had the staircase—Marilyn lived upstairs." She pointed to the floor. "This trap door is bolted shut. From my side."

"Marilyn kept her underwear in the refrigerator."
Nick's vision blurred, whether from the memory of
icy lingerie or because of his aching head, he did not
know. He blinked. "Bolted?"

"Tightly bolted."

Nick waited a beat, but apparently his sexy neighbor wasn't going to tell him the location of her
underwear. "You sure know how to squelch a fantasy,
lady."

Just as well. He had been feeling overheated and
woozy even before he had seen Magnolia Mayfair. It
would be counter-productive to weave sexual fantasies
about one of his tenants. He would need his wits
about him if he was going to catch her and the others
in an act of sabotage. "What about food?"

"Food?" she repeated, furrowing her brow.

"Yeah. I'm hungry—you know airlines these days.
Lucky if they throw you a peanut. Where can I get
something to eat?"

"It's two o'clock in the morning. There's nothing
open at this hour but a few bars. Maybe one of the
hotel restaurants on Canal Street . . ."

Nick coughed again, a harsh, wheezing cough. "I
don't feel so hot. Maybe I'll forget about food and just
go to bed."

Making a clucking sound, Maggie said, "You
shouldn't go to bed hungry. I had turkey gumbo for
dinner, and I have more in my freezer. It will only take
a minute to heat up. Wait here, and I'll bring it to you.
You do like turkey gumbo, don't you?"

"I don't know. I've never had turkey gumbo." Nick
sneezed. "But you don't have to do that. I'll go to a
restaurant as soon as I've rested for a few minutes.
Which way is Canal Street?" He sat on the naked mattress and slumped against the headboard.

"I don't think that's a good idea. Not with that cough. You shouldn't go out again tonight. I'll—"

"Yoo hoo! Maggie? What's going on?" The voice came from below.

Maggie opened the French doors and walked onto the gallery. "Hi, Shirley. Did we wake you? Mr. Gerard arrived. He's not feeling well, and he's hungry. He needs to eat and go to bed, but there aren't any sheets on his bed. I can't help him. I only have twin bed sheets."

Raising his head, Nick asked, "Twin bed? Does that mean you sleep alone?"

Turning from the door, Maggie gave him another severe look. "I have a day bed because my apartment is small, only one bedroom. I needed room for my sewing machine."

Magnolia sewed. Nick furrowed his brow. Did he know one woman who knew how to sew? He thought not. Women who sewed and cooked were old-fashioned, homey types. The type of women men felt obligated to marry.

Nick shuddered.

"Oh, dear." Maggie went out on the balcony again. "Shirley? He's shivering. I think he's got a chill. Do you have a thermometer?"

"Yes. I'll bring it. And I've got a set of sheets that will fit his bed," called the voice from below.

"Bring quilts, too. He needs to get warm."

"That's not necessary." Nick waved a hand in a feeble protest. "I can buy sheets and blankets tomorrow."

"Yes. But what about tonight? You can't sleep on a bare mattress."

"He won't have to." A woman—this one wore a silk robe even though she was well past her kittenish days—came into the bedroom through the French doors. She carried bed linens and pillows. She was followed by a shorter, thinner woman. The second woman was heavily made up and wore a tight red satin dress.

Nick got out of bed. He swayed a little, but managed to stand more or less upright. He stuck out his hand. "How do you do? I'm Nick Gerard. I didn't intend to wake the entire building."

"You didn't. The professor is still asleep." She put her bundle on the table and began making up the bed. "I'm Shirley Wyclowsky, also known as Madame Fortunata. I own Oracles and Edibles—the tea and fortune-telling shop across the street. This is Jaye Landry, sometimes called Jayne. Jaye just got home from work."

"Wake the dead, you hooligans," came a grumpy voice from the balcony.

"Uh oh," said the woman in the red dress. "Here comes the professor. You'd better sit down, Gerard. You look kind of shaky. Let's go to the kitchen—it's getting crowded in here." The woman steered Nick out of the bedroom and across the hall to the kitchen. Once Nick was seated at the kitchen table, she said, "So. What kind of books do you write?"

"Books? Oh. Yeah. I'm not sure yet. I just started writing a few months ago. Career change. What did you say your name was?"

"Jaye. Jaye Landry."

An older man with a grizzled gray beard entered the kitchen, followed by Maggie. "This is the place for it."

"The place for what?" asked Nick, distracted by seeing Maggie again.

"The place for change. And inspiration. Many authors have found their muse here in the Vieux

Carre—Tennessee Williams, for one. William Faulkner, for another." He sat at the kitchen table. "Did someone say gumbo?"

"Oh, yes. I was on my way to get it," said Maggie. "Mr. Gerard is hungry."

"I could eat a bite," said the professor.

"Me, too. Better bring it all." Jaye began opening cabinets and drawers. "We'll need bowls and spoons, too. No dishes."

"You'd think a furnished apartment would include linens and dishes, wouldn't you? Did Corinne tell you the cupboards would be bare?" Maggie asked.

"I didn't ask," said Nick, resisting the urge to rest his head on the kitchen table.

Jaye slammed another cabinet shut. "Nothing. You're going to have to go shopping, Gerard. There's a little consignment shop on Toulouse that'll have everything you need. I'll take you there tomorrow if you want."

"Thanks," said Nick, beginning to feel as if he had fallen down a rabbit hole. He hadn't had so many people fussing over him since . . . never.

"Maggie? Gumbo?" The professor prodded her with an elbow.

Nick realized that Maggie had been staring at him, a worried look on her face. She couldn't be worried about him—they had only just met.

"Oh. Right. Gumbo. I'll be back in a flash." She hurried out of the kitchen, almost colliding with Shirley in the doorway.

Shirley bustled into the kitchen. "Your bed's all made. Would you like to change into your pajamas? I think you need to get in bed as soon as possible. We can serve you your gumbo on a tray."

Nick coughed. And coughed again. "I don't have any pajamas," he said, once he could talk.

"I don't like the sound of that cough," said Shirley, frowning. She touched Nick's forehead. "And you feel warm. Too warm. Jaye, go get Doc Martin. Tell him it's an emergency."

Hitching up the red satin skirt, Jaye headed for the door. "On my way."

"Wait a minute. I don't need a doctor. I'm not that sick. Bad cold, that's all. I'm just tired. And hungry. I'll be fine as soon as I've rested. Anyway, doctors don't make house calls," Nick protested.

"Go on, Jaye," said Shirley. She turned back to Nick. "Dr. Martin is only a few steps away. He has an apartment over the Royal Pharmacy."

Not quite knowing how it happened, Nick found himself stripped to his boxers and tucked in bed. Then, almost as quickly as they had appeared, the tenants deserted him. He was alone.

Except for the guy standing in the corner of the room. Nick couldn't remember which one he was. "What did you say your name is?" he asked.

The man did not answer.

"Silent type, huh? I guess someone has to be, with this crowd. They all talk a lot, don't they?"

Nick thought the man might have nodded, but it could have been nothing more than a shift in the shadows.

"Where did the others go?" Nick closed his eyes, listening to the voices coming from the other room. He couldn't quite make out what they were saying. He could guess what they were doing from the clink of silver against china. They were eating gumbo, while he lay in bed starving. Forgotten. And alone.

Nick slitted one eye open. Not alone. The silent

man still stood in the corner. Deep shadows hid his features. "Don't you want something to eat? I do. I'm hungry." Before the man could answer, the others crowded into the bedroom.

A man who said he was a doctor asked him questions, thumped on his chest, and listened to him breathe. "Pneumonia," he pronounced, taking off the stethoscope. "Jaye, come with me, and we'll find some antibiotics in the pharmacy."

"Pneumonia? Shouldn't he be in a hospital, then?" asked Maggie.

She sounded worried. Worried about him, and she didn't even know him. Nick wheezed a contented sigh.

"Not necessary," said the doctor. "Pills, plenty of liquids, and bed rest. I'll check on him again in a day or two. Come on, Jaye. Let's get that medicine."

Nick opened his eyes in time to see the doctor and the woman in the red dress leaving the room.

"I'm going with them," said the old man—the professor. "I should know better than to eat in the middle of the night. Wait up, Doc. I need Maalox."

Nick was alone with Shirley. Where was Maggie?

"Here she is," said Shirley, smiling at him. Maggie stood in the doorway to the bedroom, carrying a tray.

Had he asked the question out loud? He must have. Nick didn't believe in psychics. "Is that food?"

"It sure enough is," said Shirley. "Now, sugar plum, sit up and try to eat some of Maggie's gumbo. We'll stay with you until you've eaten and had your medicine."

Nick struggled into a sitting position. Maggie placed the tray in his lap and sat on the edge of the bed. Her hip touched his, and Nick felt his pulse speed up. She wiggled closer, and his temperature soared. "I'm hot," he said.

Dropping the spoon into the bowl, Maggie felt his forehead. "You do feel warm." She slanted a look at Shirley standing at the foot of the bed. "Maybe one of us should stay with him all night."

"That's a good idea," said Shirley. "I don't think he's well enough to take care of himself tonight. Someone will have to make sure he takes the antibiotic. He'll need aspirin, too, for the fever. Feed the man, Maggie. His tongue is hanging out."

"Oh. Right." Maggie picked up the spoon and fed Nick a hot, spicy liquid.

Not chicken soup, thought Nick. But if Hildy could see him now. . . . She would think he had taken the first step toward A Family of His Own.

Nick shuddered.

"Oh, my lordy me. You shivered again. Did you have a chill? Shirley, do we need to get another quilt? Someone will definitely have to stay with him, to make sure he keeps warm." Maggie pulled the covers up, tucking the quilt under his chin and patting him on the chest.

Magnolia Mayfair had a motherly streak. That figured. She knew how to sew, *and* she could cook. But she still looked like a sex kitten. "I choose you," said Nick, attempting a leer.

Shirley chuckled. "Maggie, I think he likes you."

Maggie smiled at him. "I hope so. I like him, too." She fussed with the covers again, smoothing the wrinkles away. "Poor man. Imagine traveling all the way from New York City with pneumonia. He could use a little cosseting."

Cosseted. He was being cosseted, petted, and pampered. Eyes dropping shut, Nick grinned. He liked it. A lot.

A voice in the back of his head was clamoring for attention, trying to tell him there was a reason he shouldn't be alone with a woman like Magnolia Mayfair. Nick ignored the voice. Maggie was taking very good care of him, exactly the kind of care he needed. He sure didn't want to spend the night with the silent type. Nick opened his eyes and looked at Maggie. "I want you to stay with me tonight. Not that guy in the corner."

Maggie and Shirley exchanged puzzled glances.

"Nick? Mr. Gerard? What guy?" Maggie asked. Nick did not answer. He closed his eyes again, too tired to explain.

"Hush," said Shirley. "He's asleep. Who do you think he saw? A ghost, maybe?" Nick could hear the smile in her voice. "He has silver eyes."

"The ghost?" asked Maggie.

"Of course not the ghost. Our attractive new neighbor is the one with silver eyes."

"He has gray eyes," said Maggie. She sounded breathless. And slightly annoyed. "His hair is dark brown."

"I may have misinterpreted that particular card. It could have meant dark, almost black hair. My lucky silver dime says he's the one."

The one? The one who? thought Nick before he drifted off to sleep.

Shirley hustled Maggie out of the apartment, volunteering to stay with Nick for an hour or two. A few minutes after Maggie had left, Jaye appeared.

"Here's the medicine," said Jaye, handing the bottle to Shirley. "Doc said to give him one now, and then every four hours. Where's Maggie?"

"Maggie took the dishes downstairs. I told her to rest for a couple of hours, then come back to stay with Nick. We didn't think it wise to leave him all alone in his condition." Covering her mouth, Shirley yawned noisily. "I'm taking the first shift."

Jaye hitched up his red satin skirt and straddled a kitchen chair. "You look tired, old girl. Why don't you go to bed? I'll stay with Nick until Maggie returns."

"Watch your lip, queen bee. Old girl, indeed. I volunteered for this shift on purpose. After it's over, I can have an uninterrupted sleep until it's time to open up Oracles." Shirley went to the sink and filled the Mardi Gras cup she had found tucked away on the top shelf of the cabinet with water. "I'm going to give Nick his pill."

Switching on the light as she entered the bedroom, Shirley called out, "Wake up, gorgeous. Time to take your medicine."

Nick had pushed the covers off.

"What kind of idiot leaves a man with pneumonia bare-chested? No pajamas, you said, but you must have an undershirt. Not that I mind seeing pecs like yours, Nicky my boy." Shirley made a smacking sound, then chuckled. "When did I turn into a dirty old lady? Lusting after a young"—Shirley looked at him closer—"youngish man. Too young for me."

Nick turned on his side, then flopped onto his back once more. One bare foot appeared from beneath the quilt.

"Who undressed you?" she muttered as she approached the bed. "I know who—Professor Wellington. No fool like an old fool. And what did he do with your clothes? Dropped them where they fell. Just like a man."

Shirley put the cup of water and the medicine bottle on the bedside table, then busied herself picking up trousers, shirt, jacket, and one black sock. "What happened to your other sock?" She hung the clothes on the bedpost, then grabbed Nick's bare foot and shook it. "Wake up, Nick. Time to take a pill."

Nick's eyes opened wide. "Whaa?"

She dropped the pill. "Merciful heavens. Your eyes are silver." Shirley always got a pleasant shock when one of her "sights" proved to be true. Like most professional psychics, Shirley relied on intuition and a keen knowledge of body language to satisfy her clients' need to know their futures. But on rare occasions, Shirley truly "saw." She had seen a man with silver eyes in Maggie's future.

And here he was. A broad smile curved her lips. "Well, well, well. Too young for me, but exactly right for Magnolia. About time you got here. Maggie needs you."

"Aaargh," Nick moaned.

"Don't go back to sleep, sweety pie, not yet. Where did that pill go? Oh, here it is." Shirley picked the pill up off Nick's chest and put it in his open mouth. "Here, have a sip of water."

The muscles in Nick's throat worked. Opening his eyes, he asked, "What did you say about my eyes?"

"Not important. Did you get the pill down?"

"Yes. Who're you?"

"Shirley Wyclowsky. We met earlier. Go back to sleep, now."

"I'm not sick. Jus' tired. Where am I?"

"You're tired *and* sick, Mr. Nicholas Gerard. Go back to sleep, sweet pea. You'll remember everything tomorrow."

Nick's silver eyes remained stubbornly open.

"There was a girl. I remember a girl. Green eyes, dark blond hair. Pink robe. Where is she?"

"That's our Magnolia you're describing." Shirley patted Nick on his bare shoulder. "She's sleeping—probably dreaming of you."

"Dream? Why'd she dream 'bout me?"

"She saw the way you looked at her. Like you were bread pudding and she was whiskey sauce—you wanted her poured all over you."

His cheeks, flushed from the fever, turned a deeper shade of red. "It showed?"

"Sure did. Don't be embarrassed. She looked at you exactly the same way. Maggie will be back soon—we're taking turns looking after you. You'll want to follow the doctor's orders and get well soon so you and Maggie can—"

Nick closed his eyes. "Going to sleep now."

"Good. You need your sleep."

As soon as Nick's eyes fluttered shut again, Shirley tucked the quilt around him and left the room.

Jaye was seated at the kitchen table.

"Why are you still here?" asked Shirley, taking another of the kitchen chairs.

"I thought I'd keep you company. What do you think of him?" Jaye jerked his head in the direction of the bedroom where Nick lay sleeping.

"When the light strikes them just right, his eyes are silver."

"Are they? You mean the tarot cards actually predicted the correct eye color?" Jaye narrowed his eyes. "Which card represents silver eyes? You never said."

"I saw the silver eyes without the help of the cards," Shirley admitted.

"A real psychic moment?" Jaye grinned at her.

She glared at him. "Are you mocking me?"

Jaye sobered immediately. "Never. I would never tempt fate that way."

"Why don't you go change clothes? You need to wash your makeup off. Your mascara is smearing."

"It wouldn't dare. Have you got a mirror?"

Footsteps sounded in the hall. "Why is everyone still here? Isn't anyone going to bed tonight?" grumbled the professor, entering the kitchen and taking a seat at the table.

"Maggie has gone to catch a few hours sleep," said Shirley. "Why don't you do the same, you old fart?"

Ed ignored the insult. "Can't sleep. Zantac hasn't kicked in yet. I shouldn't have eaten that gumbo. How is Mr. Gerard?"

"He's sleeping," said Jaye. "Shirley gave him a pill."

Nodding, Shirley added, "His breathing still sounds wheezy, but he's not coughing as much as he did earlier."

"He wasn't too sick to notice our Magnolia. I'm not sure I approve of the way he ogled her," said Ed.

Shirley shrugged. "Nick is destined to be Maggie's next lover, according to the stars."

"Stars, humbug," said Ed. "Your inane babbling has nothing to do with the stars."

Bristling, Shirley glared at the professor. "I beg your pardon. I do not babble. I saw Maggie's future. It was foretold that her last lover will have silver eyes. And here he is."

"Last lover? When you did the reading you said, 'next lover.'" Jaye hitched up his skirt and sat down at the table.

"What's the difference?" asked Ed. "The question we should be asking is whether this man is good enough for our Magnolia? No matter what color his eyes are."

"There could be a big difference, Ed. 'Last' means forever. 'Next' implies that other lovers will follow." Jaye stared at Shirley. "Which was it, Shirley?"

"Last." Wrinkles deepened on Shirley's forehead. The vision had been brief. She had gotten only a glimpse of the man, no clear features except for his eyes. Shirley had improvised the rest of the reading, including the color of the man's hair. "Next" or "last" would have been another embellishment. "I think."

Ed snorted.

"Whichever. Nick got her juices flowing, that's for sure. Did you see the looks they were giving each other?" Jaye fanned himself with his hand. "Hot."

"The man has a fever. It follows that he would appear overheated." Ed rested his elbows on the table.

"That's not the kind of heat Jaye's talking about." Shirley rolled her eyes. Sometimes Ed's naivete was too much. No man should be that oblivious to male-female attraction. The sexual tension between Nick and Maggie had been palpable.

Jaye said, "Well, last or next, at least she'll have a lover. About time. Robert—"

"—was an ass. He hurt Maggie badly," said Shirley.

"What if this man hurts Magnolia, too?" asked Ed. "Being alone, if by alone you mean without what my students referred to as a significant other, isn't the worst thing in the world."

"The professor's right, Shirley. There are worse things—having her heart broken twice, for instance."

"I got a glimpse of his palm. Nicholas Gerard is not a cruel man. He wouldn't hurt Maggie." Shirley surreptitiously crossed her fingers behind her back. She had a vivid flashback to the first time she'd met Maggie. Her green eyes had been dull, empty, full of sadness.

Because of a man.

"No matter what color his eyes are, I'm not sure about Gerard. A writer, he said. But he hasn't written anything. He could be a bum," grumbled Ed.

"I don't think so," said Jaye, leaning back in his chair. "Nick has funds."

"What makes you think that?" asked Shirley.

"I helped Ed get Gerard out of his suit. His hand-tailored suit. Ditto with his shirt. Egyptian cotton, made to order. And his shoes—expensive. Gerard had a couple of thousand dollars on his back."

"Very observant of you," said Ed. "Add to his wardrobe the fact that Mr. Gerard paid for a trip to New Orleans and a month's rent on this place. Knowing that Ellis woman, he probably had to fork over a damage deposit, too. Perhaps he isn't a bum, after all."

"Of course he's not a bum. A bum's not good enough for Maggie." Nick had to be the one meant for Maggie.

Shirley knew Maggie thought she had had her one and only chance at lasting love, but as far as she was concerned, that particular bit of rationalization was only Maggie's way of protecting her heart from another wound. If anyone was destined to be a wife and mother, Magnolia Mayfair was that person. Sooner or later, Maggie would realize that. Sooner, now that Nick had arrived.

"Shouldn't you have known about Gerard's financial status, Madame Fortunata?" asked Ed. "From your crystal ball?"

"I don't use a crystal ball. I haven't read his cards. Or his tea leaves. And I only gave his palm a cursory reading. I'll find out more about him later."

"Humbug. You should be ashamed of yourself. It's

DREAMING OF YOU   55

bad enough that you gull the public with your phony predictions. But to do the same things to your friends, well . . ."

"Phony? Who are you calling a phony, you miserable old goat?"

"Children," said Jaye, holding up a hand. "Keep your voices down. We don't want to disturb Gerard's sleep. Think that's his real name?"

"Why wouldn't it be?" snapped Shirley, still bristling from Ed's insults.

"Why would it? Writers use pen names, don't they? And lots of people take on new identities when they come here. Look at the countess," said Jaye, referring to one of the Quarter characters. "If she's royalty, I'm the king of Siam."

"The button lady," said Ed. "No one knows her real name."

"Or the blue man's. I see what you mean," said Shirley, reflecting on several of the Quarter's more noticeable residents. "Oh, well. We'll find out more about Nick in the morning."

"Which is fast approaching. I'm going to bed. Keep the noise down, you two." Ed stomped out of the kitchen.

"Why that man ever decided to live in the French Quarter, I'll never know. Hidebound old geezer," said Shirley.

"He's a skeptic."

"He's a pain in the behind. What time is it? Maggie should be here by now."

Jaye glanced at the dainty gold watch circling his wrist. "It's a little after four o'clock. Let her sleep. I'll take her shift. You go."

"Are you sure?"

"I'm an owl. You and Maggie are the larks. And,

Shirley, don't worry about Maggie. She can take care of herself."

"I can't help but worry. What if I was wrong? What if the man with silver eyes is not her soul mate, but another Robert?"

"There couldn't be two Roberts. Ol' silver eyes will do right by our Maggie."

Shirley brightened. "You're right, of course. What was I worried about? Fate wouldn't bother signaling the arrival of Mr. Wrong, now would it?"

Three

Her first Mr. Wrong had arrived.

Heart pounding in anticipation of seeing Nick again, Maggie hurried up the stairs to the second-floor apartment. She climbed the stairs carrying a tray laden with coffeepot, coffee—Maggie hoped he liked it with chicory—two mugs, milk, and a pan for warming it.

How could she have overslept on such a momentous occasion? Why hadn't Shirley wakened her?

Maggie could not believe she had slept so late, knowing that Nick needed her—only to give him his medicine and feed him a nourishing breakfast, not for anything else. Not yet. But as soon as he was well . . .

Nick's eyes had flashed silver in the moonlight.

Maggie did not believe in tarot cards, tea leaves, or Shirley's psychic predictions. But she did believe that coincidences were or could be, on rare occasions, signs. Omens. Fate's way of agreeing that she was on the right track.

All those idle thoughts about superficial sex had done their job. Her first glimpse of a chiseled jaw and gray-not-silver eyes had Maggie jettisoning the remnants of her good girl upbringing without a backward glance.

Give lust a chance? Oh, yeah. As soon as possible.

So what if she had been raised in the Midwest, with solid Midwestern values? Those values—especially the one that said love preceded marriage which preceded sex—had left her alone and unfulfilled. After living in the sultry, sensual French Quarter for over four years, Maggie was more than ready to try a different path to happiness and fulfillment.

A sudden image of herself with Nick, replete with fulfillment, had Maggie tripping over her own feet. Her heart rate accelerated alarmingly.

Oh, lord. She couldn't be this needy. Needy was not seductive. Leaning on the banister, Maggie waited until her pulse returned to normal. When she saw Nick again, she would be caring, but cool. Not too cool. The last thing she wanted was for him to think she wasn't interested. But not too hot, either. Not until he was well.

She continued up the stairs. Balancing the tray on her hip, Maggie raised a hand to knock on the door.

Jaye opened it before her knuckles hit the glass. "Good morning, doll face." He took the tray from her. "My, aren't we dressed up this morning?"

For no special reason, Maggie had put on her favorite dress, a silky green forties number, with white lace at the collar and cuffs and a skirt that flirted with her knees. She lowered her lashes demurely. "This old thing?"

"Ha, ha. Cute. All your clothes are old." Jaye yawned. "But isn't it a little chilly to be wearing silk? You really ought to buy yourself a vintage coat."

"I'm not wearing silk. This dress is rayon. You know why I don't have a coat. I don't like coats. Coats are bulky and heavy. Besides, most of Ro's coats have fur trim. I do not approve of wearing dead animal skins."

"Any animal skins at Ro's died long before fur became passé. I think you need a coat."

"I'm fine. Warm as toast." She looked closer. "Poor Jaye. You look awful."

Jaye, in or out of costume, prided himself on his sophisticated, well-groomed appearance. Now he had raccoon eyes from smeared mascara, and his hair looked as though he had used an electric mixer as a styling brush. He arched a carefully shaped brow. *"Moi?* Awful?"

"Uh. Awful tired, that is." Maggie hastened to amend her statement. "What are you doing here? Where's Shirley? I was supposed to relieve her hours ago, but I overslept. It's after seven o'clock. Why didn't one of you wake me?"

"Not to worry, doll face. Shirley went home hours ago. I volunteered to take your shift."

"Oh. Thanks. I guess I was sleepier than I thought." Maggie swallowed a yawn. "I stayed up late waiting for Nick. Then there was all the excitement with the doctor and the midnight gumbo feast. I forgot to set my alarm."

"Humph. I'm not the only one who missed my beauty sleep. You look a little less perky than usual yourself, dearie." Jaye touched her cheek. "Put some cucumber slices on those bags under your eyes."

"I'll go to bed early tonight."

"Staying at home again on Friday night?" Jaye pursed his lips. "What a shame."

"Don't start, Jaye." She did not need any prodding from Jaye. Not this morning. Maggie's hormones were doing a very nice job of encouraging her to do something she had never done before.

"Well, if you don't have plans, you'll be available to watch over our new neighbor again tonight."

"How is he this morning?" whispered Maggie, tip-toeing into the hall. She followed Jaye to the kitchen.

Putting the tray on the counter, Jaye said, "Sleeping like a baby now. Earlier he was restless, tossing and turning. And dreaming. He kept muttering about all sorts of things. Mostly about some guy standing in the corner of the bedroom. Nick wasn't talking about me. Not in this getup." Jaye still wore his red silk dress.

"That's odd. Last night Nick said something about a man in the corner."

Jaye shrugged, then grabbed for the narrow strap that slid off his shoulder. "He must have been hallucinating. Fever does that sometimes."

"Does he have a fever?" asked Maggie.

"I don't know. I didn't touch him. Too tempting. And it's against the rules to take advantage of a man when he's sleeping. Besides, Gerard is heterosexual."

"Heterosexual? How can you be sure?"

"Puleeze. The man was all but drooling over you last night. And in his condition, too." Jaye yawned and rubbed his raccoon eyes. "In the right light Gerard's eyes are silver, did you notice? He thinks you're a sex kitten."

"Mr. Gerard's eyes are gray, and he has brown hair," Maggie said, her tone repressive. She was not ready to share her seduction plan with Jaye. Not that he wouldn't approve, but—"Sex kitten?"

"You're one of the things Nick dreamed about. You and sex, you sexy little kitty-cat you." Jaye ruffled her hair. "Politically incorrect, no doubt, but who cares? The man wants you, you lucky girl. And his hair is very, very dark brown. You can't expect the cards to get every little detail exactly right."

Maggie forced her lips into a straight line. Being wanted by a man in the throes of delirium was no reason to grin like an idiot. "Actually, it seems to me the cards get almost everything wrong. And a certain psychic we both know and love should bone up on her ethics." Maggie grumbled to cover her confusion. Nick wanted her? So soon? "Isn't there some kind of confidentiality requirement?"

"I was there the last time she read your cards, remember? The cards said your next lover would have silver eyes and dark hair."

"Oh. Right. You *were* there. I forgot. But Shirley very distinctly said black, not dark. Not that it matters. I don't need a nudge from the beyond, or wherever Madame Fortunata gets her news flashes. I am perfectly capable of choosing my own lovers." Not that she had done such a good job of that up until now, but Maggie refused to believe a deck of cards could do any better. "Sex kitten? He didn't really say that. Did he?"

"His exact words." Jaye raised his right hand. "Swear. Shortly after I relieved Shirley, Nick half woke up, looked right at me, and asked, 'Where's the sex kitten?' Trust me, dolly. The man was not talking about Shirley. Or me. I am much too sophisticated and glamorous to be mistaken for a sex kitten. And never tell her I said so, but Shirley's a bit too . . . mature to be called any kind of kitten."

"Fever must have made Nick hallucinate. I am not a sex kitten."

"Eye of the beholder, doll. You are if he thinks you are. You're not offended, are you? I'm sure he meant it as a compliment."

"What does it mean, exactly?" It had to mean something offensive, but Maggie felt anything but insulted. Being called a sex kitten made her feel . . . lusty.

"Sex kitten? Let me think. To me, the term denotes

a certain playfulness, a youthful exuberance, a joie de vivre—all wrapped up in a body to die for." Jaye eyed Maggie from head to toe. "Oh, my dear. What I could do if I had your thighs . . ."

"Jaye Landry! Leave my thighs out of this discussion, if you please. As for Mr. Gerard, the man has pneumonia. And a fever. He can't be held responsible for anything he said."

"You're right, of course. We will forgive him for that blatantly sexist remark. We would anyway, wouldn't we? After all, he has silver eyes and—"

"*Brown* hair."

"Very, very dark brown," repeated Jaye, stroking his chin. "Methinks you protest a bit too warmly. Why? It's been what? Four years since your last romance? You are free to choose your lovers, like you said. But, Maggie, when are you going to exercise your power of choice? You could use a little love in your life."

"Love?" Maggie arched her brow, even though she knew from past attempts that she couldn't win an eyebrow-raising contest with Jaye.

"Lust, then. You're definitely ready for lust."

"How did you know?" Maggie blurted. She put her hand over her mouth.

"Aha! You are interested in our new neighbor." Jaye rubbed his hands together gleefully. "About frigging time."

"I am not. It's just that lately I've been thinking about . . . things."

"Like? Come on, Maggie. Tell me."

With a rueful grin, Maggie complied. "All right. I'm not interested in falling in love again." At Jaye's artfully raised brows, she quickly added, "Honestly. I had my chance at true love, and I blew it."

"You did not blow it. Robert was an ass."

"Yes, but he was the ass I chose to fall in love with. If my relationship with Robert proved anything, it proved that I'm no good at love. But sex is a different matter. I've never tried meaningless sex."

"Never?"

"When would I have had time? I met Robert when I was nineteen; we got engaged when I was twenty; then we stayed engaged until I was twenty-four. Since I've been in New Orleans, I've spent my time earning a living and starting my business." Maggie stopped to take a breath. "Anyhow, now that business is good, I have time for . . . stuff. So. I've been thinking about experimenting with lust."

"Lust? Meaningless sex? You?" Jaye shook his head. "Are you sure that's your style? I would have pegged you for love, marriage, family. Once you recovered from your erstwhile fiancé, that is."

That got her back up. "Not again. Not a chance. I am never getting married. I am sure about that. Very, very sure." She didn't bother explaining that one chance at love was genetically programmed into her. Every woman in her family for generations had loved once, and that love had lasted forever. Hers hadn't. End of love story.

Maggie eyed Jaye. "What I'm not sure about is lust. Casual sex might be exactly my style. If it is, I could spend the rest of my life having brief, torrid affairs with any man who strikes my fancy."

Jaye did not look convinced. "Far be it from me to discourage you from coming out of your shell. But a lifetime of affairs?"

"I wouldn't be staying home on Friday night."

"There is that. I suppose you might need to test the waters, kiss a few frogs as it were . . ."

"I'm not looking for a prince. Or happily ever after. Only for . . . satisfaction."

"Magnolia Mayfair!" Jaye gasped and bit a knuckle. "I think I'm shocked."

"You are not." Jaye could pretend to be shocked, but Maggie sensed he was on the verge of agreeing with her. She began to feel a little panicky. Talking about lust was one thing. Doing something about it was another thing altogether. "Do you really think it's not my style?"

"You won't know for sure until you try." Jaye's lips curved in a sly smile.

Maggie drew her brows together. "It was Robert's style. Robert had six simultaneous affairs when he was engaged to me. He certainly seemed to be having a good time."

"Robert was a cad and a bounder. And a sex addict, to boot. That's not you, sweety. Or me, for that matter. For myself, I want a long-term, committed relationship." Jaye sighed. "If only I could find the right man."

"That's what I thought," said Maggie. "But my soul mate turned out to be a complete jerk. You only get one Mr. Right, you know. On the other hand, a woman could probably count on an inexhaustible supply of Mr. Wrongs."

"Is that what you had in mind for Gerard?" Jaye indicated the bedroom with his shoulder. "Were you thinking about seducing him?"

"Thinking is as far as I've gotten, and it's probably as far as I'll ever get. Nick is a stranger. For all we know, he's married with two point four children." Even as she voiced the disclaimer, Maggie felt her heartbeat speeding up again. A married man wouldn't dream about another woman, would he? Robert's face appeared in her mind's eye. He might.

"He's not married."

"You can't know that."

"No ring. And he has silver eyes."

"Not that again."

Jaye yawned. "If I'm repeating myself, it's time to go. The sun's up. I can sleep now. Call me if you need me to take another shift. I could get into nursing. One feels so needed. Plus, I've always wanted to date a doctor. Think Charity Hospital could use another candy striper? I'd look good in those cute little uniforms they wear."

"It would be the hospital's gain, that's for sure." Maggie waved Jaye out of the apartment, then started the coffee brewing. She put the milk in the refrigerator and left the mugs and pot on the kitchen counter. Maggie looked around, wondering what to do next. She cocked her head, listening for any sound coming from the bedroom.

Nothing.

Maggie tapped her foot—quietly. She ought to wait in the kitchen until she heard Nick stir. She certainly did not want to watch a man sleep, not even a man who thought she was a . . . sex kitten.

Instead of obsessing about sex, she could do something useful while she waited for Nick to wake up. She could go downstairs and get the mask she had been putting finishing touches on last night. Maggie took one step toward the door to the hallway, then stopped.

Maybe she ought to check on Nick first. What if he was feverish? Hallucinating? He might belong in a hospital. It was her duty to make sure he was all right.

Maggie squared her shoulders and walked to the

bedroom, halting in the open doorway. Shadows filled the room. The third-floor balcony shaded the French doors and kept most of the sunlight from entering the second-floor apartment, just as Nick's balcony kept her apartment in perpetual need of artificial light. Automatically, Maggie reached for the light switch, stopping herself just before she flicked on the ceiling light. She didn't want to wake Nick. Dr. Martin had said he needed rest.

Nick was on his back, one arm flung over his head, the other tucked beneath the quilt, which had slipped halfway down his chest. His eyes were closed. Nick's breathing sounded a bit wheezy, but much better than the night before. She hadn't heard him cough since she had been in his apartment. Surely that was a good sign.

Maggie's gaze slid from Nick's face to his shoulders. They looked broader in the daylight. And how had she missed the dark hair on his chest last night? Nick had a body to die for, and he had called her a sex kitten. Maggie had the most outrageous urge to crawl in bed, curl up next to Nick, and purr.

She blinked. All that bare, male flesh was making her light-headed. Sternly reminding herself that she was there to check out Nick's health, not his body, Maggie approached the bed. She reached out a hand, intending to feel his forehead.

Nick's eyes snapped open, and he caught her hand before she could touch him. He had a strong grip for a sick man, and his firm grip was doing intriguing things to her pulse rate. "Why're you dressed?"

"I beg your par—mumph."

With a tug, Nick pulled her on top of him. "Why're you dressed? Should be naked." He wrapped his arms around her, pinning her arms with his.

Naked? Maggie struggled to free herself. Her squirming only made things worse. Or better, depending on one's point of view. Sprawled on top of him, unable to use her hands to push free, she gasped, "What are you doing? Nick?"

"Magnolia." Nick moved one hand to the back of Maggie's head and pulled her face close. Before she could use her free hand to push herself off of him, his mouth clamped onto hers.

His hot, dry mouth. The man had a fever, he was dehydrated, and he still had her hormones doing back flips and splits. She stopped wiggling and let her body mold itself to his. One of her knees slipped between his legs.

Lust rocks, thought Maggie, sinking into the kiss. Nick slid his tongue along the curve of her lower lip, and she opened her mouth for him.

Nick used his tongue to taste, his teeth to nip, his mouth to arouse. His hands were on her face, her shoulders, her back. He cupped her bottom, holding her against his erection. Maggie's senses were filled with Nick, his taste, his smell, his touch.

The kiss ended abruptly.

Nick released her so suddenly Maggie almost fell off the bed. As he struggled into a sitting position, she did fall off of him. Maggie managed to catch herself before she tumbled to the floor, ending up perched on the very edge of the bed, her hip next to his thigh.

Gazing at her through narrowed eyes, Nick asked, "Do I know you?"

Maggie got off the bed. "Not well," she managed, still breathless from Nick's kiss. "But we have met. Last night you—"

"New Orleans." Nick interrupted her. "I'm in New Orleans. You're the mask maker."

"That's right. You arrived late last night. You were—are sick. Why did you kiss me? And why did you say I should be naked?"

"I'm never"—Nick coughed—"sick." The bed-clothes slithered lower, falling below his waist and exposing washboard abs.

Sucking in a breath, Maggie grabbed the covers and tucked the sheet and quilt under his chin. Nick gave her a quizzical look. "Uh. You need to keep your chest warm. You *are* sick—you have pneumonia. But Doc Martin said you weren't so sick that you need to be in a hospital. He prescribed an antibiotic, plenty of liquids, and bed rest. You should be fine in a few days if you take care of yourself. About that kiss—"

Nick coughed again, interrupting her. "Sorry about that. Someone else was here the last time I woke up. A woman in a red dress. Her mascara was running."

"His mascara. That was Jaye. Jaye Landry. In costume. Jaye is a female impersonator. He stopped by on his way home from work. Did you mean to kiss Jaye?"

"I didn't mean to kiss anyone. Female impersonator?"

"Yes. Is that a problem for you?" Maggie fitted her palm to Nick's forehead, irked that Nick could dismiss kissing her breathless so easily. She shouldn't be having trouble breathing—he was the one with pneumonia.

Nick shook his head. "No. How do I feel?"

"Good. I mean, warm. You must still have a little fever." Nick was radiating heat. Maggie took her hand away from his forehead. Reluctantly. Her fingers were itching to stroke his hair, which was brown, not black. And in the shadowy room, now that his passion had cooled, Nick's eyes were gray.

Nick sniffed the air. "Is that coffee I smell?"

Forcing herself to forget about the kiss—she could if he could—Maggie nodded. "Yes. Would you like a cup? It has chicory in it. I only had New Orleans blend. I can heat milk for café au lait, or do you prefer it black . . . ?"

"Café au lait sounds good." His stomach rumbled. "What's for breakfast?"

"I wasn't sure what you'd want to eat. I have oatmeal and grits. I could fix toast. I'll have to go back downstairs to get whatever you decide on. I couldn't carry everything upstairs on the tray." She was babbling, and she couldn't stop, even though she knew exactly why she was acting like a ninny. It had to do with being kissed before she had had breakfast.

Her hormones were working overtime to prove to her that her instincts were right. It was time—past time—for her to take a chance on lust. She certainly was having trouble focusing on anything but the very male body in the bed. Guiltily, she met the male's gaze. Nick was looking at her hungrily.

Oh, lord. He wanted coffee. "Coffee. Yes. I'll get it right away." Maggie hurried to the kitchen, heated the milk, and added the coffee and hot milk to a mug. She carried the steaming mug to the bedroom and gave it to Nick.

He took a sip of coffee and closed his eyes, a look of bliss on his face. "Good," he said, opening his eyes. "Thanks. You and Jaye aren't the only ones who were here last night. There were a lot of people. In the kitchen, and then here, in my bedroom. A lot of people. More people than I've ever had in my bedroom at one time."

Nick seemed fixated on that fact—the poor man must not have any family. Not even a wife. Maggie snuck a glance at his left hand. No ring. Not conclusive, but he didn't act like a married man—unless he had mistaken her for his wife when he had pulled her into bed with him. "They were the other tenants. We've been taking turns looking after you. Are you married?"

Nick shuddered. "No. Not married, engaged, or involved. Thank God." He narrowed his gaze suspiciously. "Why do you ask?"

"No reason." No reason she was ready to share, kiss or no kiss. Nick had forgotten the kiss. Hopefully because of his fever, not because the kiss wasn't memorable. "Who else do you remember from last night?"

"I remember a woman wearing a purple silk robe. She stuffed a pill down me, and then she read my palm. Said I would be a *New York Times* best-selling author."

"That's Shirley Wyclowsky, known professionally as Madame Fortunata. She owns a tea and fortune-telling shop across the street. Shirley took the first watch; then Jaye came and sat with you."

"Before that, there was an elderly man, something of a curmudgeon. I think he's the one who undressed me and put me to bed. He asked me about my muse. When I said I didn't have one, he told me I should forget about writing and get a real job."

"The professor. Edmund Wellington. His apartment is on the third floor, above yours. He taught history at Tulane until he retired last year. Ed is grumpy because he hasn't figured out what to do with himself yet."

"I remember you, too. You fed me soup, and then I went to sleep."

"Yes. But that was turkey gumbo, not soup."

"Yeah. Gumbo." Nick's glance slid to the trap door. "Your bedroom is under this room. Our bedrooms are connected by a staircase."

"That's right. We talked about *Seven Year Itch*. What else do you remember?"

Nick's gaze zeroed in on her mouth. "I kissed you. Damn."

"Damn?"

"I shouldn't have kissed you. You're not my—that is, I'm probably contagious."

She wasn't what? His type? What kind of type did he expect for a brief affair? A sex kitten ought to be just right for that. "I've had a pneumonia shot."

"That's good to know. About that kiss. I'm sorry. I don't usually manhandle women I've just met." Nick rubbed his forehead. "I had a reason . . . a dream, I think."

Nick remembered the dream. He had dreamed about Maggie. A very sexy dream. Seeing the trap door at the edge of the Persian rug brought it all back.

In his dream, he had been in bed, almost asleep. Then he had seen a dainty hand slowly push the trap door open. The hand had been attached to a slender wrist, a silky arm, bare shoulders. . . . Magnolia Mayfair had opened the trap door, walked up the last few steps, crossed the room to his bed.

She had been naked.

Nick pushed the quilt aside. He was burning up.

Maggie immediately pulled the covers up and tucked them under his chin. "You have to keep warm."

"I don't need the covers. I'm hot." Nick shoved the covers off again. He had dreamed about Magnolia

Mayfair, a marrying kind of woman if he had ever come face-to-face with one. Then he had kissed her.

Only something out of the ordinary could make him kiss a woman who cooked, sewed, and nurtured.

It had to be the pneumonia.

Or that crazy dream.

"You do need to stay covered. Otherwise, you'll get a chill. You want to get well, don't you? Here, let me fluff your pillows."

Nick eyed Maggie as she fussed with the pillows. He was being cosseted by a mask maker. With help from a female impersonator, a college professor, and a fortune-teller.

A fascinating group, his tenants.

His trouble-making tenants.

Nick remembered to be suspicious. "Why are you people being so nice to me? You don't know me."

"You're here. We're here. Why wouldn't we be nice to you? Raise up." Nick raised his head, and she replaced the pillows.

She seemed genuinely puzzled that he would ask such a question. Nick improvised an explanation. "I could be a serial killer for all you know. Or a sex maniac."

Maggie laughed. "I don't think so. Emcee wouldn't be sleeping on your bed if you were dangerous." She pointed to a black lump on the foot of the bed.

"That's a cat? I thought it was a fuzzy pillow. What did you call him?"

"Emcee—short for Marcel's cat. Or marvelous cat. Emcee prefers magnificent cat."

"M.C. I get it. Marcel's cat?"

Maggie nodded. "I inherited Emcee from his former owner—Marcel Beaulieu. Marcel lived in this apartment until he passed away."

Nick nudged the lump with his foot. It did not move. His grandfather had owned a cat when Nick had visited him. It had given him a nasty scratch when he had tried to pet it. Scowling at the lump, Nick said, "I hate cats."

"Do you really? I thought . . . How do you feel about kittens?"

A vague memory tickled Nick's brain. Something to do with . . . something. He couldn't remember. "Kittens. Cats. Same thing. I don't like felines."

"Oh." Maggie looked disappointed for a brief moment. Then she grinned. "But that explains it. Emcee hates people who like cats."

"And likes people who hate cats?"

"Perverse of him, isn't it?"

"You must like cats if you adopted him."

"I do. And Emcee tolerates me because I give him affection and food."

"Speaking of which . . ." Nick wasn't sure if he meant food or affection. There was something very appealing about Magnolia Mayfair. She had a wholesome sexiness, a combination of playfulness and sensuality he had never encountered before. Nick reached out to take her hand.

Maggie backed away from his bed, avoiding his questing hand. "I can make oatmeal or grits. Which will it be?"

"How about bacon and eggs?"

"I don't think so. I'm sure that's much too heavy for you in your condition."

Nick noted the stubborn angle of Maggie's chin and decided he was too weak to argue with her. "Oatmeal, then."

Maggie headed for the door.

"Wait. Oatmeal with brown sugar?"

She turned around and smiled at him. "Is that how your mother made it?"

Nick snorted. "Not my mother. Not any of the step-mothers, either. One of the cooks at the first boarding school I went to made oatmeal with brown sugar."

"Boarding school? Stepmothers? How many do you have?"

Nick shrugged, sending the quilt sliding off his shoulders. "I've lost count."

"Really? My goodness. That's . . . interesting." Maggie looked as if she would like to know more—curiosity gleamed in her green eyes. Curiosity, and something that looked suspiciously like pity. Pity was the last thing he wanted from Maggie. What he wanted was . . . her.

Nick's mouth dropped open. No. Not a chance. He could not want a woman who knew how to make oatmeal with brown sugar.

"Are you all right? You've got a funny look on your face."

"Fine. I'm fine," Nick croaked. "Food?"

"Oh, right. Oatmeal with brown sugar coming up."

"Toast, too, please. And more coffee."

When Maggie returned with the tray, Nick dug in. He finished the meal and leaned back against the pillows with a satisfied sigh.

"More café au lait?"

"No, thanks. Oatmeal's not so bad. I hadn't had oatmeal in, oh, twenty years. Maybe longer."

"How long have you been a writer?"

"Not very long. I'm trying to make a career change here."

"Oh, yes. You said that last night. That explains it."

"What?"

"Why we had never heard of you. And why the library didn't have any books by you. Career change, huh? Midlife crisis?"

Midlife? How old did she think he was? "I'm thirty-four. That's not middle-aged." His protest sounded defensive and weak. "How old are you?"

"Twenty-eight."

"You look younger. You checked up on me at the library?"

"Yes. And on the Internet. We Googled you. How much younger?"

"Twenty-five, tops. Must be the lack of makeup. And your clothes." Maggie was wearing a dress made of some silky material the same shade of green as her eyes. "Find anything? About me, that is." Nick kept his tone disinterested, but he was alert.

Nick jealously guarded his privacy, purposefully maintaining a low profile. Being forgettable was an advantage in his chosen profession. Not all problems showed up on a balance sheet. Sometimes Nick had to go undercover to find out why a company was losing money. Still, something could have turned up about him on the Internet.

"Not a word. You are a man of mystery. What's wrong with my clothes?"

He let out the breath he had been holding. Which made him cough. When he stopped coughing, Nick pointed out, "Your clothes are not exactly current fashion."

"No. Vintage. This outfit is from the late forties."

"Oh. Vintage. Why?"

"I like old clothes. I'm an old-fashioned girl." She smiled at him.

Momentarily dazzled by her smile, Nick blinked. "Not that. Why did you try to find out about me?"

"Shameless curiosity. Corinne said you were a

writer. We wanted to know what kind of books you write. We didn't know this was your first attempt. What did you do before?"

"Let's see." Better to stick close to the truth, Nick decided. He could tell her where he had worked, without revealing his exact position. "I've worked for a clock company, a fabric store, and a hardware company, among others." He ticked off a list of clients whose businesses he had rescued. "Most recently, I worked for a New York magazine. That's where I got the idea to write a novel."

"Lordy me. Your résumé is almost as varied as mine. Neither of us can match Shirley, though—she's been everything from a stripper to a psychic."

"Yeah? What jobs have you held?" Nick had a sudden vision of Maggie and ostrich feathers. "Were you ever an exotic dancer?"

"No. Never."

"No guts?"

"No boobs."

Nick had to look at her chest. Small, but firm and nicely shaped. Perky. Maggie had perky breasts. He forced himself to look at her face. She had turned pink. When was the last time he had seen a woman over eighteen blush? "What have you done, then?"

"The list is too long to go into right now. I've got to go to work. Don't worry about the dishes. I'll get them later. And don't forget to take your pill. If you need anything, pound on the floor."

"You're going to leave me alone?"

"I have to go. My shop opens at ten o'clock. So does Oracles. That's Shirley's tea and tarot shop. Jaye is sleeping, but I could ask the professor to sit with you if you don't want to be by yourself."

"Not the professor. What about the other guy?"

"What other guy?"

"You know. He was here last night—the one about my age. He wore some kind of costume."

Maggie shook her head. "No one else was here. Oh—maybe you're remembering the doctor. Except . . ."

"What?"

"Doc's older than you, more the professor's generation."

"I remember the doctor. But that reminds me—how did you get a doctor to make a house call?"

"There's a doc-in-the-box clinic at the pharmacy on the corner—only three doors down. Doc has an apartment above the clinic. You must have dreamed the other man."

"Maybe." Nick's eyes narrowed. "Or maybe I saw a ghost."

Maggie gave a guilty start. "G-ghost?"

"You jumped like you believe in ghosts. Is this place haunted?"

"Oh, my lordy me." Maggie glanced at her watch. "Look at the time. It's later than I thought—almost nine o'clock. I really must go. I have to put the finishing touches on a couple of masks before I open up my shop. You'll be all right alone, won't you?"

"Sure. Being alone is the story of my life."

Four

Nicholas Gerard had kissed her on the mouth.

Maggie ran her tongue over her lips as she floated down the stairs. She could taste him still. And her body retained his heat in all the places where his body had touched hers.

Nick wanted her. He must. Why else would he have called her sex kitten? And men didn't go around kissing women who repulsed them, did they? Maggie's lips curved in a smug grin. He might not want to want her—he had tried to ignore the kiss, after all—but apparently he found her irresistible.

Maggie's grin widened. She could be good at this meaningless sex business. The first kiss had already happened, and she hadn't had to do a thing but show up. Nick had taken the first step. Her hormones agreed—they were doing back flips and somersaults, signaling their readiness for step number two in the lust experiment.

Stopping one step before the bottom of the stairs, Maggie tapped her fingers on the handrail. Maybe, just maybe, she ought to think before she took another step. She knew how her hormones would vote, but it might be a good idea to get her brain cells involved.

Maggie took a deep, calming breath, stepped onto

the brick courtyard, and opened the wrought-iron gate. She wanted to skip, but she forced herself to walk down the passageway at a sedate pace. When she was in her shop, behind her counter, she felt settled enough to think clearly about what had just happened.

And what should happen next. She might have lost her one chance at true and lasting love, thanks to Robert the rat, but, hormones aside, was she really ready for a shallow, short affair?

It went without saying that she was no good at committed relationships. It did not necessarily follow that she should spend the rest of her life flitting from man to man like some nectar-starved butterfly bouncing from gardenias to honeysuckle and back again.

There was another alternative, a solid Midwestern alternative. Maggie could decide to emulate her Aunt Maureen. Aunt Maureen was a respectable spinster, a woman who had never married, but who enjoyed her single life. Her single, *celibate* life. Aunt Maureen did not have casual affairs.

Aunt Maureen had cats. Three of them.

Maggie had Emcee. Marcel's cat had chosen her as his new mistress, not Shirley, Ed, or Jaye. Maybe that was a sign, one of those omens Shirley was always going on about. Fate might be telling her that Emcee and his progeny were destined to be her future, not Nick and the nameless men who would succeed him in her bed.

How many men? asked a pesky voice in the back of her mind, sounding lasciviously intrigued. *Shut up,* Maggie told the voice, obviously her hormones' spokesperson. *I'm trying to think here.*

What did she know about Nick? Other than he possessed a lust-inspiring body and mouth designed for passion? Maggie sighed. Nick could kiss like a dream, even when he was half-awake. That was definitely a point in the pro column. If fate were involved, as Shirley believed, it might be responsible for Nick and his silver eyes showing up at the exact same time her long-dormant sex drive had reawakened.

Okay. Nick was sexy. And convenient, what with the spiral staircase leading from her bedroom to his.

But she needed to review *all* the facts before making a final decision. Deciding to have a brief affair with a man she had only just met would be a life-changing event for her. This could be the first step along a road she knew nothing about. Maggie did not want to make a mistake.

All right. What else did she know about Nick? He had arrived in New Orleans coughing and with a fever. He must have been sick for several days before he ever left New York. Why hadn't anyone there seen that he was ill? He had a family—too much family if she had understood his remark about multiple stepmothers.

Nick had a lot of family, but they were not close. His parents had sent him to boarding school. Not one of his relatives had ever made him oatmeal with brown sugar.

Maggie felt her insides begin to go mushy at the thought of Nick, alone and unloved. Ruthlessly, she sucked in her stomach. Emotions should play no part in her analysis. She had to stick to the facts.

It was a fact that Nick had been suspicious of her and the others. He hadn't understood why they had called a doctor and watched over him. Nick Gerard was not used to depending on the kindness of strangers.

So. Nick was a loner. And a man who moved from

job to job. He had a checkered employment history. Well. They had that in common. Her résumé would not stand up to scrutiny, either, not if someone was looking for focus and stability.

Focus and stability were the traits a person looked for in a mate. Surely those kinds of things had no part in selecting a temporary lover. A lover should be attractive and attracted. And available. Maggie had no intention of fooling around with another woman's man.

She was attracted. She was available. Nick was attractive. He was available. But . . . Nick had scowled ferociously when he had said he wasn't involved with anyone.

What was that about? The thought occurred to her that Nick might have recently ended a relationship. Would it matter if he was on the rebound?

What if he didn't want to be involved? Maybe Nick was morally opposed to casual affairs. Or perhaps he eschewed meaningless sex for health reasons. Chewing on her bottom lip, Maggie considered that possibility.

Could she overcome his objections? Should she? Maggie absolutely hated it when people tried to force their beliefs on her.

On the other hand, Nick had called her a sex kitten. Nick had kissed her. Those did not seem to be the acts of a man unwilling to have a harmless fling.

Nick had been asleep when he called her a sex kitten, and only half awake when he had kissed her. He said the kiss was the result of a dream. For all she knew, Nick's conscious wants could differ markedly from his subconscious desires.

He had been *almost* awake when he kissed her.

But Nick had *apologized* for the kiss. Maybe the

dream had been about another woman, and he had mistaken her for the woman of his dreams only because she had arrived at the crucial time. Maggie drew her brows into a frown. She should have asked him. She would, the very next time she saw him. Whatever the dream was, it could give her insight into Nick's feelings about—

There was a knock at the passageway door. The door opened, and the professor stuck his head in. "How's Gerard this morning?"

"Better, I think. He had an appetite. Nick ate two bowls of oatmeal and a couple of pieces of toast. I made sure he took his medicine, too. He has to take the antibiotic twice a day, with food."

"I'm glad the poor boy is feeling better. I was going to check up on him, but all's quiet on the second floor. He must be napping. If I hear him stirring around later, I'll look in on him. Who is making him lunch?"

"Shirley. And I'll take him dinner tonight."

"You seem to be doing more than your share, Maggie. We should work out a schedule, one that divides the duties relating to our new neighbor equally among all of us."

"Oh, I don't mind seeing to Nick's meals. But he could probably use some company during the day. You and Jaye could spend some time with him while Shirley and I are at work. Once Nick is feeling a little better, he'll be glad of company."

"That's a splendid idea. And if he tires of conversation, I could lend him a book or two." The professor stepped inside the door. Tugging on his collar, he cleared his throat. "Magnolia, my dear . . . Were you aware that certain people are matchmaking?"

"Matchmaking? Oh, you must mean Shirley and

her prediction about a man with silver eyes. Did she tell you about that?"

The professor nodded. "She and Jaye were discussing it last night. She has the notion that you and Gerard should . . . that is, she thinks that you and this man will become . . . close based on something she saw in her crystal ball. Humbug."

"Shirley doesn't use a crystal ball, Ed. You know that. tarot cards, palms, and tea leaves are her tools. She saw a man with silver eyes in my future when she read my cards."

"Gerard's eyes are gray, are they not?"

"Yes. But in a certain light, they do look silver." At Ed's scowl, she modified her statement. "Well. Silverish."

"And how do you feel about that?"

"What? Shirley's prediction?"

"Her blatant attempt to influence your choice of"— Ed cleared his throat again—"a significant other. Based on nothing more than her so-called psychic powers."

Maggie didn't want to be disloyal to Shirley. On the other hand, she didn't want Ed to think that she didn't appreciate his concern. "Oh, he may be an other, but I'm sure Nick won't be significant. How could he be? He's only going to be here for a short time."

"How long does it take?" Ed's cheeks turned pink. "That is to say, I've heard about love at first sight. That's why I'm concerned. I don't want to see you hurt again."

"That's sweet of you. But there's no need to worry. I won't be falling in love again. Not at first, second, or third sight. There is absolutely no chance that Nicholas Gerard will break my heart."

Ed looked dubious. "I hope you're right. Be careful, Magnolia."

"I will. Thank you."

Nodding, the professor exited and closed the door. Maggie heard his footsteps retreating down the passageway to the courtyard. What a dear man Ed was. Exactly the kind of man who should have been her Mr. Right—kind, thoughtful.

Honorable.

Ed would never have juggled multiple lovers, not before and certainly not after he had become engaged.

Even without another engagement in her future, she would never have more than one lover at a time, Maggie decided. Even a temporary alliance needed trust. She would have to make sure any man she became involved with knew that.

Now. Where had she left off her analysis of Nick? Oh, yes. She had established that she and Nick were mutually attracted. And available. What next?

Well. The first step was easy. She had to wait for Nick to recover. She could not take advantage of him while he was weak and vulnerable. But once Dr. Martin gave him a clean bill of health—

Maggie gasped. "Oh, my lordy me."

What if a healthy Nick remained vulnerable?

Nick was thirty-four, an age when a single man might be thinking about settling down. She might not be in the market for a husband, but he could be looking for a wife. What if Nick fell in love with her? Maggie sucked in a breath.

Her heart was safe, but what about his? The last thing she wanted to do was break a man's, any man's, heart. Maggie remembered all too well what that felt like. She would not do that to another human being.

Not intentionally.

And not accidentally, either. The only way to avoid that possibility, however remote, would be to tell Nick exactly what she had in mind. Before she took even one step toward her goal, she had to make her motivation clear. Lust at first sight, not love—

The grandfather clock in the corner chimed ten. Maggie got up and unlocked the Royal Street door.

Pushing Nick from her mind, she greeted her first customer of the day. But she glanced at the ceiling from time to time and listened for any sounds coming from the second-floor apartment.

Coughing woke Nick up from his nap. Someone else's coughing, not his. Raising his head off the pillow, Nick looked around. The bedroom was empty.

Except for the cat. Emcee had moved from the foot of the bed to the pillow next to Nick's. The cat's eyes slitted open. Emcee had green eyes, the same shade as Maggie's.

"Sorry I woke you. Did you cough?"

Emcee rolled onto his back, exposing his stomach. Nick rubbed it. "I'm told that you belonged to Grandfather Beaulieu. He must have done this." Petting Emcee's belly, Nick felt a connection with his grandfather he had never experienced when the old man was alive. His throat clogged, and Nick had a coughing fit of his own.

Emcee jumped off the bed and disappeared. Once the coughing had subsided, Nick decided he felt marginally better. He would feel a lot better once he had showered and shaved. Maybe good enough to do a little reconnoitering. He pushed aside the covers and got out of bed.

The bathroom contained a claw-foot tub that had to be six feet long—big enough for two—but no shower. Someone had put towels and a bar of soap on a round wooden stool next to the tub. Like all the rooms he had seen so far, the bathroom had French doors leading to the wooden balcony overlooking the courtyard. Sheer curtains obscured, but did not completely block the view.

French doors and high ceilings. Balconies and wisteria vines. Oatmeal and tub baths. Hildy would be enchanted with the ambiance. And with the sweet southern belle who lived downstairs.

Hildy had been matchmaking before there was any chance he would ever meet Magnolia Mayfair. She would be pulling out all the stops if she knew he had dreamed about Maggie. Lord knew what Hildy would think about him kissing his tenant. Nick scowled. Good thing he had left Hildy in New York, or he might be in real trouble. As it was, avoiding any permanent entanglement with the luscious Ms. Mayfair was only a matter of self-discipline.

Nick was very disciplined.

Making a mental note to call Hildy as soon as he had bathed and shaved, Nick started the water running in the tub, then went to get his razor and a change of clothes. At least no one had unpacked for him—that showed the tenants' nosiness had some limits, thank God.

Taking his clothes out of the suitcase, Nick looked for a closet. There wasn't one. Nick had a sudden memory of his grandfather explaining that the nineteenth century French Quarter buildings did not have closets because homes were taxed based on the number of rooms they contained, and closets were counted as rooms.

The razor wasn't in his suitcase.

Nick looked again but did not find it. It was possible that he had forgotten to pack it. Possible. But unlikely. His business required him to travel a lot. As a result, Nick could pack a suitcase in his sleep.

Nick hung his clothes in the armoire and slid the empty suitcase under the bed. The razor had not turned up. When he returned to the bathroom, the tub was half full of steaming water. He stepped into the tub and eased into the water. Leaning his head against the rim of the tub, he closed his eyes. He could get used to this.

After his bath, Nick dressed in jeans and a sweater. He sat on the bed, exhausted. A trip to the bathroom, not more than six or seven feet from the bed, a leisurely bath, and he felt as though he had run a marathon.

Nick coughed. Rest. The doctor had said he needed rest. The way he felt, lethargic and heavy, he didn't seem to have a choice in the matter. Stretching out on the bed, Nick pulled the quilt up and closed his eyes. He should look for evidence that would explain how the tenants had scared away every prospective buyer who had viewed the property. And he would. Later.

Nick's body ached, and he had no energy; but his brain would not let him sleep. Being in New Orleans, in his grandfather's apartment, made him wonder. What if he had made an effort to know Marcel? He had waited for his grandfather to make contact. Why? It wouldn't have killed him to send the first card, write the first letter, make the first phone call. Even if Marcel Beaulieu had not responded, at least he would have made the effort.

At the very least, he ought to have attended his

grandfather's funeral. He could tell himself he would have done exactly that had he known the time and place of his grandfather's burial, but Nick was not at all sure that was true. Given his usual attitude toward the family members he knew, he doubted he would have bothered to pay his last respects to a grandfather he had met only once.

Groaning, Nick rolled onto his stomach.

None of his family would come to his funeral. Not unless he specified that his will be read over his open grave.

At least Marcel had some people at his funeral. If the tenants had been with him when he died, it was a sure bet they had attended his grandfather's last rites.

His tenants were a friendly bunch. Considerate. And creative. He had to give them that. Nick had read all the repair reports with grudging admiration. Fake termites, phony electrical problems, bogus plumbing leaks.

And a ghost.

They were ingenious.

The ghost had been especially effective.

Ghost. Nick opened his eyes and stared at the corner of the room. There *had* been another man in the apartment last night. A man with a beard wearing old-fashioned clothes. Nick had seen him clearly. No. Not clearly at all. Now that he thought about it, the man had been kind of fuzzy around the edges.

Not a bad special effect. The fuzziness added just the right touch of otherworldliness. How had they managed that?

Why had they managed that? What kind of people were they, playing their tricks on a sick man?

The kind of people who watched over a stranger all night long.

That warm and fuzzy thought was quickly squelched. So they had been nice to him. So what? Southerners were known for their hospitality. It didn't mean they really liked him. Why would they? As far as they knew, he was an out-of-work, fledgling author. He couldn't do anything for them.

Even if he couldn't find hard proof, Nick knew for certain that his tenants were the people who were sabotaging the sale of his building. Corinne had described the horrified reactions of prospective buyers after they had heard strange noises or felt a cold spot. There were no cold spots in the apartment now. There damn well should not be. The new heating and air-conditioning unit had cost a small fortune.

He hadn't heard any strange noises, either. The man in the corner had been silent as . . . the grave. A chill ran up Nick's spine. Christ. He was letting a fake ghost give him the willies. No wonder buyers had been scared off.

There had to be something that would show him how the tenants had done it. As soon as he rested for a while, he would go over every inch of the apartment until he found concrete proof of their sabotage.

If Nick had had any doubts that the tenants were haunting his building, Maggie's face when he had said the word "ghost" would have erased them. She had had guilt written all over her face. Her very appealing face.

Maggie. The sexual tug was there. And it was mutual, Nick was sure of that. The way she had responded to that spontaneous kiss . . . He licked his lips, remembering the way Maggie's lips had softened and molded to his, the way her soft body had felt sprawled on top of him.

Sex appeal was not the only thing that made Maggie dangerously attractive. Maggie had taken care of him. She had covered him when he was cold, fed him when he was hungry. She had comforted, cuddled, and cosseted him.

Nick *liked* being cosseted by Maggie.

Resisting Magnolia Mayfair might be the hardest task he had ever set for himself. But he had to do it. She was not his type, and he sure as hell wasn't hers. Maggie was the kind of woman who required the kind of commitment Nick had sworn to avoid.

And he would avoid it. Her. He would have to avoid Maggie. No sense in exposing himself to that kind of temptation, not when pneumonia left him weak and vulnerable.

Not so weak that he couldn't use his talents, however. All he had to do was treat the problem like a turnaround consultation—Nick always had his clients set goals and match them up with priorities. First and foremost, Nick decided, he needed to get well. Then he would concentrate on exposing the tenants' plot.

His gaze strayed to the corner of the room next to the armoire. Now that he thought about it, he must have dreamed the man in the corner. None of the prospects had mentioned *seeing* a ghost. And the tenants had no reason to haunt him. No reason at all.

Yawning, Nick closed his eyes and went to sleep.

The sound of the hall door opening woke him up in the middle of a dream. The same dream. Blinking, Nick sat up and stared at the trap door. That thing was a menace. He had not dreamed the same dream twice in years, not since he had turned twelve.

The first three years he had been at boarding school, Nick had dreamed repeatedly about his mother and father coming to take him home. That dream had never come true.

This one would not come true, either. Magnolia Mayfair was not the kind of woman to walk up a spiral staircase wearing nothing but a smile. A seductive smile. Nick groaned, feeling his body begin to react to his thoughts. Aroused by a dream? He really was sick.

Shirley entered the room, giving Nick something else to focus on. Wisps of hair an improbable shade of red escaped from a green turban. The psychic wore a robelike creation with gold and purple stripes. Colorful plastic beads, also purple, green, and gold, hung around her neck. "Did you have a nice nap?" she asked.

Nick yawned. "Yeah. I did. Although how I could nap after sleeping all night, I don't know."

"Your body knows what it needs, and you need to rest. Hungry? Lunch is in the kitchen getting cold. Come on. Wait 'til you see what I've brought you. You'll think you've died and gone to heaven."

Nick followed her down the hall to the kitchen. "What have you got?"

Shirley pointed to the table. "Oyster stew. French bread. Abita Gold."

Nick eyed the long-neck bottle Shirley held up for his inspection. "That looks suspiciously like a cold beer."

"It is. You do like beer, don't you?"

"Oh, yeah." He reached for the bottle, twisted the cap off, and took a long, satisfying drink. Nick looked at the label. "I don't think I've ever had this brand, though."

"It's local. The brewery is north of the lake in Abita Springs. Don't worry. It's okay for you to have beer. Only one, though. I checked with Doc Martin. He may come by later to check on you, by the way. How do you feel about oysters?"

"I like them."

"Good. You know what they say—eat oysters, love longer." She winked at him. "How do you feel about that?"

"Aphrodisiacs?"

"Love. Are you in love with anyone?"

Nick tore off a piece of bread—the loaf was still warm—and spread it with butter. "No. Are you?"

"Not at the moment. But I'm always open to the idea. Love makes the world go round, after all."

"I wouldn't know. Are you flirting with me?"

Shirley choked on a spoonful of soup. "Good lord, no. I was only making conversation. Getting to know you. That's what neighbors do, you know."

"Oh. Well. You're succeeding at that. All of you. You sure are making me feel welcome."

"Why wouldn't we?" Shirley dipped her spoon into her bowl, capturing a plump oyster.

Nick found his own oyster and ate it, topping it off with a spoonful of creamy soup. "I don't know. Where I'm from, people wouldn't. I've lived in the same apartment for seven years, and I don't know one of my neighbors."

"Of course you don't. You're from New York."

"How did you know? Oh, I forgot. You're a psychic."

"There is that." Shirley winked at him again. "But the tag on your bag said JFK."

Nick grinned at her. "Maggie tells me the three of us have something in common—a varied job history."

"Yes. However, after several false starts, Maggie and I have found our life's work. I'm a very good psychic. And Maggie's masks are works of art. One of our local art critics called them soft sculptures." Shirley cocked her head to one side. "I think you've found your niche, too. You have the look of a writer."

"Do I? What does a writer look like?"

"Handsome, in a scruffy kind of way—"

Nick scratched his chin. "Guess I should have shaved, but I couldn't find my razor. I'll have to buy one when I go shopping for dishes and sheets and towels."

"I can pick up a razor for you at the pharmacy before I go back to work. You won't need to shop for the other items, either. Mr. Beaulieu's linens and china are packed away in the attic. The sheets and towels may smell musty, but a good washing will take care of that. The professor and I will bring the boxes down later."

"Beaulieu? The man who used to live in this apartment? Why are his things still here?"

Shirley wrinkled her nose. "Because none of his kin thought enough of him to attend his funeral. Not that he wasn't at least partially to blame. Marcel was the original grumpy old man. He claimed he hated his family."

Nick felt a stab of guilt. Shirley had verbalized his own thoughts—he ought to have attended his grandfather's funeral. But if he had, the tenants would know who he was. "Oh. Did Beaulieu have a big family?"

"Not that I know of. He mentioned a daughter a few times—Angelique Beaulieu. From the little he said about her, I gathered that they were estranged. We tried to contact her when Marcel passed, but we couldn't find a current address for her. Marcel's lawyer must have gotten in touch with her eventually, though."

"Why do you say that?"

"Angelique had to be the one who sold the building

to the present owner. Marcel wouldn't have willed his property to a New York corporation."

Nick began peeling the label off the long-neck bottle. "That would be the corporation that signed my lease?"

"Yes. Renaissance, Inc. We assumed you knew someone there."

Raising the bottle to his lips again, Nick said, "No. I don't think so." He was finding lying to Shirley harder than it should have been. He didn't owe any of his tenants honesty. They had not been honest with their landlord. To the contrary, they had been sneaky, underhanded, and dishonest.

Shirley tilted her head to one side. "Really. How did you find out about the apartment, then?"

"Ms. Ellis. A friend of mine recommended her real estate agency. I called her. She told me about this apartment—said it was one of the few that wouldn't require a minimum six-month lease."

"Oh, well. That makes sense. Too bad, though. We would like to talk to someone at Renaissance. We've tried writing and calling, but all we get is referrals back to Corinne."

"Why do you want to talk to someone at the corporation?"

"To persuade them to take the building off the market. Once it sells, all of us will have to move." The corners of her mouth drooped, and a mournful sigh escaped Shirley's lips.

"And you don't want to move." Nick managed to state the obvious without curling his lip into a sneer.

"No. We don't."

"Moving's a pain."

"Yes, especially when you've been in the same place for twenty years or more, like me and the professor.

But that's not the only reason. We're family. We don't want to be split up."

Family. His tenants thought of themselves as a family, just as Hildy had surmised. Amazing. Nick shuddered.

Shirley immediately put a hand on his forehead.

Gently pushing her hand away, Nick said, "I'm all right. Just a passing chill. The four of you couldn't find apartments together in another building?"

"We have tried. No luck so far, not for the rents we're paying here. Marcel kept the rents affordable."

Nick tore another hunk off the loaf of bread and slathered it with butter. "I suppose Maggie would have to move her business, too."

"She would. The sale of the building would hurt her most of all."

"Why? Wouldn't she be able to find another storefront for the same rent she pays here?"

"Not in the Quarter. Not anymore. Too many absentee landlords trying to wring every penny out of their property." Shirley made a disgusted noise. "They don't care about the neighborhood."

"Most people don't think of the French Quarter as a neighborhood."

"I know. Tourists think of it as an amusement park. Even the locals tend to forget that people live here. But it *is* a neighborhood. A very special one. The Quarter welcomes everyone, especially the lost souls who aren't welcome anywhere else. Be sure to write about us—the denizens of the Vieux Carre—in your book."

"I don't know if I could do you justice. I may not be a very good writer."

"I think you're better than you know. You're clear-eyed—that denotes honesty. A good writer writes the truth."

Nick managed not to squirm. Shirley couldn't be a very good psychic if she thought he was being honest with her. "The truth is . . . This is the best oyster stew I've ever had."

"I'll tell the chef. It's from the oyster bar over on Bourbon Street. They've got good oyster po' boys, too, when your stomach is ready for something more solid."

"That may be very soon." Nick coughed. "I hope."

"You still sound a little wheezy, even when you're not coughing. And you felt warm to me, too warm. Maybe you got up too soon. What have you been doing this morning?"

"Nothing strenuous, believe me. I took a bath and got dressed, that's all. That tired me out enough that I had to take a nap."

"Well. Don't push yourself. There's not much that can't wait for another day."

"That's an interesting outlook. I've always tried to do everything today, on the chance there won't be a tomorrow."

"Give me your hand."

Nick offered her his right hand. Shirley turned it palm up. "You have a long lifeline—plenty of tomorrows."

"Good to know." He took his hand back, although he had to tug to do it. Nick had the fanciful thought that his hand might tell Shirley all his secrets if he gave her enough time. "Right now, I'm feeling like I've used them all up."

"You need a pill. And a nap. Let's get you back to bed." She herded him into the bedroom, waited until he had removed his shoes and stretched out, then covered him with the quilt. "Go to sleep," she ordered. "Doc Martin is coming by later this afternoon to check on you, so you'd better follow orders and rest."

Nick had barely closed his eyes when Shirley returned. "Look what I found." She held up his razor.

"Where was it?"

"On the gallery, right outside your bedroom. What were you doing out there?"

"I haven't been outside."

"I don't remember seeing it when I brought your lunch. But that's where it was."

"Jaye. Maybe he borrowed it."

"No. Jaye doesn't shave, not even his legs. He waxes." Shirley looked at her feet. Emcee was rubbing against her ankles. "Oh. Here's the culprit."

"The cat?"

"Your razor is silver. Emcee likes shiny things. He's always stealing Jaye's costume jewelry. Or Maggie's. He leaves mine alone."

"A thieving cat?" Nick rubbed his chin. "Strange."

"Welcome to New Orleans." Shirley patted her purple turban and winked at him. "We're all a little strange."

"You're not strange. You make me feel at home." Nick did feel at home. Less than twenty-four hours with a mask maker, a cross-dresser, a curmudgeon, and a fortune-teller, and Nick felt as though he belonged.

That scared him more than any fake ghost ever could.

Five

Saturday night, Maggie closed her shop an hour early. Not a good business decision, since there were still tourists strolling up and down Royal Street. Closing the shop door almost in the face of customers, Maggie rationalized that she needed extra time to fix Nick's dinner. Feeding a sick man and making sure he took his medicine were more important than selling another mask or two.

Her true motive was not nearly so noble. Maggie simply could not wait another minute to see Nick again. Little electric shocks had been cruising up and down her spine in anticipation all afternoon. She wanted to talk to Nick, get to know him. Not that she needed to know that much about him. Only that he was basically a decent human being.

And whether or not he indulged in meaningless sex with casual acquaintances.

And if he intended to remain a bachelor for a few more years.

But she had to be subtle about it. Bluntly asking a man flat on his back with pneumonia how he felt about having a brief affair did not seem medically advisable. A shock to his system might set back Nick's recovery. As much as she would like to just come right out and ask him, she would have to be circumspect. If she played her cards right, surely she could find out what she needed to know by indirect means.

While Maggie prepared meatloaf, mashed potatoes, and green beans, she rehearsed various ways to bring sex into a conversation without being obvious. After several attempts, all of which depended on Nick giving her the right cues, she decided she would either have to give him a copy of the script she was writing in her head, or play it by ear.

Maggie ate first, barely tasting what she put in her mouth, then prepared a tray for Nick. Assuming Nick was following doctor's orders and resting, she went directly to the bedroom French doors and knocked.

Nick answered the door dressed in jeans and a navy crew-neck sweater. His hair was rumpled, and he was barefoot. He looked good enough to eat. Blinking, Maggie presented the tray for his inspection. "Dinner is served. Do you want to eat here in the bedroom on a tray, or in the kitchen? And don't you think you should put on some shoes? This floor is cold."

"I'm hot. I'll eat in the kitchen." Taking the tray from her, Nick stood aside and let her walk in front of him to the kitchen. "I've been in bed all day. Asleep most of it. I'm ready for food. And you."

"Me?" Maggie squeaked. She hadn't anticipated Nick being ready. Not in his condition. Not so soon.

"Yeah. I'm tired of talking to myself."

"Oh. You want to talk."

"And eat. I'm hungry. What's for dinner?"

"Comfort food. Meatloaf and mashed potatoes. And I brought a liter of ginger ale. You must be ready for something a little stronger than juice."

"I had a beer with lunch."

"Shirley gave you beer?"

"She checked with the doctor first." Nick eyed the single plate on the tray. "Aren't you eating?"

"I ate while I cooked. I wasn't sure if you would want company."

"I definitely want company." Nick held out a chair for her. "Stay and talk to me while I eat."

"I'll do that." Maggie took the empty tray and put it on the kitchen counter. "Oh, you've got a coffeepot."

"Yeah. Shirley loaned it to me, and she left enough coffee for me to make a pot in the morning."

"I'll get it ready now. Then all you'll have to do to-morrow is plug in the coffeepot." Maggie fixed the coffee, then sat down at the table. With her elbows on the table, Maggie rested her chin on her clasped hands. "You must be lonely. Being here all alone."

"I'm used to being alone. And I am seldom lonely. I wasn't today—I slept most of the day. The couple of times I woke up, someone was here. Shirley stayed for a while after lunch, and Ed stopped by this afternoon. He loaned me a book. This looks good." He picked up a fork and began eating.

"I bet Ed loaned you a history book. Or a biography. I prefer something a bit more . . . earthy. Like erotic romance." Maggie winced. Erotic romance? Not subtle. Not that Nick had noticed. He was con-centrating on eating, not looking at her. "Or mysteries. Give me an Agatha Christie or a Dorothy Sayers and I'm happy. Ed, on the other hand, reads nothing but history and biography."

"You know Ed well. He gave me a history of New Orleans. It's not bad. Not bad at all."

"This is a fascinating place. Especially the Quarter. Almost like a foreign country. I've been here for four years, and I still feel like I should go through customs when I cross Canal Street. The French Quarter is different from any other place in the United States, don't you think? More exotic. Sensual."

Pouring ginger ale into a plastic Bacchus cup, Nick asked, "Have you always lived in New Orleans?"

"Oh, no. I'm from Minnesota. St. Paul."

His eyebrows shot up. "Minnesota? That's a long way from here. How did you end up in New Orleans?"

"I came to Mardi Gras five years ago, and I forgot to go home." Maggie grinned at him. "That happens more often than you might think."

"Why did you stay?" He forked up a bite of meatloaf.

"I belong here." Maggie's eyes unfocused dreamily as she reminisced. "Mardi Gras was in early February that year, too. The weather was balmy like today, only warmer. Seventy degrees and sunny. I couldn't believe it, not when there was snow a foot deep back home. I *hate* cold weather." Recalling her purpose, Maggie batted her lashes at Nick. "I guess I needed someone to keep me warm."

Nick swallowed a mouthful of mashed potatoes. "Did you open your shop right away?"

Narrowing her eyes, Maggie did not answer immediately. Nick kept turning the conversation back to her. Most men loved talking about themselves. Either he was different from every man she had ever met, or Nick was trying to avoid telling her anything personal about himself. Finally, she responded. "No. I got a job at Shirley's place. Not reading cards—Shirley says I'm psychically challenged. I waitressed and worked the cash register. I've always quilted, and after my second Mardi Gras, I began playing around with quilting masks. At first, I sold them through the consignment shop on Toulouse—the shop Jaye mentioned—and continued working for Shirley. Then, three years ago, the storefront and apartment in this building became available, and voilà. Mayfair Masks was born. What about you? What made you decide to set your novel in New Orleans? The city's reputation for sin and sex?"

He shrugged. "It's as good a place as any. If you're from Minnesota, how did you get a name like Magnolia?"

"Mom. My mother always wanted to be a southern belle. She named all of us after southern flowers. My sisters are Jasmine and Camellia." She giggled. "Daddy always says it's lucky they had daughters. No way was he going to let Mom name a son of his Beauregard. Or Rhett."

"You're not an orphan, then."

Surprised, Maggie widened her eyes. "No. Why would you think that?"

"I don't know. Something someone said. All those jobs you've held. What were they?"

He was doing it again, keeping her talking about herself. "Let's see. I worked in a veterinarian's office when I was in high school—walking dogs, cleaning cages, that sort of thing. There were nice fringe benefits, though. I got to pet a lot of pets. I like petting, don't you?" She curved her lips in the sultry smile she had practiced in the mirror between customers.

"I never had a dog. Or a cat. Pets aren't allowed at boarding school. What did you do next?"

Maggie stopped smiling and began drumming her fingers on the table. Why couldn't she get Nick to talk about himself? She had never had any trouble getting Robert to wax poetic on the subject of Robert. "At college I worked as a receptionist in my dorm, announcing visitors, taking messages. My senior year I worked for one of the professors, doing his filing and some typing that his secretary didn't have time to do. Summers I did different things—camp counselor, waitress. One summer I worked in my father's office. Where did you go to college?"

"NYU. What does a mask maker major in? Art?"

"I didn't know I was a mask maker then. I have a degree in home economics. What did you—?"

Nick dropped his fork onto the empty plate. "Home economics?" He looked horrified. "I didn't know they still offered courses in that kind of thing."

"They do in Minnesota. And since I thought I was going to be a wife and mother, it seemed like a good idea at the time. I should have listened to my father and taken business courses. They would have been more useful. Then and now." A course in interrogating a potential lover would have been useful, too. How did one go about worming information out of a clam?

"Wife and mother?" Nick asked, his voice weak.

"Never going to happen. But I didn't know that then. And I did learn how to make patterns and sew, so it wasn't a total waste of time. Do you feel all right? You've gotten awfully pale."

He took a shuddering breath. "I'm all right. So. You make the patterns for your masks?"

"Uh huh. At first I did all the sewing and quilting, too, but now I employ others to help me."

"Business must be good."

"Good enough that I have time for other things. I haven't had time for much of a social life until recently. How about you? Do you date much?"

"Date? As in go out with women on a regular basis?" Maggie nodded. What else could it mean?

"Not much. Some. What does your father do?"

"He's an accountant. He wanted me to follow in his footsteps, but I didn't. What does your father do?"

"As little as possible. Did your father forgive you?"

"Sure. He really couldn't complain too much. My

sisters are both accountants. So is one of my brothers-in-law. The other one is a cop."

"Both your sisters are married?" Nick asked. There was a definite quaver in his voice.

"Yes. Jasmine has two kids, and Camellia is expecting her first. Are you sure you're all right? You're pale, and sweat is breaking out on your forehead. Maybe you should finish eating and go back to bed."

"No. I've spent most of the day in bed."

"I'm glad you're following the doctor's orders. Doc Martin said rest and lots of fluids. Would you like some more ginger ale?"

He held out his empty cup. "Yes, thank you. What made you say marriage wouldn't happen to you? It seems to run in your family."

"I was engaged for a while. It didn't work out. What about you? Have you ever been married?"

"Christ, no." He scowled at her. "I don't intend to be married. Not ever."

Finally. She had managed to get Nick to answer at least one of her questions. And he had given the right answer. Adamant. Nick was adamant about not marrying. On the other hand, a lot of men said that until they met the right woman. "Neither do I. Not that I have anything against marriage for other people. But I learned my lesson. It's not for me."

"Yeah. Right." Nick's expression could only be described as disbelieving.

"Honestly. I totally agree with you about marriage. How do you feel about love?"

Nick shoved his chair away from the table, as if he wanted to get farther away from her. "Define love."

"I don't think I can. It's one of those you'll-know-it-if-you-see-it kinds of things. Or know it if you feel it."

At Nick's blank look, she added, "What I really want to know is, are you looking to fall in love?"

"I am not. Listen, Ms. Mayfair—"

"And you're positive you're not interested in marriage? Why not? Or am I getting too personal?"

Gritting his teeth, Nick answered. "Yes, you are, but I'll tell you anyway. I don't intend to marry because I don't want any more family than I'm already stuck with."

"Oh." She had been right about that. Nick and his family were not close. "So you're not looking for a wife?"

Nick choked. "No! Look, Miss Mayfair. If you're on the prowl for a husband, you can cross me off your list of potential victims right now. I am not married. I have never been married. I will never be married. Is that clear?" His brows snapped together in a forbidding frown.

"Very clear." She beamed at him. "That's exactly what I wanted to hear."

"What?" His scowl faded, replaced by a confused look.

"I told you. I feel the same way." She made her thumb and forefinger almost touch. "I came that close to being married. It was horrible. I never intend to do that again. The last thing I want is a husband. Are you finished? Would you like anything else?"

"No. Thanks." He got up and took a step away from the table.

Nick was acting as though he was afraid of her. Maggie chewed on her bottom lip. That couldn't be right. She had done nothing to scare him. "How about a back rub?" Looking at Nick's broad shoulders had given Maggie a brainstorm. She did not have to limit her investigation to talk. Physical contact was another way to test the waters, so to speak. "Lying in bed all day sometimes makes your muscles tight."

"My muscles are fine." Nick rolled his shoulders back. "See? Loose as a goose."

"You're sure?" Maggie said. Now that she had brought it up, her fingers were itching to touch him.

"Yeah. Positive. No massage."

"How about a sponge bath? It's too bad there isn't a shower. I love my tub—I can lie down in mine—but sometimes a shower would be nice."

"I don't need a shower. Or a sponge bath. I managed to get in and out of the tub just fine. All by myself. I do not need your help." A muscle in his jaw was working.

"Well, if you're sure . . . Don't forget your pill. You're supposed to take it after eating."

"Yeah. I'll take it. As soon as you're gone."

Goodness, but he was wary. Maggie couldn't leave him to brood about her intentions, which he obviously thought were honorable. She would have to abandon subtlety in favor honesty. "I have a small television set. Would you like for me to bring it up? It would pass the time, if you get tired of reading."

Nick shook his head. "No, thanks. I couldn't deprive you of your TV."

"I wouldn't feel deprived. I never watch TV that much, especially at this time of year. Oh, sometimes I turn it on for background noise while I sew, but I have a radio. That's all I need." She slanted a look at him. "Maybe not *all* I need. I'll go get the set right now."

Maggie hurried out the door and down the stairs. It only took a minute to unplug the television set and carry it upstairs.

Nick had retreated to the front room, but he reappeared when she entered the hallway. "Where do you want this? Front room or bedroom?"

"Bedroom, I guess. I seem to be spending most of my time in there." He took the set from her.

Maggie followed him into the kitchen. "We have that in common. I spend a lot of time in my bedroom, too." She didn't bother adding that she spent her bedroom time, when she wasn't sleeping, working on her masks. "We think alike about things, too. That's nice, don't you think?"

Nick placed the small set on the kitchen counter. Slanting a wary look over his shoulder, he asked, "What things do we think alike about?"

"Well, for one, we both have an aversion to marriage." Maggie waited a beat before asking, "How do you feel about affairs?"

"Affairs?" Nick turned around and leaned against the counter. He rubbed his face with both hands. "You're losing me here."

"Oh. Sorry. I guess that wasn't clear. Are you opposed to casual affairs?"

Nick stared at her over the tops of his fingertips. "Why do you ask?"

She shrugged. "No special reason. Just trying to get to know you better."

Dropping his hands to his sides, Nick asked, "Why? I'm not going to be around for long. There's no need for us to become bosom buddies, much less lovers. I don't get involved with—"

"You are opposed to casual affairs." Maggie tried to hide her disappointment. "I knew that was a possibility, but I had hoped—never mind. I'll leave you alone now." She started for the kitchen door.

"Wait. You can't leave now."

When she looked back at him, Nick had a peculiar expression on his face. As if he hadn't meant to ask her to wait. He sat down at the kitchen table, then got up again, keeping the table between them. "Define casual affair."

"I can do that. Casual means brief, no strings, no emotional attachment. Affair means sex. Lots and lots of hot sex." Maggie watched as Nick's eyes turned silver. Interesting. Just the words "hot sex" could arouse a man. She would have to remember that for future use. Parting her lips, she moved closer to Nick, backing him up against the table. "How do you define it?"

He cleared his throat. "About the same." He raised his arms.

For a heart-stopping moment, Maggie thought Nick was going to take her in his arms. Instead, he reached behind him and grabbed the kitchen table with both hands. "And? Are you for or against sex?"

"You can put me in the pro-sex column. I am not opposed to casual affairs. With the right kind of woman."

"And she would be . . . ?" Maggie moved a centimeter closer, looking up at Nick with wide eyes.

Nick turned his head. "A woman who is not and does not want to be married." That muscle in his jaw twitched again.

"That's me," she said, beaming at him. She backed away from him and sat down. "So. I have this plan I wanted to run by you, if that's all right."

"A business plan?"

"No. A personal plan."

"How personal?"

"Pretty personal."

"Then, no. It's not all right."

Ignoring his plea, Maggie blurted, "The reason I brought up the subject of casual affairs is because I want to have one. With you. But not if you're involved with someone else, and not if you would expect an affair to turn into something more, and not if—"

"Wait. One. Minute." Nick began coughing.

"Oh, my lordy me. I've upset you. I'm sorry. I wasn't sure how to bring this up, but I thought you should know what I had in mind. I mean, you did kiss me, but I couldn't just jump you. Not when you're recovering from pneumonia. It wouldn't be fair. Or healthy. But I spoke too soon, and now you're coughing again, and it's all my fault."

Nick caught his breath. "No, it's not your fault. I'm coughing because I have pneumonia. Nothing to do with you. But, Maggie—"

"What?"

"I am not in the market for an affair."

Her face fell. "Oh. There is someone else."

"No, there is not someone else."

"I don't appeal to you, then."

"I find you very appealing. Hell, I dream about you every night."

"You dream about me?" Maggie got that mushy feeling inside again. "Then, why—?"

"I thought I made that clear. I am not in the market for a w-w-wi—"

"Wu-wu-wu? Oh, wife. But that's good. We have that in common, remember? I'm not ever going to marry, either."

"Of course you are. You've got w-w-wi—"

"Wife."

"—written all over you."

Maggie was outraged. "How can you say that? I just asked you to have a brief, no-strings-attached affair with me."

"It's a trick. Old as the hills. You don't expect me to fall for that, do you? One-night stand turns into brief affair turns into a *relationship*." He sneered the word. "And we all know what that means, don't we?"

"It is not a trick. I wouldn't trick you. I don't want a husband. All I want is sex. Hot, sweaty, mind-blowing sex. And, just to set the record straight, I did not say anything about a one-night stand." Maggie stood up fast, so fast she almost tipped the chair over. "Listen to me, Nick. I am not playing tricks. I'm doing the opposite. I'm telling you *exactly* what I want."

"Uh huh." Leaning against the counter, arms crossed in front of his chest, Nick nodded. "And if I fall for that, you'll sell me the Huey P. Long Bridge."

"I don't own the bridge, and why would you want it anyway? It shakes. I'm not talking about bridges. I am talking about sex. Meaningless yet mutually satisfying sex."

"Why me?"

"What?"

"Why did you choose me? There must be plenty of men right here in New Orleans who would jump at the chance to jump your bones. Why pick a stranger?"

"Because you're here now, but you won't be around for long. You're the perfect lover. Convenient, and temporary."

"Perfect, hmmm? A perfect chump, you mean." He took a step toward her. Looking down at her, Nick said, "Listen, Maggie. I mean it. I do not want to have an affair with you. Not today. Not tomorrow. Not ever. Is that clear?"

Maggie felt her chin begin to tremble. Oh, lord. Being turned down was bad enough. Was she going to be a cry baby about it, too? Snatching up Nick's empty plate and silverware, she slammed them on to the tray. "Couldn't be clearer. Sorry I bothered you."

She swept from the room, head high.

* * *

Magnolia Mayfair was out to get him.

Casual affair? Bull.

Miss Mayfair could say she wasn't interested in marriage until the sky turned green. He was not buying it. She had majored in home economics, for Christ's sake. Probably made the dean's list, too. And she thought she would trick him into having an affair with her? A woman made to be a w-w-wi—a married woman?

He had been right about her. She was dangerous.

Nick lugged the small television set into the bedroom and put it on the chest of drawers. Maybe he would stay up all night watching the tube. At least he wouldn't dream.

But he wouldn't get well that way. He had to get well. Well and strong. Resisting Maggie's overtures would be hard work for a healthy man. When she had backed him against the kitchen table, it had taken every ounce of strength to keep from hauling her against him. He had wanted to kiss those soft lips one more time. Groaning, he modified that wish. He had wanted more than one kiss from Magnolia Mayfair. A lot more.

Nick returned to the kitchen and took the antibiotic. While he was at it, he swallowed a couple of aspirin.

Once in bed, he fell asleep quickly.

Sunday morning, Nick woke up with a headache and an erection. That damn dream again. He could use a cold shower. He wasn't going to get it, not unless he gave up on his plan to expose the tenants' plot and checked into a hotel.

Barely suppressing a groan, Nick got out of bed. No green-eyed home ec major was running him out of his own building. He could handle Magnolia Mayfair.

If he were well, he wouldn't find Magnolia tempting at all. Not a woman who cooked, sewed, and cosseted. His illness made him weak, and it kept him dependent on her. As soon as he felt better, Nick told himself, he would have no trouble resisting Maggie's blatant overtures.

Until then, he could use a little help.

The next time Dr. Martin came by to check on him, he would ask for something to make him sleep.

Sleep, and not dream.

Maggie and her talk about casual affairs and hot sex should have added erotic overtones to his dream. Instead, her questions about love and marriage had turned his dream into a nightmare. The dream had begun as usual, with Maggie walking up the spiral staircase in the buff. But then the staircase had flattened into an aisle, with Maggie walking toward him completely dressed.

In a wedding gown.

That kind of nocturnal fantasy should have given him a relapse. The fact that he actually felt better must mean that he was well on the way to recovery. At the very least, he felt well enough not to spend the entire day in bed as he had on Saturday. He could begin looking for evidence of tenant sabotage.

Nick bathed and shaved, then dressed in khakis and a New York Yankees sweatshirt. When he went for his watch, he couldn't find it. He was sure he had left it on the bedside table the night before. It wasn't there.

Giving up, Nick went into the kitchen and plugged in the coffeepot. While he waited for the coffee to brew, he stared out the kitchen French doors. He heard footsteps on the stairs from the third floor. The professor walked by the French doors.

Nick tapped on the glass and opened the door.

"Good morning. You're up early. At least, I think it's early. I can't seem to find my watch."

"Morning, Gerard. You look like hell. Bad night?"

"Bad dream."

"Antibiotics sometimes induce vivid dreams."

So do spiral staircases and green-eyed mask makers, thought Nick. "That could be it. Join me for coffee? It's almost ready."

"Thank you, but not this morning. I'm on my way to mass at St. Louis Cathedral. When you're feeling better, I'll take you there. A church has been on that site since 1724. That first church was destroyed by the fire of 1788. And, of course, the cathedral was extensively remodeled in 1850, when—good lord. Here I am, boring you with history. Why didn't you tell me to stop?"

"I wasn't bored. Your students must have enjoyed your lectures."

The ex-professor turned a healthy shade of pink. "I don't know about that. I enjoyed teaching. I hope my students got some pleasure out of learning." Ed glanced at his watch. "Oh, my. Look at the time. I must be on my way."

"What time is it? I seem to have misplaced my watch."

"Seven o'clock. Maggie will probably be here around eight or so. If you're hungry now, I could tell her to hurry things up on my way out."

"Maggie's bringing me breakfast? She brought me dinner last night."

"Did she? We had better have a meeting and draw up a schedule that spreads the work around. Not that looking after you is a chore. Glad to be of assistance, all of us. But if Maggie is doing more than her share . . . well. I'll speak to the others later."

"I'm feeling much better today. I shouldn't need so much of everyone's time in a day or two."

"That's good to hear. But don't be in a hurry to be independent. Take all the time you need to get well."

"I'll do that." Nick saluted the professor as he continued on his way. Interesting old codger. Too bad he had had to retire. Ed had obviously enjoyed teaching.

Pouring himself a cup of coffee, Nick decided he felt good enough to do a cursory search of the apartment before Maggie arrived with breakfast. Looking for traces of the tenants' ghostly tricks would have the added bonus of giving him something to think about other than the mask maker downstairs.

Nick shook his head. Why she should be on his mind, awake and sleeping, made no sense. Magnolia Mayfair was not his type. She was a bride-in-waiting if ever he had met one. That should be more than enough to squelch the lustful feelings she and the dream inspired. Gritting his teeth, Nick focused on hunting for evidence.

He found nothing. Except his watch. Right on the bedside table where he had put it the night before. Why hadn't he seen it earlier? Maybe pneumonia had affected his eyesight. He would have to ask Dr. Martin about that, too.

Giving up the search for the time being, Nick unpacked his computer and cell phone and took them both to the front room. There was a desk next to the doors leading to the balcony. He set up the computer there, but he did not turn it on. It was only a prop, after all. He had no intention of writing a novel.

Sprawled on the surprisingly comfortable red velvet sofa in the front room, Nick stared at the ceiling. There was a reason he hadn't found anything incriminating. He should have figured that out sooner, before he had wasted time and energy searching every inch of the apartment.

Corinne Ellis must have told the tenants the second-floor apartment had been leased. Knowing the apartment was about to be occupied must have made the tenants remove whatever technology they had used to create the ghostly antics.

Ellis had said there were unexplained noises—terrifying moans, heart-wrenching groans—and a bone-chilling cold. If he had wanted to haunt someplace, how would he have gone about it?

After giving the problem some thought, Nick concluded that the noises could have been a voice-activated tape recorder concealed behind a loose brick. The tenants could have manufactured a cold spot with some kind of compact, heavy-duty air conditioner.

The "ghost" who had sat in the corner that first night had probably been nothing more than a friend of theirs, dressed in old-fashioned clothes. A trick of lighting—Jaye was in show business and would know about such things—could have made the man appear blurry.

If the tenants had removed the tape recorder and the chiller, why had they left the "ghost" behind? An oversight? And why hadn't any of the prospective buyers reported seeing a ghost?

Something odd was going on. The tenants and their fuzzy friend were haunting *him*. But why? As far as they knew, he was one of them, temporarily at least.

Unless Maggie had lied, and they had found out who he was. He hadn't bothered to use an alias, although he sometimes found that necessary in his work. Joining the staff of a company as a regular employee could be very useful, especially if the company was failing because of personnel weaknesses or personality clashes—things that would not necessarily show up on a balance sheet or a profit-and-loss statement.

But Nick had never worked in Louisiana. His connection with Marcel Beaulieu was not known. Or was it? What if his grandfather had talked to the tenants about his grandson? Nick immediately discarded that possibility. After that one visit, he had never seen Marcel Beaulieu again. The old man had never sent him so much as a postcard.

Nevertheless, his grandfather might have mentioned him in passing. Nick groaned. Why hadn't he thought of that possibility? He would have if he had planned the trip with his usual attention to detail. Instead, he had impulsively decided to visit New Orleans. Nick never did anything impulsively. He could blame that on being sick, too, he supposed. Blame didn't get the job done, however.

Suppose the tenants knew who he was?

That could explain Maggie's attempt to seduce him. She probably thought a man wouldn't sell a building out from under his lover. Nick felt a twinge of disappointment. He didn't want Maggie to have an ulterior motive for seduction. He hadn't wanted her to use sex as bait in a marriage trap. Nick didn't want saving her home and business to be Maggie's reason for coming on to him, either. Not even if that would explain her actions.

It did not explain the ghost.

Nick rubbed his forehead. His brain was as fuzzy as the man in the corner had been. If the tenants knew who he was, they would not haunt him. Putting a fake ghost in his bedroom would only give him the ammunition he needed to evict them. He must have imagined the silent man in the corner.

He had been feverish. Fever caused hallucinations. That made more sense than imagining the tenants had created a ghost just for him.

"Priorities, damn it. Get well, Gerard. Then maybe you'll be able to think straight."

Once he was himself again, he wouldn't be seeing fuzzy guys in the corners of rooms, and he wouldn't be dreaming about Magnolia Mayfair.

Six

"Seen the patient this morning?" asked Jaye.

Maggie shook her head in lieu of speech. Her mouth was full of beignet. Maggie and Jaye had a standing date for breakfast at Café du Monde on Monday mornings. Jaye did not perform on Sunday nights, and Monday was Maggie's day off. Once Maggie had swallowed the sugary bite, she asked, "You?"

"No." After Nick had practically thrown her out of his apartment Saturday night, Maggie had stayed well away from him. She had asked Shirley to take him Sunday breakfast.

"I saw Shirley in the courtyard earlier this morning. She said he seemed better than yesterday."

"Mmmm." Maggie had talked to Shirley late Sunday night. According to Shirley, Nick's fever had spiked alarmingly Sunday afternoon, prompting another visit from Doc Martin, and a stern warning not to get out of bed again for at least twenty-four hours. Maggie had a hard time not blaming herself for Nick's relapse. If she had kept to her plan of subtlety, it might not have happened.

Shirley and Ed had kept watch over him and had reported that he was resting, although not comfortably. Shirley had told Maggie that Nick tossed and turned a lot Sunday night.

So had she. Nick had rejected her before she had done anything but talk, in the most general of terms, about making him her lover. It seemed prudent to rein in her libido and wait for another man to come along. Her hormones had not agreed. Determined to make her crazy with lust, they had cooked up a disturbingly erotic dream for her Sunday night.

Maggie had dreamed she wore a cat costume like Michelle Pfeiffer had worn in one of the Batman movies. Nick had figured prominently in the dream as an animal trainer.

An animal trainer who specialized in sex kittens.

Good lord. She hadn't thought about sex for almost four years. But ever since Nick had showed up, flashing his silver eyes at her, Maggie couldn't seem to think of anything but sex. She wanted Nick.

But he did not want her.

Because he thought she was the marrying kind.

Feeling her face growing warm, Maggie hid behind her mug of coffee. She took another sip, then asked, "What if they both forgot?"

"I'm sure one of them looked in on him. What are you going to do today?" Jaye asked, licking powdered sugar off his top lip.

"What I always do on Mondays—grocery shop, laundry, clean my apartment. Plus, I've got some new patterns to send to my ladies." Maggie employed several women to sew and quilt the masks she designed. "I need to take those to the post office."

"All work . . . You know the rest."

Frowning in mock outrage, Maggie asked, "Are you calling me dull?"

Jaye shook his head. "Not dull so much as . . . unused."

That surprised her. "Jaye Landry! You think I should let someone use me?"

"For pleasure, Maggie. For pleasure. And you could use him right back. I thought you were going to give casual sex a try?"

"*You* thought that was a bad idea."

"I changed my mind. You need to live a little."

"I'm alive," Maggie protested.

"Alive, but asleep. Wake up and smell the roses."

"I thought it was wake up and smell the coffee. I can do that—see?" Maggie inhaled the rich aroma of her café au lait. "I'm alive, and I'm awake." She almost told Jaye about her cat woman dream. That would show him she was alive—even when she was asleep. But it would also reveal her unrequited attraction to Nick, something Maggie wasn't sure she was ready to share. It was too ego deflating.

"Are you? Let me rephrase my question. What are you going to do for fun today?"

Setting her empty coffee mug on the table, Maggie scowled at Jaye. "I don't know. It's such a pretty day, I may take a walk on the levee this afternoon after I mail the patterns. I'll probably drop by Second Hand Ro's on the way home." Jaye's disappointed look forced Maggie to add, "Shopping is fun."

"Solitary pursuits. That's what I mean. You're sleep-walking through life. Alone. You need a playmate."

"We play. You and I. What do *you* want to do today?"

"I have a lunch date, and this afternoon I'm going for the second fitting on my Mardi Gras ball gown. Why don't you ask the boy upstairs that question?"

"Nick?" Maggie's heart stuttered a beat. "I don't have time for Nick today."

"Maggie, Maggie, Maggie. Make time."

"What about my laundry? My dust bunnies? My groceries?"

"Like I said. All work . . ."

"Making masks is fun. I *like* making masks." A pattern for a cat mask blossomed in Maggie's mind. She could use black silk, pink velvet for the inside of the ears, outline the eyes with silver thread, and—

Jaye interrupted her design daydream with a wave of his hand. "I like dressing up like a girl. But they call it 'work' for a reason—I have to wax my legs and pluck my eyebrows, and my feet always hurt."

"You shouldn't wear such high heels. I can't spend the day with Nick. Nick doesn't like me." Hearing the tone of her voice, Maggie winced. She was whining.

"What? Where did you get that idea?"

"He told me, more or less. No, not less. More. Nick didn't even give me a chance to make improper advances before he rejected me."

"How? When?" Jaye leaned forward. "Tell me exactly what he said. No. First, tell me what you said. And did."

"Saturday night, when I took Nick dinner, I brought up the subject of meaningless sex. I was very open and direct. I asked him to have an affair with me and—"

"Magnolia Mayfair! You came right out and asked him? I'm in awe. That took guts. What did Nick say?"

"He said no. End of story."

"There's more to it than that. Why did he say no?"

"He thinks I have honorable intentions."

"What does that mean?"

"He seemed to think meaningless sex would be some kind of trick to get him to propose. Marriage, I mean. Nick thinks I'm wu-wu-wife material."

"What's with the stutter?"

"I was imitating Nick. He's so paranoid about marriage he can't even say the word wife. Nick says wu-wu-wu."

Jaye frowned. "Nick must have fallen fast and hard if he's got marriage on his mind."

"Jaye. The man told me to take my offer and—"

Waving a hand under her nose, Jaye shook his head. "He's running scared. As any red-blooded, afraid-of-commitment male would. Nick only just met you, and already he's got wedding bells ringing in his ears? Trust me, kitten, he's yours for the taking. All you have to do is make it clear you're not after a wedding ring. You aren't, are you?"

"After Robert? No way. I was smart enough not to marry my Mr. Right. I'm certainly not walking down the aisle for Mr. Wrong. But I did make it clear, Jaye, as clear as glass."

"With words." Jaye shook his head.

"Well. Yes. How else could I have made it clear?"

"Actions speak louder, doll. You won't mind a little critique of your methodology, will you?"

"I guess not. What do you think I did wrong?"

"Like I said, too much talk, not enough action. Next time, instead of asking Nick to have sex with you, make it impossible for him to avoid it."

"How? I don't own a gun."

"Maggie. Touch him."

"Touch him?"

"Come on. You know how to do this. Put your hand on his arm, brush against him in the hall. Stroke his fevered brow with your fingertips."

"As it happens, I thought of that. I offered to give him a massage and a sponge bath. Nick turned me down."

"Right idea. Wrong approach. Instead of asking him

if he wanted you to rub his back, you should have just done it."

"Oh. I'll remember that." Running her finger around the rim of her empty coffee cup, Maggie sighed. "For someone else. Nick is not the man for my experiment."

Shooting her a disgusted look, Jaye threw his paper napkin on the table. "Magnolia Mayfair. I am disappointed in you. One little setback, and you give up. Where's your fighting spirit?"

"Gone. Being rejected is not fun. Fun was the main object of this exercise, remember?"

"Think of it as a challenge. What kind of man walks away from a no-strings affair? We've already established that Nick is not gay. And that you turn him on. He called you a sex kitten, remember? I'll bet you any money he's kicking himself for turning you down."

"I doubt it. He thinks I'm after a proposal. I'm telling you, Jaye, the man is demented on the subject of marriage." She frowned. "Plus, I don't think he remembers the sex kitten thing."

"Yes, but you're not after marriage. Make nice. Be friends. Nick needs all the friends he can get right now." Jaye sighed dramatically. "Poor guy. All alone. Not knowing anyone in town. You really ought to spend the day with him. See what develops."

"I know what will develop. A serious case of low self-esteem. Mine. It's humiliating to have a man turn down an offer no man should be able to refuse."

"You didn't hear my subtext. I said be friends. I meant *pretend* all you want is friendship. Then, when you've lulled him into a sense of security, pounce."

"Pounce?" Her hormones formed a cheering squad. Pom-poms waved at the idea of pouncing on Nick. "Trick him, you mean? That's what Nick thinks I'm doing."

"Not exactly. He thinks you're trying to trick him into a wedding. The truth is you'll be tricking him into bed. Period. That is all you want, right? His body?"

"Oh, yeah." Maggie took a napkin from the holder and began dusting powdered sugar off the front of her Tulane sweatshirt. Her pulse was doing funny things, and she kept forgetting to breathe. If only thinking about approaching Nick again could do that to her, what would happen if she actually did it? On the other hand, nothing ventured. . . . Maggie eyed the last beignet on the saucer. "Are you going to eat that?"

"No. I've had my sugar fix for the week. You?"

"No. It would be a shame to waste it, though." Capitulating, Maggie grinned at Jaye. "I know—I'll take it to Nick. I'll toss it in his door, and if he doesn't toss it back out, maybe, just maybe, I'll try again."

"You go, girl." Jaye's expression could only be called gleeful.

"I knew you would say that. But don't get your hopes up—it could be that he really doesn't like me."

"Don't be silly. What's not to like?" said Jaye, continuing to smirk.

No more naps, Nick thought, rolling out of bed for the second time that morning. He had gotten up at eight o'clock when Shirley had brought him breakfast. The minute he had finished, he had gone back to bed. And he had dreamed that dream. Again. Every time he closed his eyes, he saw Maggie emerging from that trap door.

A man could only take so much mental foreplay.

He could have lived the fantasy—if he had taken her up on her offer. Once the fantasy became reality, the dream would go away.

Yeah. But what would be left behind? A woman who expected him to do the right thing. Maybe he could walk away from Maggie and her "brief affair." Maybe not. Nick could not forget the character flaw that made him do things he did not want to do. Like help his family every time they asked. What if Maggie—?

Hearing a faint knock, Nick made his way to the hall and opened the French doors. Maggie stood on the gallery holding a white paper bag. He opened the door a crack.

"Were you napping? Did I wake you?" Maggie asked, taking a step backward. She appeared wary. He couldn't blame her for that. He had been downright nasty to her Saturday night. Nasty enough that he hadn't seen her all day Sunday.

Nick looked closer. Maggie might be nervous, but she had a suspicious glint in her green eyes. A determined sort of a glint. Was she going to renew her offer? Bracing himself against another seduction attempt, Nick opened the door wider. "I've had enough naps to last me for a while. What's in the bag?"

"A beignet. Jaye and I went to Café du Monde this morning. We go every Monday, for café au lait and beignets. My shop is closed on Monday. There are three beignets per order, and we had one left over; so I thought you might want it." Maggie thrust the bag in his hand and slipped across the threshold. "Do you have any coffee?"

"No."

"I'll make a pot."

"No, thanks. I've had enough coffee this morning to float a barge. Was there something you wanted?"

"Well. Yes. I wanted to talk to you. To apologize, actually."

"Apologize? What for?"

"For making improper advances. To a man in your condition. It was thoughtless of me. I'm really sorry."

She lowered her head, the picture of shame.

Nick wasn't buying it. "Apology accepted. Anything else?"

Maggie walked through the kitchen door, brushing against him. "I don't want an affair. Not with someone who doesn't want me. But we are neighbors, temporarily. We ought to be friends." She sat down at the kitchen table. "Aren't you going to see what I brought you?"

Taking the chair across from her, Nick opened the paper bag, revealing a square, flaky pastry heavily dusted with powdered sugar. Nick removed it and took a bite. "Mmmm. Good. Shirley brought me blueberry muffins for breakfast. But only two." He took another bite, finishing the pastry. "I needed this. Thanks."

"You've got powdered sugar on your mouth."

"Where?" He rubbed the right side of his mouth.

"Other side," said Maggie, leaning across the table. She touched his left cheek with her fingertips. "Here."

Nick put his hand on top of hers, keeping her fingers on the corner of his mouth. He almost nibbled, but stopped himself in time.

Maggie's fingers lightly traced his jaw. "The sugar is gone. I should go, too, I guess. Today is the day I do my chores."

"Chores?" Nick muttered, gazing into Maggie's eyes. Maggie had the greenest eyes he had ever seen. He could drown in those emerald pools. Abruptly, Nick pushed his chair away from the table and stood. Emerald pools? Where had that sappy phrase come from? He had never compared a woman's eyes to jewels in his life.

Pneumonia must have done something to his immune system. And his brain.

"Chores. You know. Laundry. Grocery shopping."
Maggie eyed him as he began pacing the length of the
kitchen. "That reminds me. You don't have any food.
Make a list and I'll get you what you need."

He stopped pacing. "I don't *need* anything from you."
The words came out harsher than he had meant.

She blinked, then shrugged. "Just a thought. I'll
leave you alone, then." Pushing back her chair, Maggie got up.

"Wait. About those groceries—I guess I could use a
few things. I can't expect you and the others to keep
feeding me."

Maggie sat down again and pulled a small pad and
a tiny pencil from the pocket of her jeans. "Okay. Coffee? Or did Shirley leave you more?"

"No. I mean, yeah. Put coffee on the list."

"Do you want pure or chicory?"

"'Pure' being without chicory, I presume?"

"Yes."

"Pure, then. Chicory must be an acquired taste."

"You'll need milk, too, for your coffee. Or would
you rather have cream?"

"Milk's okay."

Continuing to make notes, Maggie said, "And
bread. Something to make sandwiches, maybe? You
can make a sandwich, can't you?"

"Yeah. I can make a sandwich. And I guess I could
use something for breakfast." Nick snapped his fingers.
"I know—donuts. You don't have to cook donuts."

A tiny frown appeared on Maggie's brow. "Cereal
would be better for you than all that sugar."

Raising his eyebrows, Nick asked, "Who just
brought me a powdered sugar treat?"

Her cheeks turned pink. "Once a week is okay. But
not every day."

Maggie had blushed—Nick couldn't remember the last time he had seen a woman over twenty blush. A sudden surge of desire caught him by surprise. A woman who blushed, who made meatloaf and mashed potatoes, and who had her original parents and two married sisters was *not* his type. Nick wiped his forehead. It was not hot. He must be feverish. "All right. Put cereal on the list. Can I have chips and dip? Popcorn? Beer?"

"It's your grocery list." Maggie gave him a severe look, adding, "And your arteries. Fruit would be a better choice. Apples and oranges?"

"Okay, Miss Mayfair. I didn't know I was dealing with the cholesterol cops. Have it your way. Apples and oranges." Nick felt hard desire change into something else, something . . . softer, cozier. No one gave a damn about his arteries, with the possible exception of Hildy. Hildy had never made a grocery list for him, however. Who would have thought that making a list could be seductive?

Maggie chewed on the end of her pencil. "Anything else?"

Pulling the list toward him, Nick looked it over. "That looks like more than enough. I don't want to overdo it."

"I guess not. I forgot you won't be here that long." She gave him a look . . . a calculating look. The kind of look a predator might give its next meal.

Nick blinked. Friends? Maggie had lied to him. She wanted more than friendship from him.

As he did from her, he reminded himself. He wanted information, and now was as good a time as any to get it. Concentrating on business might just get him through this. "Long enough. I was thinking about you. How far do you have to go for these groceries?"

"Not far. The A&P is on the corner of St. Peter, about six blocks from here."

"Do you have a car?"

Maggie shook her head. "In the Quarter? Not likely. Do you have any idea how hard it is to park around here?"

"At a guess, about as hard as it is in New York City."

"Right. So I don't have a car. I've got one of those two-wheeled grocery carts, though."

Nick looked at her list. "I know the kind you mean. It won't hold all that—and that's just my list. I'd better go with you. To help you carry the groceries."

She caught her bottom lip with her teeth. "I don't know. Doc Martin said you should stay in bed for at least twenty-four hours."

"I did. Now I think I'm suffering from cabin fever. A short walk will do me good." And it would be just the opportunity he needed to grill Maggie. Gently. He didn't want to make her suspicious.

"It is a nice day. Sunny, temperature in the sixties." Green eyes twinkling, Maggie smiled at him. "Perfect January weather."

"There must have been something besides the weather that made you stay here." A man, maybe. Nick bristled at the thought. Not that it was any of his business, but Nick found the idea of Maggie with another man—any man—distasteful.

"The charm of the place. There's no place like New Orleans, especially the French Quarter."

"And you didn't mind leaving your family behind?"

"I miss them, of course. But they visit, and I go home every year, in August. We e-mail almost every day and talk on the phone at least once a week."

She and her family were close. Very close, considering the distance between them. And Maggie expected him to believe that she wasn't interested in marriage. Ha. "What do you do about your shop in August?"

"Close it—lots of the shop owners take August off. Not a lot of tourists brave the heat and humidity of August in New Orleans. What about you? Are you from New York?"

"I was born there. I went to school in Connecticut. Until college—then I moved back to New York." Nick stood up and held out his hand. "Let's go."

Maggie put her hand in his and let him pull her from the chair. "You'd better get a jacket."

"It's sunny and sixty, weather girl."

"You're recovering from pneumonia. You don't want to get a chill."

"All right, Nurse Mayfair. I'll get my jacket." Nick walked to the bedroom and got a tweed sport coat from the armoire. He shrugged into the jacket and returned to the kitchen, reminding himself again that this trip was to gather data, data that would prove the tenants were interfering with the sale of his building.

Maggie was standing by the hall door. "Jaye said I should ask you to come out and play today. I'm glad I did. But I hope you don't have a relapse."

"Not likely. Not with all of you taking such good care of me." Nick put his hand on Maggie's elbow and walked her down the stairs.

Maggie stopped at her apartment door. "I'll just pop in and get my grocery cart. It's right inside the door."

Nick took the cart from her. "Let me carry it. You are very special, Magnolia Mayfair. As are Ed, Jaye and Shirley. I'm glad you all are my neighbors."

"Oh, Nick. That's so sweet. I'm glad you're our neighbor, too." She hugged him.

Hugging her back, Nick grinned. As long as he remembered what she was up to, he could indulge himself in a little harmless flirting. Pneumonia or not, Nick was sure he could resist Maggie. All he had to do was think about real estate. Nick pushed the door open and followed Maggie onto Royal Street. "Too bad the building's for sale. You'll all have to move when it does sell, won't you?"

"Yes." Nick followed Maggie's gaze to the FOR SALE sign in the storefront window, almost completely hidden by her display of masks.

"How long has it been for sale?"

"Since last spring."

"I guess there isn't much demand for property in the Quarter."

Maggie shrugged. "I don't know much about real estate. That's Corinne's job. I do know it's a nuisance having people poking about, looking at the place. One morning I woke up and people were standing outside the bedroom French doors staring at me."

"Doesn't the agent tell you when the building is going to be shown?"

"She's supposed to. But Corinne doesn't always give us fair warning. I know she's only the agent, but sometimes I almost hate her. I do hate the owners of the building. How could they just decide to sell? They haven't even bothered to look at the place."

Nick cringed inwardly. He had suggested to the realtor that she try to catch the tenants unaware, so they wouldn't have time to play their dirty tricks. If the fact that strangers would be invading the tenants' privacy had occurred to him, he had ignored it. Abandoning his interrogation for the time being, Nick changed the subject.

"How did a family of accountants end up with a mask maker among them?"

"I'm the Mayfair misfit. Every family has one. Mom says she'd think I was a foundling if not for her vivid memories of labor. It wasn't always easy, being different. But now that I've found my place and my profession, everything is all right."

Nick winced. Parents, sisters, brothers-in-law, and Maggie was about to become an aunt for the third time. Misfit or not, she was a walking advertisement for the American family. "You said you were engaged. Tell me about that."

"I was engaged for four years and—"

"*Four* years?"

"Yes. When Robert kept putting off setting a date, I should have realized—" Maggie shrugged. "But I didn't."

"Robert? Is he the four-year fiancé?"

She nodded.

"Why did you dump him?"

Maggie wrinkled her nose. "He was seeing . . ." Her chin trembled ever so slightly.

"Another woman?"

"Women. Six to be exact. Robert was having affairs with six other women while he was engaged to me." Maggie grinned, a wobbly kind of grin.

"Six? He had six women at the same time?"

"Seven, including me." She tilted her head and gave him a sideways glance. "You've got that look. It must be a guy thing."

"What look?"

"Sort of appalled admiration. You don't approve of Robert, but you admire his . . . stamina?"

"I find nothing admirable about deceit."

"I don't care for it much myself—"

A tap on the shoulder stopped him. "Charms? Potions? Lucky beads?"

Nick looked over his shoulder. A woman dressed as a voodoo priestess stood behind him.

"Good morning, Alcira," said Maggie. "We don't

need anything today, thanks. We're on our way to the A&P. This is our new neighbor, Nicholas Gerard."

"Monsieur. You do not look well. Have you a need for gris-gris? Or perhaps a potency potion?"

"I sincerely hope not."

"Nick is recovering from pneumonia. Do you have anything for that?"

The woman nodded. "A tisane for good health. I will prepare it and leave it with Shirley." Alcira held out her hand. "Twenty dollars."

"Twenty dollars?" said Nick, outraged.

"Fine. Get it from Shirley and tell her I'll pay her back."

The woman walked away.

Nick turned to Maggie. "Twenty dollars for a potion? Are you nuts?"

"No, but Alcira is. Well, crazy may be a bit strong, but she's . . ."

"One brick short of a load?"

"You could say that. She thinks she's a descendant of Marie Laveau. Have you heard of her?"

"No."

"Marie was a famous voodoo priestess. She's buried in St. Louis No 1. People still leave prayers at her crypt."

"You don't believe in that nonsense?"

Maggie shrugged. "Many people do. The thing is, Alcira refuses any kind of treatment for mental illness, and she won't take charity. So we help her out by buying her charms and potions. Quarter people look after their own."

"Just one big, happy family." Nick shuddered.

"Exactly. If you don't want the potion, I'll pay for it."

"No. I'll pay Shirley the twenty. The tisane is for me, after all. Who knows? It might help. Unless . . . Alcira doesn't poison people, does she?"

"Not that I know of." Maggie stopped at the corner of St. Peter. "Here's the A&P."

Nick followed her into the store. "Are you sure we'll find everything on the list? This place is awfully small."

"Small, but nicely crammed." Maggie exchanged her cart for one of the store's four-wheeled variety. She stopped by the coffee display. "Do you want French roast or something else?"

"French roast is okay." Nick followed Maggie down the narrow aisles. Every time they met another shopper, he and Maggie had to squeeze together to let the person past. Nick suspected that Maggie crowded him closer and more often than was strictly necessary, but he didn't call her on it. If investigating tenant trickery included having a soft, feminine body rub against him—well. A man had to do what a man had to do.

Maggie checked items off the list as they put them in the cart. "This is fun. I can't remember the last time I grocery shopped with a man. Except Jaye. Not the same. This is more like a date." She reached around him to snag a loaf of bread, squashing her breasts against his chest.

"No. It is not a date," Nick snapped, feeling sweat break out on his upper lip. "I thought I made it clear. I don't date women like you."

"Women like me?" Maggie bristled. "What does that mean? What kind of woman do you think I am?"

"W-w-wi—"

"Wu-wu—? Oh. Wife. Oh, my lordy me. I thought we had gotten past that. You have a real phobia about marriage, don't you? Read my lips, Mr. Gerard. I do not want to get married. Ever."

"So you say. But you can't deny that you're the kind of woman men marry."

Maggie lifted her chin. "Not me. The only man who ever wanted to marry me got over it. Why do you think I'm wife material?"

"You cook. You sew. You nurture."

"You said that before. Most women cook, don't they? A lot of men do, too, for that matter. Not everyone wants to eat in restaurants all the time. As for sewing, that's the way I make a living. I'm sewing masks, not baby clothes. I'm a businesswoman, not a potential bride."

"You nurture," Nick repeated stubbornly. "You cosset. You're taking care of me."

"So are Jaye and Ed and Shirley. They're not potential mates, are they? We're being neighborly. Why don't you relax and enjoy it?" Maggie shoved the cart down another aisle. "What kind of lunch meat do you want? Turkey?"

"Ham." Nick was beginning to feel foolish, seeing brides lurking behind every bush. Maggie must think he was as crazy as Alcira.

"We'll need to get you some mustard, then. Condiments are one aisle over."

He made one last attempt to prove his instincts were right. "You don't want to get married? Ever? I don't believe you."

Maggie stopped, turned, and looked him in eye. "If you can't believe that, believe this: I don't want to get married to you, Nicholas Gerard."

She must have known by the look on his face that he wasn't buying it.

Maggie blew a lock of honey-colored hair out of her eye and tried again. "Look. Think of love and marriage as a swimming pool. An Olympic-size pool. Five years ago, I fell in that pool—some people call it falling in love. What happened? I almost drowned, that's what happened. How likely is it that I would jump back into the big pool?"

Nick raised a brow.

"All right. I will admit you've reactivated my interest in swimming. But I intend to wade before I swim. As far as I'm concerned, if you hadn't turned me down, you would have been the kiddy pool."

"I think I'm insulted." Nick wasn't sure why—Maggie was telling him exactly what he wanted to hear.

"I don't see why. You turned me down. I'll have to look elsewhere for someone to go wading with." She gave him a smile full of regret. And promises.

"Have anyone in mind?"

"No. I don't meet many eligible men for some reason. But I got a flyer from a computer dating agency in the mail today. Maybe I'll try that. Or a personal ad."

"You'd take that kind of chance? On a stranger?" His vision clouded.

"You were a stranger. But having you turn up just when I decided to experiment with lust seemed so . . . fortuitous. Shirley would say we were meant to be. And then there's that staircase connecting our bedrooms. It would be so easy to be discreet. Discretion is important, don't you think?"

"Uh huh." Nick blinked to clear his vision. "I don't think a personal ad is the way to go. That dating agency might be safer. Make sure they check out the applicants, though."

"Don't worry. I'll be careful. And I'll try to be patient." She giggled. "You'd think, after four years without . . . you know . . . it wouldn't be so hard to wait a few more days."

"Four years? You haven't had sex in four years?"

"Pitiful, isn't it? I am definitely, as they say, hot to trot."

Nick coughed to give himself an excuse not to respond to that outrageous statement. He managed to keep quiet for the rest of the shopping trip.

Once they were back at eleven-thirteen Royal Street, Maggie reached in her shopping cart and handed him his bag of groceries. "Put up your groceries, then take a nap. And don't forget your pill."

Nick clenched his teeth together. He wasn't falling for her tricks. Magnolia Mayfair was the marrying kind, and he was not going to touch her.

Like hell, he wasn't.

Nick set the bag of groceries on the bottom step, then turned to face Maggie. Her green cat eyes opened wide. Her soft pink lips formed a startled O as he approached.

"Nick?" she managed, before he hauled her against his chest and clamped his mouth on hers.

Damn, damn, damn. He should have kept his mouth to himself.

Nick would have ended the kiss, but Maggie's lips clung to his, then parted. Nick could not resist the invitation. Plunging his tongue inside her mouth, he tasted her sweetness.

Magnolia. Sweet, but not southern, and definitely not an idiot.

He was the idiot.

Kissing a woman like her. Exerting every ounce of his willpower, Nick ended the kiss.

Maggie looked up at him, her emerald eyes clouded with desire. "Wow. Does this mean you've changed your mind about meaningless sex?"

Seven

"No, it does not mean I've changed my mind. I did not mean to kiss you. Not the first time, not this time. It's that damn staircase." With a jerk of his head, Nick indicated the French doors leading to her bedroom. The spiral staircase was visible through the sheer curtains.

"The staircase?" Maggie looked at Nick's hands, still grasping her shoulders.

"Yes. The staircase. A fantasy maker if ever there was one. You told me about it that first night, and I've dreamed about it every night—and nap—since."

"You dreamed about the *staircase?*" Swallowing her disappointment, Maggie gazed at him. "I—I thought you dreamed about me."

He gave her a shake. "I do dream about you. About you coming up the staircase, through the trap door."

"Oh. That's it? That's what you dream about? I could do that, I suppose. Next time I come upstairs to check on you, I'll use the spiral staircase. It's a little rickety, but I don't think it's dangerous."

"Oh, it's dangerous, all right. When you walk up those stairs in my dream, you are not coming to remind me to take a pill, or to bring me food. You're bringing me you. In my dream, you're naked. You emerge from the staircase like Venus emerging from the sea."

Maggie gasped. "Naked? As in without a stitch?"

"Yeah." His fingers kneaded her shoulders.

After a pause, while the image Nick painted indelibly painted itself on her mind, Maggie nodded. "Okay. I could do that. Now that you've agreed we're going to have an affair, I could do that. Not even a wispy little bra?"

"No bra."

"Panties?"

"No panties."

"How about a thong?" She didn't own one, but she could remedy that. There was a Victoria's Secret at the Riverwalk.

"Nothing, not a stitch. And I haven't agreed to anything. I am explaining why I keep grabbing you."

"And kissing me? Well, finish the explanation. I climb up the stairs to your bedroom. Nude. What happens next?"

Nick let her go. "What do you think happens next?"

Maggie felt her face grow hot. Other body parts followed suit. "Sex?"

Nick nodded. "Exactly. Hot, sweaty, mind-blowing sex."

"Oh, my lordy me." Maggie fanned herself with her hand. "That's some dream."

"Yeah. But. I don't want to dream about you. I do not want to kiss you. I do not want to have an affair with you."

"You sound like you mean that. Almost."

"I do mean it. You're the one who keeps egging me on."

"Me? I beg to differ. I told you I would be satisfied being your friend. Oh. 'Satisfied' may be the wrong word. Content. I would be content to be a neighbor and a friend. I'm going to sign up at that computer dating agency, remember?"

"Good. You do that." Nick turned away from her.

"Although . . ." Maggie said. "Maybe you would stop dreaming about me if your dream came true."

Nick's back stiffened. "That had occurred to me. I'm not taking that chance."

"I don't see why not. If you dream about me every night, your subconscious obviously wants me."

"Fortunately, my subconscious is not in control when I'm awake." Scooping up the bag of groceries he had left on the bottom step, Nick stomped up the stairs.

"It's not? Then, why did you kiss me? I mean, you are awake now."

He did not answer her. Nick was angry.

He had melted her bones with one awe-inspiring kiss. What did he have to be mad about?

It had to be that wu-wu-wife business.

Maggie tossed her head. She wanted only his hormone-inspiring body, not his heart. His well-protected heart. The man was so paranoid about love and marriage that he couldn't even say the word "wife." She had told him flat out she wasn't interested in becoming Mrs. Nicholas Gerard, and he hadn't believed her. Nick had jumped like a scared rabbit when she had casually referred to their trip to the A&P as a date.

Nick hadn't liked being compared to the kiddy pool, though. That must have been what had driven him to kiss her silly. The kiss had made him mad, though. With a flash of insight, Maggie realized that Nick had been angry at himself, not her. He hadn't wanted to kiss her, but he couldn't resist. Maggie's heart beat faster. Nick found her irresistible.

Humming "When the Saints Go Marching In,"

Maggie opened the French doors and pulled her cart inside the kitchen. She could be on her way to bagging her first Mr. Wrong.

Emcee rubbed against her ankles. "Hi, Emcee. If I'm wrong, and I fail at this seduction business, I will still have you. Come on, big fellow. I have cat treats in here somewhere."

She set the bag of groceries on the counter. Emcee jumped up and began pawing the plastic bag. Tickling the cat behind his ears, Maggie said, "I got your favorite flavor of cat food, too. Salmon and crab." She opened the bag of treats and counted out three. Emcee took one, crunched it, then chewed. And chewed. Emcee never swallowed anything before he chewed it to dust. When the first treat had been pulverized, Emcee swallowed and reached for another.

Someone knocked at her door, then entered without waiting for Maggie to answer. Shirley rushed into the kitchen, waving a section of newspaper. Her emerald green turban was askew, as if she had attempted to put her hands through her hair. "Did I see Nick go up the stairs just now? Where have you been?"

"At the A&P." Maggie took a carton of milk out of the grocery bag, keeping her back to Shirley. She was sure Nick's kiss had left some kind of mark on her mouth, and she was not ready to talk about it, not even with Shirley. "Oh, Nick ordered a potion from Alcira. She's dropping it off at Oracles later."

Shirley put her hands on Maggie's shoulders and turned her around. "Fine. Maggie, I've had a revelation."

"Have you? That's nice." Shirley had revelations at least once a week. Maggie shrugged Shirley's hands away and reached in the grocery bag again. She found the tub of margarine and put it in the refrigerator.

"A big one." Shirley waited until Maggie had closed the refrigerator door. "Listen to me, Magnolia. This is important. I know who Nick really is."

"Who he really is?" Her mind on the kiss she had shared with Nick, Maggie barely heard what Shirley said. She took a can of mushroom soup out of the bag. "Isn't Nick who he says he is?"

"No, he is not. Nick Gerard is"—Shirley paused dramatically—"Norton Graves."

Maggie almost dropped the soup can. She whirled around. "Norton Graves? The mystery writer?"

"The mysterious mystery writer. No one knows what he looks like, or even if Norton Graves is his real name."

"What makes you think Nick is Norton?"

"This little blurb in the *New York Times* Book Review section—I only got around to reading it this morning. See? Norton Graves's next book is set in New Orleans." Shirley pointed to the article and quoted, 'The author is believed to be in Louisiana researching the location of his next book.' Nick is here soaking up atmosphere for his book."

"Nick told us he's a beginning writer. It could be just a coincidence that both he and Norton have chosen to set their books here."

"I don't believe in coincidences. Nick—Norton wouldn't tell us he's the author of nine *New York Times* best-sellers, now, would he? Not if he wants to keep his identity a secret. Here, read it for yourself." Shirley thrust the newspaper into Maggie's hands.

She scanned the article quickly. "But, Shirley, it says 'Louisiana,' not 'New Orleans.' Norton Graves could be lots of places besides here. Maybe he's writing about the Cajuns. He could be in Lafayette or New Iberia or Cocodrie."

"He's here, all right. In apartment 2B." Shirley pointed to Maggie's ceiling.

"I don't think so." A flock of butterflies had taken up residence in Maggie's stomach. She didn't want to believe that Nick was someone else. That would mean he had lied to her. "Nick told me he doesn't care much for deceit."

"Who does? A writer probably wouldn't look on a pseudonym as deceitful—more of a business decision." Shirley was looking at her expectantly. "Think about it, Maggie—we could have a best-selling author right here."

"So? What if Nick is Norton Graves? Why are you so excited about it? I didn't know you were that much of a fan of his."

"I'm not. My genre of choice is fantasy, not mystery. But Norton Graves gets seven-figure advances for his books. Not to mention what he pulls in from the movie deals. The man is rolling in money."

"So?" The butterflies turned into bats. Now she knew why she had found the idea that Nick was Norton Graves so disturbing. She did not want a famous, wealthy man for a lover. Famous people did not have discreet affairs. Their love lives were plastered all over the grocery store tabloids.

Plus, people always assumed that a woman who slept with a rich man was a gold digger. Or worse. After four years of living in the Quarter, Maggie had acquired a gloss of sophistication. Enough that she was prepared to become what her grandmother would have called a fallen woman.

But Maggie hadn't planned on falling *that* far.

Shirley continued, "If Nick is Norton Graves, he has money. Lots and lots of money. Don't you see what that means? He could buy this building with his pocket change."

"Why would he want to do that? He won't need an apartment in the Quarter for long."

"Long enough for us to convince him that eleven-thirteen Royal Street is exactly what he needs. A little hideaway, far from the hustle and bustle of New York. And not just any hideaway, but the French Quarter. A magical, creative place, a place that has inspired countless artists and authors."

"How are we going to do that?" Maggie turned away from Shirley and the fanatical gleam in her eyes. She opened the pantry and stuck the soup can on the second shelf. "*Why* are we going to do that?"

"Because. It's the best shot we've got at keeping our homes and your business right where they are. Are you finished?"

She was finished, all right. Just as she had gotten started. Maggie realized Shirley was looking at her half-full grocery sack. "No."

"You've put the perishables away. The rest can wait. I'm calling a tenants' meeting. Jaye is back from his fitting, and Ed is upstairs. Let's go get them."

Shirley hustled Maggie outside and up the stairs to Ed's apartment while she went to find Jaye. As soon as the four of them were assembled in Shirley's apartment, Shirley opened her mouth. Ed, who had taken his usual seat in one of the twin wing chairs facing Shirley's camelback sofa, forestalled her with a raised hand.

Ed rapped on the coffee table with his signet ring. "I call this emergency meeting of the Beaulieu Building Tenants' Association to order. Old business?"

Arms akimbo, Shirley stood in front of Ed and

glared down at him. "Forget Robert's Rules, you old coot. I have something important to say."

Ed scowled at Shirley. "New business? The chair recognizes Shirley Wyclowski."

"About time," Shirley muttered. She stood in front of the sofa and spread her arms wide. "We have a chance to buy the building."

Jaye snorted. "Do we really? Did someone die and leave you a pot full of money?"

Lowering her arms, Shirley scowled at Jaye. "No one died. Not yet, anyway. Are you ready to listen to me?"

Jaye, standing next to the corner fireplace, held up his hands, palms out. "I'm listening. Tell us how we're going to buy the building, Madame Fortunata."

"Our new tenant is rich. Very rich. All we have to do is convince him to buy the building for us."

"Explain yourself, woman," said Ed. "As usual, you are making no sense."

"Shirley thinks Nick is really someone else," said Maggie, sinking onto the sofa across from Ed. "She thinks Nick is Norton Graves."

"The mystery writer?" asked Jaye.

"That's the one," said Maggie.

Shirley repeated her theory.

Nodding his head, Jaye said, "It makes a weird kind of sense. I thought Gerard dressed more like a tycoon than an out-of-work, fledgling author. Nick Gerard, Norton Graves. They have the same initials. I think you're on to something, Shirley."

Ed shook his head. "Harumph. Seems far-fetched to me. Why would an author conceal his identity in the first place?"

"No one knows for sure," said Shirley. "Some people say Norton is CEO of a *Fortune* Five Hundred company—the stockholders might not be pleased to know he wasn't focusing all his attention on business."

Jaye added, "Others speculate that it's nothing more than a publicity stunt."

"Or that he's obsessively protective of his privacy," said Maggie.

"Well. What if Nick is this writer?" asked Ed.

"Norton Graves is rich." Shirley paced back and forth in front of the sofa, waving her arms. "More than rich enough to buy this building."

"You expect him to buy the building?" Ed asked. "Why would he? For that matter, why hasn't he? He knows the building is for sale. I haven't heard him making an offer."

"He's ill, Ed. Nick—Norton hasn't had real estate on his mind. If he doesn't think of it, we'll ask him to buy the building," Shirley said.

"That's a cockamamie idea, even for you, madam. Why don't we just send out letters to every multimillionaire in the country? There could be dozens of wealthy men who need an apartment in the French Quarter."

Shirley stopped pacing. "There well may be. But those other millionaires aren't here, already living in the building—in the owner's apartment. Nick—Norton is. We're going to have to make an effort to be nice to Nick. I mean Norton."

"We have been nice to him," said Jaye. "Maggie, especially." He pushed away from the mantel and patted Maggie on the head.

Maggie shoved Jaye's hand away. With a rueful grin, Jaye returned to his spot by the fireplace.

"Why should we be nice to him?" asked Ed, scowling.

"Because," said Shirley, glowering back at him. "We

want him to think of us as his best friends. He has to like us before we ask him to buy the building."

"We're off to a good start," said Jaye. "We have been taking care of him while he recovers."

Maggie squirmed. "I don't like this. It seems . . . cold and calculating." The more Shirley talked, the more Maggie realized she couldn't seduce Nick, Norton, whatever his name was. If she did, and then the tenants asked him to buy the building, he would think she had done it for something other than pure lust. Nick would think *she* was a gold digger. Or worse. "It's mean."

"Mean? How is taking care of him mean? The man is ill. He needs us." Shirley began pacing again.

"Maggie objects to the motive, not the deed," said Jaye. "Isn't that right?"

"Yes. How would you feel if someone was nice to you only because they wanted you to do something for them? To *buy* something for them?" If Nick was Norton, there would be no more of those knee-buckling kisses. Maggie almost wept at the thought. She blinked her eyes. "You'd feel awful, wouldn't you?"

Shirley came to a halt in front of the sofa. "But, Maggie, sweet pea, all we're going to do is make sure that Nick absolutely falls in love with New Orleans. Plus, we'll be helping him with his research. What's wrong with that?"

"Not a thing," said Ed, surprising Maggie. The professor never agreed with Shirley. "Letting New Orleans charm Graves shouldn't be difficult. And the Quarter has nurtured many literary figures." Ed patted Maggie on the knee. "Exposing Nick to the rich history of this town would not be mean. And if it turns out that Shirley's theory is correct, it won't hurt to ask him to buy the building. He can always refuse us."

Ed sounded downright excited. Maggie hadn't seen him so animated since before he had retired.

"That's the idea," said Shirley, throwing a grateful look Ed's way. "Ed, you show Nick the city's literary landmarks. Play up the opportunity for inspiration."

"I can tell him about the more interesting murders that have taken place here. Grist for the mill, as it were." Ed was positively beaming.

"I never knew you liked murder stories," said Maggie.

"Harumph. For your information, madam, history is full of murder and mayhem. How do you think I kept my students' interest? Not with hearts and flowers, I can assure you."

"Amazing," said Shirley. "You think you know all there is to know about a person, and then—well. You surprised me, Professor. Jaye, you can show him the night life. Take him to the jazz clubs, the restaurants."

"Maggie should do that. Nick is attracted to her. And the feeling is mutual, I do believe. Maggie could seduce Nick into buying the building. If she wanted to, that is."

Ed and Shirley stared at her.

"Is he?" asked Shirley. "Are you?" Shirley slapped her forehead with the heel of her hand, knocking her turban completely off. She grabbed it before it fell to the floor. "Of course you are. How could I have forgotten? Nick has silver eyes. And that's not all. Maggie, remember that reading I did before Nick arrived? I told you he had a secret."

"I remember," Maggie muttered, feeling more and more agitated. "But I'm not seducing Nick Gerard or Norton Graves." She glared at Jaye. "Certainly not for a building."

Jaye grinned at her. "Admit it, Maggie. Seducing Nick will do you good, building or no building. And it's what you want. *He* is what you want. You said as much this morning at Café du Monde."

"You can't fight fate, Magnolia dear. The cards predicted that your next lover would have silver eyes," said Shirley, conveniently forgetting the card that had indicated Silver Eyes would have black hair.

Maggie stuck out her chin. "I don't care what the cards said. I won't do it. It wouldn't be fair. And there is certainly no guarantee that it would work. If Nick and I . . . got involved, he might not want to hang around after the fling is over. He could be a love-em-and-leave-em kind of a guy." Considering his attitude toward marriage, that had to be exactly what Nick was—a man who would leave a lover without a backward glance. A hollow feeling replaced the bats in the pit of her stomach.

"Aw, Maggie—"

Shirley interrupted Jaye. "Magnolia, dawlin', you can't ignore fate. The cards foretold—"

The two advanced on her. She put her hands over her ears. Maggie refused to listen to one more argument in favor of her pillow talking Nick into buying the building.

"Stop it, both of you," Ed ordered. "Your teasing is upsetting Maggie."

Jaye ruffled her hair. "Sorry, doll. Couldn't resist. You're so cute when you're flustered."

"Maggie, sweety. We're certainly not expecting you to do anything you don't want to do," said Shirley. "But if the opportunity arises, and if you are attracted to him, well, what's wrong with killing two birds with one stone? Especially since the cards predicted that you and Nick would . . . you know."

"Screw the cards. I'm not killing anything," growled Maggie.

Shirley backed away, a hurt expression on her face. "But, Maggie, dawlin'. You can't ignore your destiny."

"Oh, yes, I can."

"I think we should forget about asking Maggie to bear the brunt of this campaign. We will all do our part." Ed stood up and walked to the French doors. Looking out at the courtyard, he said, "I will offer my services as a guide to the historical and literary landmarks. Jaye can show Nick the nightlife. Shirley, you can expose him to the fringe elements that give the Quarter its reputation for tackiness."

"Fringe? Tacky?" Shirley picked up her turban and replaced it on her head, tucking in stray bits of red hair. "Sometimes, Ed, you go too far."

"Nonsense. tarot cards, tea leaves, and psychic mumbo jumbo are far from the modern American mainstream."

"What would you know about modern, you old coot? You've been stuck in the past since puberty." Shirley advanced on Ed, who sank back into the chair, eyeing her warily.

"That's enough, children," said Jaye. "I swear to God. You two argue like married people."

"Bite your tongue, Jaye," Shirley snapped. "When do we start?"

Maggie shook her head. They were going to do it. And, even if the professor had left her off his list of marching orders, at some point they would expect her to do her part.

Well, she wouldn't participate, no matter what they wanted. She would forget all about seducing Nick. Now that she knew what the others intended, enticing Nick to be her first Mr. Wrong seemed . . . wrong.

Nick might or might not be lying about his identity, but she would be lying about her reasons for wanting to make love—have sex with him. She could tell herself over and over that she would never prostitute herself for a building, but the motive would be there lurking in the dark recesses of her mind. Like a purple elephant. It was a well-known fact—the minute a person was told not to think about a purple elephant, that was all that person could think about.

"A cruise on the *Natchez* would be romantic," said Shirley, with a sigh. She slanted a hopeful glance at Maggie.

Maggie ignored her.

"A swamp tour. Nick ought to go on a swamp tour. I'll do that," offered Jaye.

"No, let me," said Ed. "The swamp offers grisly opportunities for murder and mayhem."

"Let's not spend too much time away from eleventhirteen. We've got to make him think that any writer worth his salt must have a pied-a-terre in the French Quarter. This is a charming building—the courtyard, the fountain, the wisteria. Not to mention the colorful characters who inhabit the other apartments. We'd make fabulous additions to any story Graves might write, don't you think?" Shirley sat down on the sofa next to Maggie.

"When is this campaign going to start?" asked Jaye. "Don't forget—Nick's still recovering. We don't want him to overdo and have a relapse."

"Point taken," said Shirley, nodding. "For the next couple of days, we'll go on as we started. Taking care of Nick. Norton."

"We must continue to call him Nick," said the professor. "If we refer to him as Norton even among ourselves, we might slip up and call him that to his face."

"I think you're right, Ed." Jaye moved away from the fireplace and came to stand in front of the sofa.

"I think you're moving too fast," Maggie said, a little desperately. "We should make sure that Nick really is Norton Graves before we do anything."

Three pairs of eyes focused on her.

Ed cleared his throat. "Magnolia has a point. We are getting ahead of ourselves. We should establish that Shirley's premise is correct before we go galloping off in all directions."

"How?" asked Jaye.

"We could call his publisher," offered Ed. "Inquire if Norton Graves is currently in New Orleans or elsewhere in Louisiana."

Shirley shook her head. "That won't work. I doubt that they would tell us."

Ed half turned and eyed Shirley. "The newspaper reporter found out somehow. Why not call the reporter?"

"A reporter wouldn't reveal his source. However, maybe we could get a peek at what's on Nick's laptop. Graves has a very distinctive style. You've read his books, Ed. You could do that." Shirley got up and began pacing again.

"I'll try."

"And we could ask Corinne about him," said Maggie, anxious to find a way to disprove Shirley's theory. "Find out who made the arrangements for Nick to come here."

"That's a good idea," said Jaye. "Nick must have a return ticket. He would have used his real name to book a flight, wouldn't he?"

"I don't know. Maybe not. But it's worth a shot," said Shirley. "In the mean time, we'll go on as we started. Being neighborly. Maggie, why don't you help him put up his groceries?"

"I'm sure he's finished with that. We didn't buy all that much."

Shirley wagged her finger. "Maggie. He may have forgotten to take his noon pill. One of us needs to check on him."

"Not me," Maggie said, sticking out her chin.

"Don't bully the girl," said Ed. "Is that it? Are we finished?"

"For now," said Shirley.

"Fine. Meeting adjourned."

Maggie was the first out the door. She was feeling raw and unsettled. Disappointed and guilty. Her first attempt at a casual affair had turned into a French farce, complete with mistaken identities, convoluted plots, and star-crossed lovers. Her star and Nick's were double and triple crossed. No chance for romance there, not now.

Maggie blinked, surprised to feel tears welling in her eyes. What was that about? She didn't know Nick well enough to cry over him. And romance had never been a part of her plan.

It had to be the way she had behaved toward the others. For the first time since she had met them, she was on the outs with her friends.

Maggie bit back a moan. History was repeating itself. She had isolated herself from her family after Robert because she hadn't wanted to admit the terrible mistake she had made in falling in love with him. Now she was withdrawing from her friends because she didn't want to take part in the seduction of Norton Graves. What was it about her relationships, or attempted relationships, that set her at odds with those closest to her?

Maggie wondered if Emcee's veterinarian had any kittens to be adopted.

Nibbling on an apple, Nick stood at his bedroom French doors and watched the tenants gathered in Shirley's apartment. They were having a party, and they hadn't invited him.

Story of his life.

Nick had never been invited to his siblings' parties, or to his parents' parties for that matter. Not that it mattered. He hated parties. And this was just what he needed to remind himself that he was not one of them. They were his troublesome tenants, not his best friends. They kept sucking him in, making him feel at home. Making him want things better avoided.

Mind-blowing sex, for example. With a woman who had marriage on her mind, no matter how much she denied it.

Nick looked closer. He had an unobstructed view of Shirley's living room. Maggie and the professor were sitting on a sofa. Shirley was speaking, waving her hands in the air. Jaye was standing next to the fireplace, leaning his shoulder on the mantel.

They weren't having a party. They were having some kind of meeting.

About the building. It couldn't be anything else. The tenants were plotting new ways to keep his building from selling. He would bet his reputation on it.

And they hadn't invited him to join in. Why not? He was a tenant, too. He should have been included. They must not trust him.

That hurt.

Tossing the apple core into the wastebasket, Nick continued to watch. A few minutes later, the meeting broke up. Maggie came out into the courtyard first. She glanced up at his apartment, then disappeared under the balcony. Nick heard her door open and close.

Ed and Jaye came out next. They crossed the courtyard together and climbed the stairs to the second floor. A knock sounded on Nick's door. He opened it.

"Hey, old buddy," said Jaye. "Busy?"

"Hardly. Come in." Nick motioned the two men over his threshhold and led the way into the front room. When Jaye and Ed were seated on his red velvet sofa, Nick took the chair opposite and asked, "What's up? I saw you all gathered in Shirley's apartment. Were you having some kind of meeting?"

"Yes. An emergency meeting of the Beaulieu Building Tenants' Association," said Ed. He frowned. "Remind me, Jaye. At our next meeting I will put forth a motion to change the name. Beaulieu is no longer appropriate."

Jaye nodded. "Sure thing, Professor. Now, Nick, about the meeting—"

"I'm a tenant," Nick pointed out, his tone mild.

The professor looked embarrassed. "So you are. In the normal course of things, if we had followed Robert's Rules of Order, you would have been invited to attend the meeting. However—"

Jaye interrupted. "We didn't invite you, Nick. We couldn't. The meeting was about you."

Nick raised a brow. "About me? What about me? Wait—I get it. You were working out some kind of schedule for taking care of me. That won't be necessary. I feel well enough to take care of myself."

"Good. We're glad to hear that. But that was not what the meeting was about, no indeed," said the professor, beaming at him. "You are an author here to familiarize yourself with the French Quarter and New Orleans, in preparation of writing a novel set here."

Nick said, "Yeah, that's right."

"At our meeting we considered how we might assist you in that endeavor. Since we were talking about your work in progress, you might think we had an even more compelling reason to have included you. However, first we had to agree among ourselves to take on this project. Your presence might have inhibited a free and fair discussion of the pros and cons of—"

"Of showing you around town," said Jaye.

"Exactly. We voted to offer our services as tour guides, as it were. If you're amenable to our plan, I will take you to the museums and historic sites. I thought we could start close to home. The Gallier House is in the next block—an excellent example of how people lived a century or more ago. When you're up to it, we can range farther afield. I thought, perhaps, a swamp tour might be of interest?" The professor looked at him anxiously.

"I would definitely be interested in a swamp tour," said Nick. He already felt as if he was up to his ass in alligators. He might as well see them in their native habitat.

"I'll show you the night life on Bourbon Street. We can hit the jazz clubs and the bars. And you can see my show."

"That sounds good," said Nick.

"Madame Fortunata volunteered to read your palm and take you to the Voodoo Museum. She wants to take you on a cruise on the *Natchez*—the riverboat," said the professor. "And, although she didn't mention it, you might easily persuade her to take you on a street car ride up St. Charles Avenue."

"What about Maggie? What part of town will she show me?"

"Harumph. Well." The professor, looking embarrassed, turned to Jaye. "You explain."

"Uh. Maggie's not going to show you anything, Nick."

Ed chimed in. "I regret to say that Magnolia objected to our plan to assist you with your research. For herself, that is. This is her busy time of year, you see."

"What with Mardi Gras right around the corner," Jaye added.

"Maggie doesn't have time for me, is that what you're saying?"

"Exactly. Nothing personal, you understand," said Ed.

"Not at all," Jaye insisted. "Maggie needs to have a good season, especially since it may be her last before she has to relocate."

"If the building sells, that is. You do know that the building is for sale?" Ed asked.

"I saw the sign in the shop window," said Nick.

"All our lives will be disrupted, of course, once a sale takes place. Our leases require us to move within a very short time thereafter."

"Maggie's life will be disrupted most of all, since she has both her home and her business here," Jaye pointed out.

"Perhaps a new owner will keep the status quo," Nick suggested, squelching guilt feelings. He had nothing to feel guilty about—it wasn't up to him to keep his tenants sheltered for the rest of his life.

Ed shook his head. "Doubtful. The trend is to convert apartments into condominiums or single-family residences. Although, there is a rumor that the Vieux

Carre Commission is considering a temporary ban on condos."

"Even if a new landlord kept the building as is, he'd want to raise the rents. He wouldn't be able to do that if we remain as tenants."

"He would have to either recognize our leases, with the rents specified therein, or evict us. Which he could do if we don't vacate the premises within thirty days after the sale," Ed explained.

"Considering the escalating value of Quarter real estate, that's a no-brainer. Eviction is the only thing that makes financial sense." Jaye got up and moved to the French doors.

"Yeah. I can see that."

"Now, back to you. When would you like to begin your tour of our fair city?" asked Ed. "If you're feeling up to it, that is."

"How about tomorrow? I went out today, with no adverse effects. Maggie and I went to the grocery store."

"The A&P is a Quarter fixture," said Ed. "Tell me, Nick. Is your novel set in the past or the present?"

"The present." At the professor's disappointed look, he added, "However, the story involves the past as well. Something that happened in the past is important to the plot. I'm not sure what that something is at this stage. A look at the historic sites may give me exactly what I need."

The professor nodded. "The muse may strike at any moment. It will be interesting to see where."

"What kind of story is it?" Jaye asked, staring out at the balcony. "A mystery?"

"Not exactly," said Nick, grinning. "It's a ghost story."

Eight

Nick's fingers came to rest on the computer keyboard. He had spent the afternoon at the computer. When he had sat down, he had meant to work on Renaissance, Inc.'s, five-year business plan. Instead, he had made a list.

A list of the reasons he should not go near Magnolia Mayfair, no matter how tempted he was. Nick stared at the screen, then blocked the list and deleted it. There was only one reason that mattered. If he got close to Maggie, he would not be able to walk away from her. Nick wasn't sure how he knew that, but the knowledge had invaded his bones.

For four days, since the tenants' meeting Monday afternoon, Maggie had ignored him.

Diabolical. That was what she was. Diabolical and determined. She was toying with him, like Emcee might toy with a mouse. Offering him sex, then, after he turned her down, pretending to want nothing but friendship. Yeah. Right. That was why she had been all over him at the grocery store, rubbing her body against his, touching him, making him kiss her. Again.

Now she was playing hard to get.

And it was working.

The less he saw of Maggie, the more he wanted her. Nick had to make a decision. Go, and hope distance would cool his desire, or stay, and risk letting Maggie have her affair.

What kind of heel would he be if he took her to bed, knowing she was the marrying kind? It had taken Maggie four years to get over Robert's betrayal. Nick wasn't about to be the next man to walk away from her.

He had tried telling himself that he could ignore the facts and take Maggie at her word. He could agree to exactly what Maggie had offered, a casual affair. Casual sex was what she said she wanted. That was what he would give her. Nothing more.

Except Nick knew she was lying. Even if she believed her lies, he couldn't justify taking advantage of her.

Christ. He sounded so damn noble. Protecting Maggie was not the only reason he couldn't get close to her. Not by a long shot. He was looking out for number one, too. Maggie made him think about wedding rings and happily ever after.

Magnolia Mayfair was diabolical, all right. Diabolical and a danger to herself and others. She ought to be locked up.

Since that wasn't going to happen, there was only one viable option. He had to leave. Picking up the cell phone, Nick prepared to dial Delta and make a reservation. A knock at the door interrupted him.

Jaye was at the door, holding a gold gift bag tied with purple and green ribbons. "I have bad news and good news," Jaye said.

"Come on in," said Nick, standing aside and gesturing for Jaye to enter.

"No time. As it turns out, I have two shows at the Foxy Lady tonight. I won't be able to go with you to Preservation Hall."

 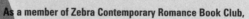

To start your membership, simply complete and return the Free Book Certificate. You'll receive your Introductory Shipment of FREE Zebra Contemporary Romances. Then, each month as long as your account is in good standing, you will receive the 3 newest Zebra Contemporary Romances. Each shipment will be yours to examine for 10 days. If you decide to keep the books, you'll pay the preferred book club member price of $15.95 – a savings of up to 20% off the cover price! (plus $1.99 to offset the cost of shipping and handling.) If you want us to stop sending books, just say the word… it's that simple.

BOOK CERTIFICATE

Yes! Please send me FREE Zebra Contemporary romance novels. I only pay for shipping and handling. I understand I am under no obligation to purchase any books, as explained on this card.

Name _____

Address _____ Apt. _____

City _____ State _____ Zip _____

Telephone (___) _____

Signature _____

(If under 18, parent or guardian must sign)

Thank You!

CN122A

THE BENEFITS
OF BOOK CLUB
MEMBERSHIP

- You'll get your books hot off the press, usually before they appear in bookstores.

- You'll ALWAYS save up to 20% off the cover price.

- You'll get our FREE monthly newsletter filled with author interviews, book previews, special offers, and MORE!

- There's no obligation — you can cancel at any time and you have no minimum number of books to buy.

- And — if you decide you don't like the books you receive, you can return them. (You always have ten days to decide.)

lll..l..lll...lll.l.l..l.l..l.l..l.l.ll.l..l.ll.l..l

Zebra Contemporary Romance Book Club

Zebra Home Subscription Service, Inc.

P.O. Box 5214

Clifton , NJ 07015-5214

"No problem. After every place I've seen this week, I have more than enough background for my book. I can skip Preservation Hall." Shirley, Ed, and Jaye had been generous with their time and knowledge, so generous that Nick was feeling guilty about deceiving them.

And about selling the building out from under them.

When he got back to New York, he would consult with the lawyers first thing. There had to be a way for him to get rid of the building without displacing the tenants. Maybe structure some kind of sale with installment payments so that the tenants could afford to buy the building.

"You won't have to skip anything. The good news is, Maggie will go with you instead."

"Maggie? I thought she was too busy for me." Before Nick had decided to be noble and cowardly about the whole thing, Maggie's turning from hot to cold in the blink of an eye had annoyed him. It still grated, apparently. "At least, that's the line you and the others have been giving me all week."

"She won't be busy tonight. Maggie finished all her special order masks last night. And she closes up shop at six. Plenty early enough to make the first set at Preservation Hall."

"I don't know," said Nick. "I really ought to get some writing in tonight." Cold sweat popped out on his forehead. He and Maggie together at Preservation Hall in the dark, hot jazz pounding in their ears? No way. He could resist Maggie when she was behind the counter of her shop. But there were limits to his control. Nick wondered if Delta had a red-eye flight. If Maggie had decided to stop ignoring him, he needed to get out of town fast.

"You have to go, Nick. You can't get a complete picture of New Orleans without sampling the music. New Orleans and jazz go together."

"I don't think so, Jaye."

"Well. If you're sure. Maggie will be disappointed. She feels really bad about neglecting you all this week. It wouldn't take much time—the first set is at eight o'-clock, and each set only lasts about forty minutes. You could be home by nine. Get your writing in then."

Nick gave in. "All right. Tell Maggie I'll come by for her at seven-thirty." He would treat it as a test of his character. He owed it to Maggie to tell her good-bye in person and to wish her luck with her business.

As long as he was being forthright and honest, he ought to tell Maggie and the others that he was their landlord. And he would. Later. His cowardly streak kept him from telling them face-to-face. Nick did not want to see the shock and disappointment in their eyes when he admitted that he had lied to them. But as soon as he figured out the best way to structure their takeover of the building, he would call and spell it out for them.

Nick surfaced from making plans for a hasty retreat when Jaye waved the gift bag under his nose. "What's this?"

"Mardi Gras present. Ya'll have a good time tonight." Jaye handed him the bag and waved good-bye. "See ya."

Nick opened the bag. It contained a box of condoms.

Maggie rested her elbows on the counter and stared out the shop window. It was almost closing time, and the steady stream of customers had stopped. She was alone. Maggie sighed. Ever since the other tenants had begun their campaign to get Nick to buy the building, Maggie had felt alone, even when customers crowded the shop.

All alone and left out.

Emcee, in his usual place on the counter, began purring. His purr sounded like a Humvee in need of a new muffler. Absently, she stroked the cat behind his ears.

It wasn't fair. She had been the first one to think about seducing Nick. Well, the second, if the tarot cards counted.

Then came Shirley's revelation about Nick's identity, and a simple foray into the world of casual sex had turned into something complicated.

She had been right to refuse to participate in the seduction of Nicholas Gerard, aka Norton Graves, but that didn't keep her from feeling although she had let the team down. The tenants had always acted together from the day she had moved into her apartment at eleven-thirteen Royal Street. Maggie couldn't help feeling guilty about letting them down.

She couldn't help feeling jealous, either.

Monday, she had seen Ed escort Nick across the street and down the block to tour Gallier House. They had not returned home after that, but had continued down Royal Street. Ed had been talking, waving his hands, pointing. At least the plot to charm Norton Graves would have one positive outcome. Ed was having a good time, and he was feeling useful again.

When they returned home late Monday afternoon, Ed had stopped by and given her a report on their day. After the Gallier House, they gone to Jackson Square to see the Cabildo and the 1830 house in the Pontalba apartment building. The professor had described Nick as a prize student, attentive, intelligent, quick to understand and appreciate the past.

Maggie didn't know how Nick felt, since he had returned to his apartment without so much as a glance in her direction, but Ed had been charmed out of his argyle socks.

While on their tour, Nick had pointed out to Ed that other people were following along, hanging on Ed's every word. Nick had suggested that Ed start up a tour service, one that would give the tourists the true history of the Quarter, instead of the garbled version the tour guides and the carriage drivers used.

"Have you ever listened to what some of those tour guides spout as history?" Ed had asked her, indignant. "Or what the carriage drivers say? It would be a service to set the record straight, don't you think?"

Maggie had nodded agreement, smiling wistfully as Ed wandered out the side door and down the passageway, muttering to himself.

Tuesday, Shirley had taken Nick on a riverboat cruise, then to dinner at Commander's Palace. They had come home late. Maggie had heard them in the courtyard, giggling like a couple of teenagers. Since Shirley rarely giggled, Maggie could only surmise that Nick had charmed her, too. Shirley had confirmed Maggie's impression the next morning on the way to work. Nick had given Shirley several ideas on how to increase her business.

"Maggie, he said I should offer classes in tarot card reading. I could use the stockroom. It's practically empty. Three or four tables, some chairs—instant classroom. I could have a blackboard, too. I always wanted my very own blackboard. Besides the fees for the course, think of all the tarot card decks I would sell. Do you know what the markup on tarot cards is?"

Shirley had grinned at Maggie, an avaricious gleam in her eyes.

Wednesday had been the professor's turn again. He had taken Nick on a swamp tour, a trip that had taken all day. They had not returned before Maggie closed her shop, but she had heard them talking as they climbed the stairs. Nick had been asking Ed if he had thought any more about setting up a tour business. She hadn't heard Ed's words, but from the excited tone of his reply, she guessed that the professor had decided to do it.

Thursday, Nick had gone to see Jaye's show at the Foxy Lady Club. On their way out, Jaye had popped his head in the door to tell her that after his performance he planned to take Nick on a tour of French Quarter bars, from the tourist traps on Bourbon Street to the seamen's bars on Decatur. Nick, waiting outside the storefront, had waved at her. They must have been at it all night, because Maggie hadn't heard them return.

Jaye hadn't dropped in to give her a report today. Maybe she would catch him on his way to work. Maggie groaned. She was pathetic, desperate for any crumb of information about Nick. Norton.

Nick was Norton Graves, wealthy *New York Times* best-selling author. Not the man for her experiment. Not now. Not ever.

Why not? asked a testy voice, the voice of her long-suffering hormones, no doubt. Why the hell not?

Nick or Norton wouldn't be around long. Since he was traveling under an assumed name, the chances of the tabloids picking up on their affair were slim to none. Come to think of it, the tabloids didn't seem to waste much ink on famous writers.

No matter what his name was, Maggie had to admit that she was mightily attracted to him.

Maggie sighed. She couldn't do it. She could not make love with Nick and turn right around and ask him to buy a building for her. That would be beyond tacky.

Even if she stepped aside and let Shirley and the others do the asking, Nick would think she had traded sex for a long-term lease. Even if she would never see him again, Maggie couldn't help wanting Nick to think well of her. Which he wouldn't, if—

A knock on the side door brought her out of her reverie. Jaye entered the shop from the passageway. He sauntered over to the counter. "Hey, Maggie. How's business?"

"Good. Very, very good. I will definitely end up in the black this year—if we don't have to move, that is. Are you on your way to work?"

"In a little while. I thought I would drop by for a schmooze. Haven't seen too much of you lately."

Maggie busied herself restocking the displays. Her masks had been flying out of the store all week. "I know. I've been busy. Lots of customers this time of year."

Jaye looked around at the shop, currently devoid of customers. "Yeah. I can see that."

"This is the first time all day that I haven't been swamped with customers. Lulls happen."

"I know that. Changed your mind yet?"

"About what?"

"About doing your part."

Shifting a Saints mask to a more prominent place on the counter, Maggie said, "I don't know what you mean."

"Oh, yes, you do, doll face. I mean helping out with Nick."

"I don't have time. I'm really very busy."

"Not after closing, you're not." Jaye leaned on the counter. "We're doing it for you, you know."

She knew Jaye and the others thought she had the most to lose if the building sold—both her apartment and her shop. "I don't want you making sacrifices for me."

"Taking Nick around town isn't a sacrifice. Seeing the Quarter through a newcomer's eyes is fun. Not to mention, Nick gave me some dynamite advice about my career."

"Really? What did he advise—that you shave instead of wax?"

"Meow. The sex kitten has claws."

"Sorry. What did Nick think you should do?"

"He said I should see about getting some bookings at the Gulf Coast casinos. Talent scouts from New York and Los Angeles check out the acts there. Nick is sure that if one of them saw my act, I'd get an offer for the big time."

"How did Nick know about talent scouts and casinos in Mississippi?" asked Maggie.

"He said he worked for an agency that booked acts for a while. Nick has had a lot of different jobs."

"Or maybe Norton has researched different careers for his books."

"Maybe not. Listen up, doll. Nick wants to go to Preservation Hall this evening. Why don't you go with him? I've got two shows tonight, as usual, so I can't do it. Shirley is painting her storeroom tonight. And Ed's going out to dinner with a former student."

"I can't go. I have a date."

Jaye arched a brow. "Magnolia Mayfair. You do not."

Maggie abandoned her lie. "I don't want to go to Preservation Hall. It's dark and crowded. And those benches are uncomfortable."

"Those benches mean you'll be sitting hip to hip, thigh to thigh, with Nick. He'll probably have to put his arm around you to support your back. Doesn't that sound tempting? Nick has noticed you're avoiding him."

Maggie ignored temptation and concentrated on Jaye's last remark. "I'm not avoiding him. Not exactly. What makes you think he's noticed?"

"Oh, I don't know. It could be the way he drops your name into the conversation every two minutes."

"Nick talks about me?" Maggie felt a little tremor slide down her spine.

"Incessantly."

She took a roll of paper towels and the spray bottle of Windex from under the counter. "What does he say?"

"He asks questions. Where you are, what you're doing, that kind of thing. He wanted to know more about Robert."

Maggie made a face. "Why would he want to know about Robert?"

"I got the impression he was trying to figure out if you were over him."

"Well. I hope you told him I was over Robert years ago."

"Magnolia. It's a sin to tell a lie. Even to yourself."

"I am not lying. I was over Robert about five minutes after I gave him back his ring. The man was a slug. Why do you think I would waste time mooning over Robert?"

"I don't think that. I think Robert did a number on your self-confidence. You lost your trust in your ability to choose the right man. So you're not going to make a choice at all."

"When did you get your degree in psychology?"

"Never mind. About Nick. He wants to know why you persist in ignoring him. We make excuses for you, but I can tell he's not buying them. You're hurting his feelings."

"I doubt that." Maggie sprayed the countertop with Windex and began rubbing the glass vigorously with a paper towel. "Why would a rich, famous author care what I do or don't do?"

"Nick cares. He's attracted to you."

"Yeah. Right." Using a thumbnail to scrape away a stubborn spot, Maggie avoided looking at Jaye.

"He is. Reluctantly attracted, maybe, considering he thinks you're a wife-in-waiting. But definitely attracted. Admit it, doll. The same goes for you."

Forcing herself to look Jaye in the eye, Maggie insisted, "I am not going to sleep with Nick."

"That, naturally, is your call." Jaye pointed to a streak on the glass. "Missed a spot."

Maggie rubbed the spot clean. "Jaye, you know that's not true. You all think I should have a fling with Nick." She would have done it, too, if Nick had been who he claimed to be.

"I don't deny it. My personal opinion is that it would do both you and Nick a world of good. Nick seems lonely. He and his family aren't close."

"I know. He told me that."

"Did you know his parents divorced when he was nine and shipped him off to boarding school?"

"Yes. He mentioned that, too."

"His mother and father both remarried and started new families. Nick was the forgotten child." Jaye blinked rapidly. "Sad, isn't it?"

Maggie shrugged. "If it's true. Maybe it's Norton's cover story. Trying to make me feel sorry for Nick isn't going to work, Jaye. I am not going to seduce Norton—Nick—for a building. That's . . . prostitution."

"Prostitution?" Jaye's eyebrows shot up. "Ah ha! So that's what made you change your mind about using Nick for your experiment with lust. I should have realized . . . But you were up for having a little exploratory fling with him when you thought he was just plain Nick, weren't you?"

"Maybe. But, if you will recall, Nick was not interested."

"I didn't believe that then, and I don't believe it now. Nick might be wary, but he was and is interested. So were you, until Shirley stopped you in your tracks with her theory."

"So?"

"The theory is unproven."

"You said he wouldn't let you look at the files on his computer."

"That doesn't prove anything one way or the other. No writer, especially not a beginner, wants to show his work to anyone else. Not the first stumbling efforts."

"Did Shirley ever talk to Corinne? What did she say?"

"Nothing useful. Think about it, Maggie. If Nick is Norton Graves, why would he tell Corinne? You know as well as I do, if Corinne had the tiniest inkling that Nick was someone who could afford it, we wouldn't have to do a thing to convince him to buy the building. She would be here every day with her hard-sell hat on."

"I suppose so. So, we still don't know whether or not Nick is Norton Graves."

Jaye leaned over and planted his elbows on the

counter. "I know. No matter what Shirley thinks, Nick can't be Norton Graves."

Maggie's heart stuttered. "He can't? Why can't he?"

"I did a little research. Norton Graves writes a book a year, has done ever since he first published. He's on his seventeenth book. Nick is what? Thirty-five?"

"Thirty-four."

"You really think Graves wrote his first mystery when he was sixteen?"

"It could happen. He could be a prodigy."

"Not likely. I'm sure Nick is exactly who he says he is: Nicholas Gerard, unpublished author."

"Jaye. At the meeting, you agreed with Shirley and Ed. All of you were convinced that Nick was the answer to our problem. Now you're sure that Nick isn't Norton Graves after all. What's going on?"

He shrugged. "Shirley's theory made a weird kind of sense at the time. But, after reflection, one completely lacking in factual support. Put the idea out of your mind, Maggie."

"Why? What difference does it make? I'm not going to seduce Nick even if he isn't Norton. I've come to the conclusion that you were right. I am not the type to have affairs."

"I was wrong about that. *You* said I was wrong. And I was. Maggie, last Monday at the Café du Monde, you were on the verge of coming out of the cavern of celibacy you've been in for the past four years. That was a good thing. Then Shirley sent you running for cover with her Norton Graves scenario. One way or another, you need to get out. You can't spend the rest of your life hiding behind that counter."

"I don't intend to. And I am not hiding. Cavern of celibacy? And the way out would be what? The path to promiscuity?"

Jaye shrugged. "You're not promiscuous until you've had more than six lovers. When Shirley came up with the plan to charm Nick, I thought that would give you the push you needed to take that first step. Now I see it had the opposite effect."

"You made that up. The thing about six lovers."

"No, I didn't. I saw it on a sitcom. *Mary Tyler Moore*, I think. Forget about celibacy and promiscuity. You aren't the kind of person who will be happy alone. You are a people person. Look at what happened when you and your parents were on the outs. You came to New Orleans and found yourself another family."

"Yes, but—"

"No buts. But you're still letting your experience with Robert keep you in—"

"The cavern of celibacy."

"Exactly. I don't want you to spend the rest of your life alone."

"Having an affair with Nick is not going to fill up the rest of my life."

"No, but it will get you out of the house. That's a start."

Maggie felt her resolve weakening. She wasn't sure about affairs, but she was positive—almost positive—that she didn't want to be celibate for the rest of her life. Robert had been a cad, but he had been a good lover—he would have had to be, wouldn't he? To satisfy seven women. And Robert had satisfied her, in the bedroom anyway.

Maggie liked sex. And she missed it.

Directing her gaze to a spot over Jaye's left ear, Maggie said, "Oh, well. I guess I can spare an hour or two this evening."

Jaye made a fist and pumped his arm twice. "Yahoo!

Now. On to the important stuff. What are you going to wear?"

"What difference does that make?"

"Maggie. This is your first date in five years. It makes a difference."

"This is not a date. It's a . . . a research trip."

"Maggie, doll. It will look like a date to outsiders. You don't want to embarrass Nick. He cleans up real good. Let's go check out your closet."

"I don't have a closet. And it's twenty minutes to closing time."

"Close early for once."

"No." As soon as she had agreed to see Nick again, Maggie began having second thoughts. She needed at least twenty minutes to think about where a date with Nick might lead and if she really wanted to go there. She handed Jaye the key to her apartment. "Here. You go look. I'll be there as soon as I close up."

When Maggie joined Jaye, every item of clothing she owned was out of her armoire and on her bed or hanging from the railing of the spiral staircase.

Jaye shook his head. "Nothing, Maggie. Too bad it's too late to go shopping. You could use a few new clothes, and I do mean 'new.'"

"I can't afford to buy clothes, new or vintage. Not now. Not when we're on the verge of eviction."

"We've got to find something suitable for you to wear."

"People go to Preservation Hall wearing everything from jeans to sequins. What would you consider suitable?"

"Something covertly sexy."

"Covertly sexy." Frowning, Maggie eyed the pile of clothes on her bed. "I don't think I have anything like that."

"I know you don't. Your clothes all scream 'whole-some.' Not to worry, I know exactly what you need. I'll let you borrow my favorite outfit."

"You will? Will it fit?"

"It should. That ball gown I loaned you last year for the Bacchus Ball fit you perfectly. And the outfit I have in mind is mostly Lycra."

Jaye's favorite outfit turned out to be tight-fitting black pants that hung low on her hips and showed Maggie's navel. Standing in front of Jaye's cheval mirror with him standing behind her, Maggie gave his reflection a dubious look. "Jaye. Margaret Orr said it was going to be in the low forties tonight. I hope the top is long enough to cover my midriff."

"It is. Almost. Here, put on the sweater. Cover up that sad excuse for a bra. I can't believe you don't have any underwear that isn't white cotton."

"My panties aren't all white. They have pink roses embroidered on them," said Maggie, pulling the sweater over her head. The sweater was black cashmere, shot through with silver metallic threads.

"Pink roses." Jaye put one hand on his heart, the other on his forehead, palm out. "Be still my heart. Oh, well, by the time Nick gets to see them, he won't care."

"Nick isn't going to see my underwear." The sweater reached the top of the pants. Barely. As long as she didn't breathe deeply, her navel stayed discreetly covered, but the slightest movement gave anyone looking a peek at her belly button. "I get the covert part. But sexy? What if Nick is not a navel man?"

"Doesn't matter. The sexy part is letting Nick think he's seeing something he shouldn't. Could be a shoulder, could be a navel or an ankle. Or a boob, but that's so obvious."

"How did you learn all this stuff?"

Jaye grinned at her reflection in the mirror. "I was born knowing, doll."

"No wonder Robert had to go out with six other women," Maggie muttered. "I must not have that gene."

"Maggie. We do not let others define who we are. Especially not others like Robert. Nor does your choice of clothes say anything about your worth as a woman. Got that?"

"Yes. Thank you. On the other hand, my choice of men says a lot, don't you think?" She gave the sweater a tug. "Maybe I should forget about this and proceed to plan B."

"Which is?" asked Jaye, giving her a critical once-over.

"To forget about men and get another cat. Or two."

"Don't be silly. You're not destined to be a spinster, with or without cats. You're a sex kitten, remember?"

"I remember, but I don't think Nick does."

"Oh, he remembers. Not the phrase, maybe. But he is still attracted to you." He motioned for her to turn around. When she faced Jaye again, he said, "The ensemble is perfect. Except for shoes." He shook his head. "The outfit needs strappy sandals with four inch heels, but these were the best your armoire had to offer." Jaye handed Maggie the silver flats she had worn to the Bacchus Ball last year. "Now, let's do your makeup."

"I know how to do that."

"No. You don't."

"Well, gee. I suppose the wrong makeup doesn't say anything about my worth as a woman either. Why didn't you tell me this before now?"

"No need. The scrubbed midwestern look worked

fine for a wholesome shop owner. But you need to add a little pizzazz for a date. Go wash your face while I get out the war paint."

Maggie threw up her arms, but she did as Jaye told her. When she exited the bathroom with her face scrubbed clean, Jaye escorted her to his dressing table. Jars, tubes, pots, and brushes lay in wait on the table. "Sit."

Maggie sank onto the plush cushion of the stool. Large butterflies began to have a party behind her bare navel. "This will be a date, won't it?"

"Yes, Magnolia. There really is a Santa Claus." Jaye screwed the top off a jar and handed it to her. "Here, smooth this moisturizer on your face."

Maggie followed instructions, then sat back and let Jaye do the rest. When she had been creamed, powdered, and rouged to his satisfaction, she barely recognized herself. Her skin glowed, her eyes were dark and mysterious, and her lips were begging to be kissed. "How did you do that? I still don't look as if I have on makeup, but I look different. I look good."

"Better than good. Sexy. Makeup's not supposed to show, doll face. Unless you're on stage, that is. Stand up. Let's have a look at you."

Maggie stood and twirled around. "I feel pretty."

"You look gorgeous, Gorgeous. I've done my part. Now you do yours. Go get him, girlfriend." Jaye gave her a playful push toward the door.

Maggie dug in her heels. "Wait. We're forgetting something."

"Perfume? You don't need it. Think pheromones."

"Not perfume. Nick. We forgot about Nick. I haven't asked him out yet. What if he turns me down?"

Jaye grinned at her. "He won't."

"You can't be sure of that."

"Yes, I can. I already asked him for you. Or, rather, I told him you would be the one taking him to Preservation Hall. Nick will be calling for you at seven-thirty."

With her hands fisted on her hips, Maggie glared at Jaye. "And how did you know I would go?"

"I know you, doll. You're ready for this. Or you will be." Jaye went to his armoire and took out a shocking pink coat and held it out to her.

"This is fur." Maggie stroked the coat. It was softer than Emcee. "Real fur. I don't wear fur."

"You'll need a coat tonight, for the walk to Preservation Hall. And this is the only coat I have that goes with the outfit. Come on, Maggie. The nutria have already given their all. Do you want their deaths to count for nothing?"

Maggie jerked her hand away. "Nutria?"

"Wild nutria. No farmed animals made this fur."

"Oh. Well. I do need a coat." Maggie let Jaye help her into the fur coat. Her principles were toppling like pine trees in a hurricane.

Maggie had a feeling she knew which one would be the next to fall.

Nine

Maggie answered the door at his first knock. Nick stared at her, his gaze moving from her eyes down to the toes of her silver flats. She had on a shimmery black sweater and pants so tight he wondered how she could breathe.

As if she wanted to show him how, Maggie sucked in a deep breath. The sweater parted company with her pants, exposing a narrow strip of bare skin. He could see her belly button. Nick swallowed hard, but resisted the urge to tug on his tie. "Are you ready to go?" he asked, his voice husky.

"Yes. Just let me get my jacket." She reached for a coat hanging on the hall tree.

Nick took the coat from her and held it while she slid her arms into the sleeves. "Soft. What kind of fur is this?"

"Nutria."

"Nutria? Those huge rats that live in the swamp? I saw several when the professor and I went on the swamp tour."

Maggie nodded. "That's the rodent."

"The ones I saw were not hot pink."

"Dyed fur. Maybe I should get another jacket. I don't really approve of fur coats. Although, rodent fur doesn't seem as politically incorrect as, say, mink."

"No. And it is very soft." Nick slid his hands from her shoulders to her forearms. Fur was as sexy as silk. Sexier, maybe. Nick jerked his hands away. "If you don't approve of fur coats, why did you buy one?"

"Oh, I didn't buy this. Jaye loaned it to me."

"Ah. That makes sense. Jaye seems more the hot pink fur coat type than you do."

"Oh, really? What type am I, then? Sensible wool?"

"Cashmere."

"Oooh, nice. I like cashmere. Good recovery, Gerard. As it happens, I don't own any kind of coat."

"Why not?"

"I don't like cold weather. Mainly because I don't like wearing all those extra clothes. Coats, fur-lined boots, gloves, scarfs, hats. I think it started when I was a little girl. Snowsuits made me claustrophobic."

"If you don't own a coat, how do you keep warm?"

"It's never that cold here. Not for long, anyway. When it is cold, I manage with sweaters and jackets. I can always borrow a coat from Jaye. We're the same size, more or less."

"I like your more," Nick said, unable to stop himself from ogling her chest.

Maggie pulled the coat closed, hiding her bare midriff. "Thank you. I think."

Taking her by the arm, Nick led her down the passageway and onto Royal Street. "Where are we going?"

"St. Peter. Preservation Hall is on St. Peter, between Royal and Bourbon."

Tucking her hand in the crook of his arm, Nick walked Maggie up Royal Street. After a few blocks, he said, "Look, we're back at the A&P."

"Turn right at the grocery store," said Maggie. "Where we had our first date."

An alarm bell sounded faintly in the back of Nick's head. "Grocery shopping isn't dating," he said.

She slanted a look at him. A sly look. "You should agree that our trip to the A&P was a date. That would make this our second date."

"First date, second date. What difference does it make?" The bell was ringing louder now.

"Well. I always thought of myself as the kind of girl who doesn't go to bed with a man on their first date."

Nick dropped her arm. "Maggie—"

"Don't worry. I'm probably still that kind of girl. I'm not making any promises, though. It has been a long time since I dated. We'll just have to wait and see, won't we?" Maggie looked at him. "You're shivering. Am I making you nervous?"

"I am not shivering. Nor am I nervous. Why would I be nervous?" To prove it, Nick took her arm again. "I see it. Preservation Hall. Across the street, in the middle of the block. I thought you changed your mind about that. About me. You were going to wait for another guy to have your affair."

Maggie opened her eyes wide. "Who said anything about an affair?"

"You did. You said this was our second date, and that you didn't go to bed on the first date."

"I was making conversation, not expressing my intentions." She batted her lashes at him as they entered the jazz club.

"Uh huh. Here we are. Preservation Hall." The clanging in his head was making thinking difficult. A change of subject was in order. "Do you like jazz?"

"I love jazz, especially the traditional kind they play here. Have you been to the Jazz Museum yet? It's on Esplanade at the old mint, close to the French Market."

"No."

"I could close up early, and we could go there tomorrow."

"You can't close up for me. This is your busy season. Jaye explained that to me. Shirley, too. And the professor. They all said the time between Thanksgiving and Mardi Gras was the busiest time of the year for you."

"Actually, it starts with Halloween." Maggie began shrugging out of her coat. As she twisted around, her sweater rode up again. "This is the only place I've ever lived where the adults have more fun than the kids at Halloween. They have costume parties at all the bars. I sell a lot of masks at Halloween."

"That's interesting," Nick said absently. He couldn't take his eyes off her middle. He handed her the coat, pushing it against her chest. Maggie draped the coat around her shoulders and sat down.

As more and more people came in, Nick found himself squeezed closer and closer to Maggie. Hip to hip and thigh to thigh. Heat surrounded him—hot music, hot bodies.

The bench was hard, hard and uncomfortable. Maggie squirmed. Nick guessed that she was trying to find a more comfortable position. She twisted around and leaned her back against his shoulder. He stiffened, and started to pull away.

He couldn't do it.

Nick put his arm around Maggie's waist. "Stop wiggling," he hissed. "Your sweater is riding up. I can see your belly button. And so can everyone else." Over the top of her head, Nick glared at the man seated on her other side. The man was staring at Maggie's exposed navel.

Nick found the hem of the sweater and tugged. He meant to withdraw his hand as soon as she was decently covered, but his fingers had other plans. They traced the warm, silky skin above the low-riding waist-band of her pants, from her spine to just above her hip bone. Nick's hand came to rest on her bare tummy. He splayed his fingers and felt warm, smooth skin. Skin with the same properties as Super Glue. His hand was stuck to Maggie's middle.

When the set was over, Nick managed to free his hand. He pulled Maggie to her feet and stuffed her into her coat. "Let's get out of here. I'm burning up. I need air."

And he needed to get Maggie to her apartment and leave her there. Alone.

Maggie had other ideas. As he tugged her out the door, she said, "Do you want a drink? Pat O'Brien's is right next door. Or did you go there when you and Jaye went bar hopping?"

"We missed that one."

"Well. You ought to see it. For your research. And I would like a drink, too. A Hurricane. I've never had one."

For a little thing, she was strong. She had dug in her heels, keeping him from steering her toward home.

"Jaye said Pat O'Brien's was a tourist trap."

"It's a landmark. A tradition." She grinned at him. "And a tourist trap. You're a tourist. Feel like being trapped?"

"No." Nick could hear iron bars clanging shut. The alarm bell in his head was screeching a warning: marriage trap. Marriage trap.

Maggie's bottom lip came out. "Please? It's too early to go home."

Before Nick could utter a protest, Maggie had pulled him into the bar. Once they were seated at a copper-topped table, a green-coated waiter listed the ingredients of a Hurricane—four ounces of dark rum, passion fruit juice, and lemon juice.

"She'll have that," said Nick to the waiter. With any luck, the drink would make Maggie tipsy. He wouldn't take advantage of a woman impaired by four ounces of rum. "And I'll have an Abita Gold."

"Passion fruit and rum. Sounds like a dangerous combination to me. Was Abita Gold the beer Shirley gave you when you were sick?"

"Yeah."

"I thought so. It's a local brand. You should try Purple Haze. That's another Abita beer—it has raspberries in it."

"I don't like fruit in my alcohol."

The waiter returned with their drinks. Maggie's Hurricane was garnished with a slice of orange and a cherry. "Oh, well then. I guess you wouldn't like this." She took a sip of the Hurricane. "Not bad." She pushed the glass toward him. "Have a sip."

"No, thanks." Nick settled back in his chair and lifted his beer to his lips.

Maggie waved a hand in front of her face. "Hot. Help me with my coat?"

Setting the beer bottle on the table, Nick helped her out of the coat. "That sweater is too short."

She raised her arms, taking the sweater up and away from her pants. "No, it's not. It's supposed to—"

Nick reached across the table and pulled her arms down to her sides. "You have to stop this, Maggie. It's not going to work."

"I don't know what you're talking about. Stop what?"

"Trying to make me want you."

"Why should I stop?" She scowled at him. "You're not still worried about my intentions, are you? I promise, Nick. I do not want to marry you."

"I believe you. But I don't believe that you're the kind of woman who can go to bed with a man for nothing more than sex. I think you have to care about someone before you do that."

"Well, of course I care about you. I like you. I wouldn't consider having sex with a man I didn't like."

"Maggie. I'll hurt you."

"No, you won't. How? Because you'll leave? But that's part of your charm. That you won't be around for long." She drew her brows together. "Didn't I explain this to you before?"

"It took you what? Four years? Five? To get over that ass you were engaged to? You're not the kind to walk away from someone you care about unscathed."

Her brow smoothed, and she took one of his hands in hers. "Okay. Let's suppose you're right. It took me four years to get over a four-year relationship. Following your reasoning, it will take me two weeks to get over you. Assuming it takes any time at all, that is." Maggie stroked the back of his hand. "I think it's sweet of you to worry about me."

"I'm not sweet, Maggie. I was trying to let you down easy. The truth is, I don't want you. I don't even dream about you anymore."

"You don't?"

"Nope. Must have been the pneumonia. I haven't had the dream since I finished the antibiotics. Ed said antibiotics induce vivid dreams."

Maggie dropped his hand. "What are you saying? That wanting me was some kind of medical side effect?"

"I think so. I will admit that I was attracted to you. While I was sick. Now that I've recovered, I'm not."

"Oh, really?" She arched a brow. "Then, why did you agree to go out with me tonight?"

"To make sure."

Her shoulders slumped. "Oh. Well. That's not very flattering."

"I wasn't trying to flatter you." Nick threw some bills on the table. "Let's go."

They were out of the bar and back on Royal Street in record time. Nick kept up the brisk pace all the way back to eleven-thirteen. He almost made it safely to his apartment.

But halfway down the passageway, Maggie stopped suddenly. Nick bumped into her back.

"Maggie?"

She leaned her back against him. "I don't believe you. I think you're lying."

"Lying? About what?"

"Not dreaming about me anymore. I dream about you. Every night. The same dream, over and over. It's maddening."

"You dream about me? Coming down the staircase?"

"No staircase. In my dream you're an animal trainer. With a whip."

"A whip? Kinky. What are you? My assistant?"

She shook her head. "I'm a sex kitten. You tame me." She turned around and pushed Nick against the wall. "Kiss me, Nick."

"Maggie. Stop. I'm leaving tomorrow."

"Leaving? Tomorrow? Why? You have a month's lease. You'll miss the Mardi Gras parades."

"Something's come up. I've got to go back to New York. I can't have an affair with you, Maggie."

She opened her mouth, but no words came out. He had managed to shock her silent by telling her he was leaving.

Torn between regret and relief, Nick walked Maggie to her door.

And left her there.

Maggie pressed her nose against the pane of glass in the French door and watched Nick take the stairs two at a time. He really wanted to get away from her. Fast. Not only for tonight. For forever. He was leaving.

So much for her powers of seduction.

Pushing away from the door, she slid the fur coat off and hung it on the hall tree. Maggie walked to her bedroom, slithering out of the Lycra pants as soon as she was in her room. Emcee was curled up on her pillow. He slit one eye open.

"I'm a failure as a woman." She crossed her arms and grabbed the hem of the sweater, pulling it over her head and tossing it on the bed.

Emcee closed his eye, uninterested.

"Some friend you are. Maybe I should get a dog."

Emcee rolled on his back, inviting her to rub his tummy. She did. Maggie felt a tear roll down her cheek. She touched her cheek. It was wet. She was weeping.

"Out of frustration. That's all. I had other plans for tonight. I am not crying because he's leaving. Only because he's leaving before we—"

Maggie sat on the bed and dragged Emcee onto her lap. "You know what, Emcee? I think Mr. Gerard is leaving because he's afraid. Of me. And not because I'm wu-wu-wife material. I've made it very clear that I am not the marrying kind. I think Mr. Nicholas Gerard is the one who is the marrying kind, not me. He may not want to be, but he is."

Nick could say he wanted nothing to do with family,

but his actions didn't follow his words. Look at how he had taken to the tenants. Nick had cured Ed's retirement blues, given sound career advice to Jaye, and offered Shirley suggestions on how to increase her business. He had been a good friend to all of them. A man who made friends that easily was not a man meant to be alone.

He hadn't wanted to be alone with her.

Why hadn't he?

Maybe it was her fault. In part, at least. She had been avoiding him, until tonight. But he hadn't had his mind on business tonight. She was sure of that. He had had his hands all over her bare skin. Heat pooled between her legs as she remembered the feel of his hand on her stomach.

Maggie stood up, dumping Emcee onto the floor. He meowed in protest.

"Sorry."

She picked up the clothes she had discarded, hanging Jaye's sweater and pants on the staircase railing. Her gaze followed the spiral staircase up to the ceiling. Nick had dreamed about her entering his bedroom from the staircase. Even if he had told the truth about not dreaming about her now, he had dreamed that dream more than once.

A man wouldn't dream about a woman unless he was interested, would he?

On the other hand, he could have dreamed about her because she was the one currently occupying the apartment below his. Maybe Nick's dream didn't depend on her, specifically. It could be that any woman emerging nude from the staircase would fulfill his fantasy.

Maggie shook her head. "No way, Emcee. That's my staircase. If anyone uses it, it will be me. me."

But she wouldn't. Not for a one-night stand. Nick wouldn't be around long enough for a brief affair. Maggie sighed mournfully. She had a right to mourn the loss of her first Mr. Wrong. Nick had seemed so perfect for her.

For her experiment, she meant. No silver-eyed lover for her after all. The tarot cards had lied.

Emcee meowed loudly and jumped onto the window-sill. Maggie reached across the narrow bed and opened the window. "There must be a meeting of Quarter cats tonight," Maggie mumbled, watching as the black cat disappeared into the dark.

Maggie pulled back the covers on her bed and slid between the sheets. She let her gaze circle up the spiral stairway. Was Nick dreaming about her now? What would he do if she really did come through the trap door wearing nothing but a smile? Closing her eyes, Maggie tried to imagine his reaction.

Nick would be in bed, asleep. The creaking of the trap door as it swung open would wake him. She would emerge slowly, rising through the opening one deliberate step at a time. First her head, then her shoulders, then her bare breasts would come into view. His gray eyes would turn to molten silver as she crossed the room. Nick would sit up, holding the covers aside so she could slide in beside him.

Maggie pushed the quilt off and fanned her face with her hand. "Whooee. That's some fantasy. Should I do it? Could I?" She shivered. A one-night stand might be as good a way as any at finding out about lust. Maybe the best way. No time for anything but hot, mind-blowing sex.

No time for strings to develop.

No time for emotions.

No time for love.

Definitely no time for love. She had her chance. Robert had been her soul mate, her one love.

Nick would be her first—and probably only—one-night stand.

She looked down at herself, still wearing her serviceable white bra and the cotton bikinis embroidered with tiny pink roses. "Maybe complete nudity isn't really necessary. I could go like this." No wonder Jaye had made a face. Her underwear was not sexy.

"No. This underwear is too . . . wifey. I'd spoil the fantasy and remind Nick what he thinks—what he *thinks* he thinks about marriage. If I'm going to do this, I have to do it right."

Maggie took a deep breath. Sitting up in bed, she reached behind her and unhooked her bra, letting it fall to the floor. Standing, she shimmied out of her panties. Taking a deep breath, she walked to the bottom of the staircase. Before she put her foot on the first step, Maggie stopped.

"I can't do this. I can't go up those stairs completely naked." Her gaze fell, and she found herself staring at her sewing machine. The cat mask was on the table next to the machine. She had finished the black silk mask on Thursday. Maggie snatched it up and put it on. She sighed, relieved. The mask gave her the illusion of invisibility.

Maggie put one bare foot on the first wrought-iron stair, then the other. Up she went, step by step, higher and higher. The ceiling was twelve feet from the floor, but it seemed farther. The staircase groaned and shifted as she climbed higher, and she kept one hand on the handrail.

At the top, Maggie struggled with the latch. When she succeeded in getting it open, she pushed on the trap door, letting it fall to the floor. If her fumbling with the latch hadn't wakened Nick, the noise of the trap door crashing open surely would.

Maggie took another step, resisting the urge to hurry up the last few stairs. She had to go slowly. Nick had dreamed that she emerged from the stairwell like Venus emerging from the foam.

The cat mask had shifted slightly during her battle with the latch, and Maggie could not see clearly. She didn't want to straighten it—that would detract from the spectacle she was performing for Nick.

Maggie took the last step, the step that would put her completely inside Nick's bedroom. She avoided looking at the bed until the last possible minute, terrified that he might be staring at her with disgust, not lust.

Finally, tossing her head to reseat the mask, she made herself look.

The bed was empty.

His dream had come true.

Nick almost pinched himself, to make sure he wasn't asleep and dreaming. But he knew he was awake. He had gone to the kitchen to get a drink of water. Standing at the sink, he had heard a loud crash from the bedroom. He had loped across the hall, and now, standing in the doorway, Nick watched as Maggie slowly emerged through the trap door. When she reached the top, her back was to him.

And a lovely back it was, too. Nick's gaze slid from her bare shoulders, down the curve of her spine to her round bottom, where it lingered awhile. Then he looked lower, down long, shapely legs to dainty ankles and delicately arched feet.

He must not have drunk enough water. His mouth

was drier now than when he had gotten out of bed to go to the kitchen. Not only that, a strange kind of lump in his throat made it difficult to swallow.

Maggie had done this for him. She had climbed those stairs, naked and vulnerable, for him. He cleared his throat.

Maggie whirled around.

She was wearing a mask, a cat mask.

Nick held out a hand. "Maggie—"

"I can't do this," she whispered, not looking at him. She crossed her right arm in front of her breasts, and her left hand hovered over the juncture of her thighs. "I thought I could, but I can't." Her gaze shifted from his eyes to his body. "You've got clothes on." She made it sound like an accusation.

Nick looked down. He had on a pair of white knit boxers. His erection was stretching the cotton. "I'm sorry," he said. "I wasn't expecting company."

The whiskers on the mask twitched. "Are you laughing at me?"

"Never. Come on, Maggie. Finish the fantasy. Come to me." Nick held out a hand.

She remained standing next to the trap door. Maggie appeared to be frozen in place. "I—I can't move."

"Sure you can. You've already done the hard part." Dropping his hand to his side, Nick took a step inside the bedroom.

"I thought I could. But you weren't there." She pointed to the bed, then quickly covered her breasts again. "You didn't see."

"Oh, I saw, all right. Just from a different angle. You have a very sexy back, Ms. Mayfair." He set the glass on the bedside table and advanced. "Look what you've done to me."

Maggie's gaze went to his crotch. "Oh. I did that?"

"Nobody but you. Come here, Maggie. You're shivering."

Her head jerked up. She looked him in the eye. "Of course I'm shivering," she said, her voice shrill. "It's cold and I'm naked."

"Come here, Magnolia," he coaxed, moving closer. "I'll warm you up."

Maggie took a tiny step toward him. "I'm very cold. Especially my feet."

"I'll bet. Come on, Maggie. Just one more step."

Maggie took the step, and Nick wrapped his arms around her. She snuggled closer. "Your body is hot, hot, hot. It feels good."

"Things are going to get hotter." Nick picked her up and carried her to the bed. He set her on the edge of the bed and knelt in front of her. Taking one foot in his hands, he began rubbing it. "Your foot is like a block of ice."

"I know. Those wrought-iron stairs are frigid."

Nick took her other foot and rubbed briskly. "Better?"

"Much. Thank you," she said primly, crossing her ankles.

Nick stood up and touched the curly whiskers. "I like your mask. The Sex Kitten mask?"

She nodded. "You gave me the idea for it."

A sudden flash of memory made him groan. "The first time I saw you, coming down the passageway to let me in, I thought you looked like a sleepy sex kitten."

"I know. Jaye told me. You talked in your sleep."

"I'm sorry." He wasn't sure why he kept apologizing.

"I'm not. I like being a sex kitten." Maggie made a purring noise. "My feet are warm now, but the rest of

me needs attention. I've got goose bumps all over."
She lay back on the bed, holding the covers aside.

Nick slid in beside her. He leaned over her and
kissed her on the nose. "Your nose is cold."

Maggie wrapped her arms around his neck. "Not
anymore."

"Your lips are blue. I can fix that." Nick kissed her
on the mouth.

The kiss lasted until Maggie's mouth felt warm.
Nick stared at her chest. "Your nipples are like mar-
bles. Cold?"

"Cold," she agreed. "Very, very cold." She gave an
exaggerated shiver.

Lowering his head, Nick took one nipple into his
mouth. Maggie's back arched, and she threw her
head back and moaned.

"One more time," Nick whispered, moving his
mouth from one breast to the other.

Nick's mouth moved over her body, licking, kissing,
sucking. Everywhere his lips touched heated. Nick
Gerard was better than central heat. Her skin glowed
with heat; her blood was a river of fire.

"Nick! I'm going to spontaneously combust. In another second I'll be nothing but a pile of ashes."

"Not yet. I'm not through with you yet."

Nick opened the drawer in the table by the bed. It
was empty. He fumbled around, frantically seeking
what he had put there earlier.

"What are you doing?"

"Condoms. Looking. Gone."

"Gone? You had a condom in that drawer?"

"Condoms. Box. Stop. Now. Can't go on."

"What do you mean, we can't go on? We have to go
on." Maggie sat up and pushed her hair out of her
eyes. "Let me look." Leaning across him, she pulled

the drawer completely out of the table and turned it upside down. Nothing fell out. "Are you sure you put the box in this drawer?"

"It's the only drawer in the room, Maggie."

"Maybe you put the box in a kitchen drawer."

"Who puts condoms in the kitchen?"

"I don't know. A chef, maybe?"

"Emcee took them."

"What?"

"That damn cat took my razor. And my watch. Why not the condoms?"

"Emcee didn't take your razor or your watch. What makes you say that?"

"Shirley told me he takes things."

"Not *big* things. Emcee has taken some of my earrings. One at a time, not even a pair. Once he stole one of the professor's cuff links. The biggest thing he ever managed was Jaye's tennis bracelet. Emcee likes shiny stuff. He uses his mouth, Nick. Emcee couldn't carry a razor or a watch in his mouth. Well, maybe the watch, if he dragged it by the band. But a razor? I don't think so."

"Condoms are shiny—foil wrappers."

"Were they loose? Had you taken them out of the box? He might have taken one. If he's learned how to open drawers, that is."

"The box hadn't been opened. But if not Emcee, then who? I had the damn condoms. I put them in this drawer this afternoon." Nick got up and pulled on his jeans.

Maggie narrowed her eyes. "This afternoon? Why did you buy condoms today? You said you were leaving."

"I didn't buy them. They were a present from Jaye.

A Mardi Gras present. He knew we were going out tonight. He must have thought—"

"—that we would end up in bed?"

"Yeah."

"That's why I came up the spiral staircase. I wanted us to be together. I wanted to make your dream come true."

"You did that."

"I'm not done yet. Now, about those condoms. Maybe they're in the bathroom."

"I'll look."

Nick returned. "Not there. We're screwed."

"Not literally. Unfortunately. I guess we are done, then." Maggie sighed mournfully.

"No, we are not done. I'm going to the pharmacy."

"Nick. It's the middle of the night. The pharmacy is closed."

"I'll wake up Dr. Martin. He has a key, doesn't he? He must have one. He got my antibiotics in the middle of the night."

"That was an emergency."

"Trust me, Maggie. So is this." He pulled the sweater over his head and shoved his bare feet into a pair of loafers. "You. Stay. Do not move."

"I'm not going anywhere."

"One box may not be enough. I'd better get two."

"Oh, my lordy me."

Nick almost ran out of the room, not stopping to turn on a light. Maggie heard a thump, followed by a muffled curse. "What was that?"

Nick reappeared in the bedroom door. "Me. Tripping over this." He held up a box of condoms.

"Oh, good. Where were they?"

"On the floor in the hall."

"How did they get there?" As he advanced toward

her, Maggie became aware that Nick was angry. More than angry. He was in a towering rage. With a supreme effort, Maggie resisted pulling the covers over her head.

Nick shook the box under her nose. "The correct question is, who put them there?"

"What?"

"Condoms don't walk themselves out the door. Emcee is not the culprit. He may be a smart cat; but he can't open drawers, and he can't carry a box in his mouth. Which one of your buddies moved the condoms?"

Maggie sat up and drew the quilt tightly around her. "I don't know what you're talking about."

Nick sat on the foot of the bed. "What I don't get is why you're doing this. Are you trying to make me think I'm nuts? Moving things around. Coughing and sneezing in my ear. That fuzzy guy in the corner that none of you will admit you saw. I just don't get it."

"Nick—"

"You take care of me when I'm sick. Then you ignore me for a week. Tonight, you act out my favorite fantasy." He waved the condom box under her nose. "Then you pull a trick like this. Care to explain?"

She pushed his hand away. "First, you needed us to take care of you. Second, I did not ignore you. Not for a week. For three days. I was busy. You were occupied. Okay, to tell the truth, I was scared to take the next step with you. This step. But so were you."

Nick leaned closer, almost nose to nose with her. "You don't scare me. You make me crazy."

Maggie closed her eyes to block out Nick's fury. "Lastly, I did not move the condoms. How could I? You've been with me ever since I climbed those stairs."

"I know you didn't do it tonight. But you could have done it earlier, before we went out."

Her eyes popped open. She was beginning to believe Nick was right. He was crazy. "I didn't even know you had condoms. If I didn't know you had condoms, how could I have moved them? *Why* would I have moved them?"

"You knew. You and Jaye and the other two are a team. If you didn't move them, one of the others—"

"No! No one moved the condoms. You must have done it."

"Right. Blame it on the outsider." Nick jerked the quilt out of her hands. "That's it. We're done. I don't know what your game is, but I'm not playing. Out. I want you out of here."

"Nick—"

"Now."

Nick watched Maggie disappear down the spiral staircase. As soon as she was out of sight, he closed the trap door.

His dream had almost come true. Would have come true if he hadn't tripped over the box of condoms and gone ballistic. What kind of stupid idiot kicked a woman out of bed *before* he finished with her?

Nick shook his head violently. Never would have happened. It took two to tango, and Maggie would have ended the dance if he hadn't.

Why? Why had she come up those stairs? It hadn't been easy for her. He sat on the bed and dropped his head into his hands. What if he had been wrong? What if Maggie hadn't known anything about the condoms?

Then he would have found out once and for all how the dream ended.

Sucked in again.

A group of people had pretended to like him. Then they began playing tricks on him. Clearly, they wanted him out of the apartment. Something incriminating had to be hidden there. Something they had used to scare off potential buyers.

Nick dropped his head onto his hands. Ah, well, it could be worse. At least they hadn't asked him for money.

But Maggie had come up the stairs wearing nothing but her Sex Kitten mask. And she would have made love with him if he hadn't lost the condoms and his temper.

Nick snapped his fingers. She had planned to seduce him, and she had almost succeeded. She wanted him, and not for a brief affair. His instincts had been right. Maggie was angling for a wedding ring. And he had almost fallen for her. It. For that trick women used to confuse and befuddle poor unsuspecting males. Sex. If he had gone through with it, Maggie would have expected him to do the right thing, make an honest woman of her. That meant marriage.

Nick wiped away the beads of sweat that had popped out on his forehead. Talk about your narrow escapes. He ought to thank whoever had moved the condoms. But for that, he would have violated his principles and made love—had sex—with Magnolia Mayfair.

Nick picked up the cat mask. It was made of silk. Sex kittens ought to wear silk. Maggie did know that, after all.

Ten

Maggie woke to the sound of rain.

The sound was not loud enough to drown out the beat of her heart. She was still alive.

Not fair. She ought to be dead from shame.

Maggie squeezed her eyes shut, blocking out the sight of the spiral staircase. Even with her eyes closed, she couldn't block out the memory of walking up those stairs. Naked.

Going up the spiral staircase had been embarrassing. Coming down had been humiliating. Worse than humiliating. There was not a word in the English language to describe how awful she had felt when Nick had ordered her out of his bedroom.

Not only out of his bedroom. Nick had thrown her out of his bed.

And he had stripped the quilt away, forcing her to leave as she had arrived. Naked.

From the bed to the staircase could not have been more than three or four steps, but it had seemed like a mile. Her knees had knocked together with every step.

And Nick had been watching her.

Maggie had wanted to run, but she had forced herself to go down the stairs slowly, taking care not to trip. Nicholas Gerard was not worth breaking her neck over.

Or her heart.

"Noooo." Pulling the down comforter over her head, Maggie tried desperately not to think or feel. She succeeded only in not breathing. Fighting her way free of the comforter, she gasped for air.

The ache in her chest had nothing to do with her heart. Nothing. Not a thing. Her pride had suffered, her pride and her hormones. Both would recover, as soon as she—

Emcee appeared at the window, his fur shiny from the rain.

Maggie sat up and opened the window. A cold blast of air followed Emcee inside. Great. A cold, rainy day exactly matched her mood. With any luck, she could freeze the memories of last night. Or drown them.

"Come on, Emcee. Let's get a towel and dry you off."

Maggie picked up the soggy cat and walked to the bathroom. Taking a towel off the shelf, she began rubbing Emcee dry. The cat settled down on her lap, purring loudly.

Someone had lied to her. She didn't remember who, but someone had told her that meaningless sex didn't hurt. More than one person had assured her that love affairs were playtime.

A one night-stand should have been a walk in the park. She hadn't had a one-night stand, a tiny voice whispered. Even an affair as brief as one night required a completed sex act. She and Nick had not had meaningless sex.

"Right. Nick kicked me out of his bed before we got that far." Meaningless foreplay, then. Whatever it was called, it had hurt. As much as the end of a four-year engagement. More.

Just as Nick had predicted.

Tears gathered in her eyes. Maggie dashed them away with her hands. "No. No. No. I am not going to cry. I'm not going to feel sorry for myself. I refuse to wallow in misery. Why should I?"

Because a man she cared for had rejected her in the most mortifying way possible? That was no reason to cry.

Nick was mean. And crazy.

Nicholas Gerard was the one with a problem. Not her.

At least she had learned one thing from the fiasco. Lust was not the answer. Not for her.

Maggie quickly suppressed the thought that lust was not all that had sent her up the spiral staircase. She refused to allow herself even a fleeting thought that the other *L* word might be involved.

Emcee wiggled out of the towel and jumped to the floor. He began drying his fur with his tongue.

"Kitten. I've got to get a kitten. I hope Dr. Hector has one left. I'll call right away." And on the way to the vet's, she would stop by one of the sex shops on Bourbon Street and buy herself a new vibrator. Electrical sex would have to do—barring a power surge, she wouldn't get hurt.

Maggie's hormones wept.

She told them to get a grip. Kittens had much to recommend them—Aunt Maureen had a full, happy life. And so would she, hormones be damned.

As Maggie dressed in her brown gabardine trousers and Eisenhower jacket, she remembered that it was Saturday. That was good. Saturdays were traditionally her busiest day. With any kind of luck, she wouldn't have time to think about her mortifying experience for hours and hours. By the time her day was over, she would be over Nick.

As soon as she got to her shop, Maggie busied herself rearranging the window display. She had to do something until it was time to open up. But fooling around with the window display left her way too much time to relive her walk of shame.

Maggie had about decided to open up early, even though she hadn't seen one person walk by the window yet, when Shirley entered the shop by the side door. She took one look at Maggie's face and said, "What's wrong?"

"All the k-kittens were gone." Maggie bit down hard on her bottom lip to keep from bursting into tears. Shirley would smother her with sympathy, and sympathy was not what she wanted or needed. What she wanted was to hit someone. Hard.

"What?"

"I called the vet this morning, but I was too late. They gave away the last kitten yesterday."

"Are you coming down with something? Your nose is red, and your voice sounds funny, like you're congested."

Maggie pulled box of Kleenex from under the counter. She took one and blew her nose. "I'm okay. I got chilled last night, that's all."

"What were you saying about a kitten? Why would you want another cat? You've got Emcee."

"One is not enough. I'm going to be like my Aunt Maureen. She has three cats. I only have Emcee. And Emcee doesn't like to snuggle. Probably all those years of living with Marcel. Marcel didn't seem like the snuggling kind."

"No," agreed Shirley. "Marcel was more the prickly

sort. Aunt Maureen. Isn't she your mother's younger sister? The one who never married?"

Maggie nodded. "I'm never going to marry. And I'm not going to have affairs, either. I've got to face it. I'm not good at relationships."

"Of course you are. You're sweet and kind and adorable. Perfect for the right kind of relationship."

"And that would be with cats. Not with men. I don't do well with men."

Shirley tapped the side of her chin with her finger. "Men, or Nick? Jaye said you went out with Nick last night. What happened?"

"Nothing happened. Something almost happened, but then Nick couldn't find the box, and then he did, and he got mad and kicked me out." Maggie stopped, breathless.

"What box? He kicked you out? Of his apartment? Why would he do that?"

Maggie gave a shuddering sigh. "I don't know. He's crazy. He thinks we're playing tricks on him. Hiding his things—his razor and his watch. Scaring him with a fuzzy figure."

"That doesn't make any sense, Maggie. Why would we play tricks on Nick? What kind of figure?"

"Fuzzy. Ghostly. Remember the man in the corner Nick mumbled about that first night?"

Shirley nodded. "He had a fever then. He imagined the man in the corner when he was delirious."

"Nick doesn't think so. He thinks we did it. Put a man in the corner, and then pretended that we didn't see him."

"As if we'd do something like that to a sick man." Shirley tossed her head, sending her turban askew. Her eyes widened. "But I remember the razor. When I took him lunch that first morning, he hadn't shaved.

Nick told me he couldn't find his razor. I found it outside his bedroom door, on the gallery. He thinks one of us moved it? Has he come up with an explanation for why we would do such a thing?"

"He thinks we're trying to get rid of him."

"Why would we want to do that? We don't want him to go. We want him to buy the building and stay." Frowning, Shirley shook her head. "I don't understand."

"Of course you don't. How could you? You are sane. Nick isn't. I'm telling you, Shirley. Nicholas Gerard is nuttier than the proverbial fruitcake."

"Surely not. Nick has been ill. Maybe we pushed him too hard this week, took him too many places too soon. Nick must have been having some kind of reaction."

"Oh, he reacted all right. Like a madman. Shirley. I went up the spiral staircase naked. Nude. Without a stitch. Nick ordered me to go back down the stairs."

"Up the stairs? Naked? You? Why on earth?" Shirley paused and took a breath. "Not that I think it was a bad idea. Just not one I would expect you to come up with."

"It wasn't my idea. Nick told me that he dreamed about me coming up the stairs naked. So I did."

"And he told you to leave? Why?"

"He couldn't find the condoms. I will never understand men. Never. Do you know what Nick said? He said he didn't want to make love with me because I would get hurt. He thinks I'm a wimp."

Frowning, Shirley said, "Maggie, if he's only worried about hurting you, well, that's not crazy. That means Nick cares about you. And you shouldn't make love without protection. He was right about that."

"No. I mean, yes. But that was before he couldn't

find the condoms. Before I went up the stairs. Once I was there, he forgot all about me being too fragile for an affair. I guess he thought if I was brave enough to climb the stairs naked, that I was fair game. But he changed his mind again, when the condoms turned up missing."

"I need to sit down," said Shirley, sinking onto the bench next to the passageway door. "What happened next? After he couldn't find the condoms. Why did he have condoms, anyway?"

"That is a very good question. If he was so concerned about my getting hurt, why was he prepared to hurt me?" Maggie asked, righteously indignant until she remembered what Nick had said. "Oh. I forgot. Jaye bought the condoms and gave them to Nick. But how he got them isn't the point."

"It isn't?"

"No. Things didn't get weird until the condoms disappeared. Nick left to go get more condoms. Then he found them, in the hall. That's when he went nuts and started yelling about razors and watches and the fuzzy man in the corner. All the time he was yelling, he was waving the box of condoms under my nose. He thought I had hid them. I don't care if he does have silver eyes, he is not the man I thought he was."

Moving behind the counter, Shirley gave Maggie a fierce hug. "Maggie, sugar, don't give another thought to that reading I did for you last year. Nick cannot be the one predicted to be your next lover. His eyes are gray, and his hair is brown. He's all wrong for you. I see that now. Don't worry, sweet pea. The right man will come along."

Maggie shook her head violently. "Good lord, I hope not. The last man I want to see right now, except for Nick, is Robert."

Shirley scowled at her. "Robert wasn't your Mr. Right. I know you think he was, but he wasn't."

"Yes, he was. Robert was perfect. Handsome, smart, funny."

"He wasn't honorable."

"No. Robert didn't know the meaning of the word 'honorable'. But I didn't know that until after I fell in love with him. Every female in my family, my mother and both sisters, fell in love once, with the man they married. I fell in love once with Robert. He was my Mr. Right."

"What does that make Nick?"

"I thought he was my first Mr. Wrong, but I was wrong about that. Right or wrong, there's not going to be another one. I've learned my lesson."

"You've lost me again, sugar. If Nick isn't right or wrong, what is he?"

"Nick is nuts. I don't want—" An electronic ringing interrupted her. "What is that noise?" Maggie looked around the store.

"Sounds like a cell phone," said Shirley, moving things on the counter.

"I don't have a cell phone," said Maggie.

"Maybe a customer left one behind—look, here it is." Shirley handed the ringing cell phone to Maggie.

"Do you think I should answer it?" asked Maggie.

"Yes. Ask the caller who the phone belongs to so you can return it."

"Good idea." Maggie pushed the button. "Hello?"

"Hello. Who is this?" The voice was female, with a pronounced New York accent.

"Who is this?"

"Hildy Adams. Is Mr. Gerard available?"

"Nick? Oh, is this his phone?"

"I assume so. I called his number. Wait a minute—

where is Nick? Who are you? Why do you have his phone? Is Nick all right? I thought he had gotten over the pneumonia. Ohmigod. Did he have a relapse?"

"No. Nick—Mr. Gerard is fine. How did you know he had pneumonia?"

"He told me." There was a pause. "With whom am I speaking?"

"Magnolia Mayfair. I live in the same building where Nick—Mr. Gerard—is staying."

"Ah, yes. Nick told me about you, too. You've been taking care of him. You and the other tenants. That was very kind of you. Nick could use some kindness in his life." The woman sniffed. "He certainly doesn't get any from his family."

"I don't know about that, but Nick—Mr. Gerard—is well. I don't know how his phone ended up in my shop. I'll tell him you called, Ms. Adams."

"Thanks. Nick has my number." The connection was broken. Maggie looked at Shirley. "This is Nick's phone."

"I got that. Who was calling?"

"Hildy Adams. How did Nick's phone get here?"

Shirley shrugged. "He must have left it here. Who is Hildy Adams?"

"She didn't say. Someone close to him, it seems. She knew he had pneumonia, and that we had been taking care of him." Maggie eyed the phone again. "Shirley. Nick hasn't been in my shop all week. I don't understand how—"

Someone knocked on the side door. Shirley opened the door. Nick stood in the passageway. "I thought I saw you come in here. Shirley, I need to use your phone to call the airlines. I can't find mine."

"Please tell Mr. Gerard his phone is here," said Maggie. She refused to look at Nick.

Scowling, Nick advanced toward her. "Why did you take it?"

Maggie turned her back on him. "I did not take it."

"She didn't take the phone, Nick. It was here, on the counter underneath a mask, when—"

Nick glared at Shirley. "Then, how did it get there? If one of you didn't take it?"

"I don't know," said Shirley. "It was just there."

"Yeah. Right. Like my razor was nowhere, and then it was there." Nick glared first at Shirley, then at Maggie. "And my watch. First, it wasn't on the bedside table where I left it, and then it was. And last night, that box of—"

"Nick! Stop it. What are you accusing us of?" asked Shirley.

"Tricks. You're all playing tricks on me, and I want it to stop. I want you, both of you, and your two buddies to stop playing your silly games."

Shirley bristled. "Games? What games? No one is playing games. I do not appreciate being accused of . . . whatever you're accusing us of. Maggie did not take your cell phone, and neither did I."

Nick sneered. "It didn't walk down here all by itself."

"I didn't say it did. Do you sleepwalk?" asked Shirley.

That wiped the sneer off Nick's face. "Sleepwalk? No. Never."

"If you're asleep, how would you know?" Maggie asked, gazing at the Mardi Gras masks hanging on the wall. She refused to look Nick in the eyes. His ordinary, unexceptional gray eyes.

"I know that I do not walk in my sleep," said Nick through clenched teeth. "Give me the damn phone."

Maggie turned and slapped the phone into his hand. "Take it. And call your girlfriend."

"My what?"

"Girlfriend. Hildy Adams. She called. She's worried about you."

"Hildy is a married woman, fifty years old. She is not my girlfriend. Hildy is my—" Nick broke off abruptly.

"Your . . . ?" asked Shirley.

"None of your business." Nick headed for the door to Royal Street.

"Where are you going?" asked Shirley.

He rattled the doorknob. "Out. Away from you crazy people. I need to think."

"You can't go out that door," said Shirley. "It's still locked. Maggie hasn't opened for business yet."

"I can see that." Nick glared at Maggie. "Unlock the door, Miss Mayfair."

"You can't go out," Maggie echoed. "It's cold and raining. You're recovering from pneumonia, remember?"

"I am fully recovered," said Nick, his hand on the doorknob. "Open this door."

"I won't," said Maggie. "You're not even wearing a coat."

"I don't need a coat. And I don't need you telling me what I can and cannot do. I'm going out. I'm going to find a place where I can get a cup of coffee, and I'm going to call the airline and make a reservation to leave this place as soon as possible."

"You're leaving?" asked Shirley.

"Yes, he is. Good riddance. I, for one, am overjoyed that you're leaving."

Nick bowed. "I live to make you happy."

Shirley stepped between them. "Maggie. Nick. Cut the crap. Maggie, you know you'll miss Nick if he leaves. And, Nick, if you go out in the cold rain without a coat and an umbrella, you will risk a relapse. Go upstairs. You have your cell phone now. You can call the airline from your apartment. If you decide you really want to leave."

"Wasn't that the point of your silly tricks? To scare me out of the apartment?"

"Scare you?" asked Shirley.

"Yes. Your little tricks are all designed with one thought in mind—to make me think that the damn apartment is haunted. But I know that you're the ones doing the haunting."

Maggie and Shirley exchanged guilty glances. "Haunted?" They asked the question in unison.

"Haunted," repeated Nick. "Things disappear. Then reappear."

"You could be misplacing things," said Shirley, her voice soothing. "Or forgetting where you put them. If that's all you're basing your accusations on, then—"

"There's more. As you well know. Someone coughs in my ear and wakes me up. Sometimes he sneezes. Then there was the blurry guy in the corner that first night—no one saw him but me. At least, none of you will admit seeing him."

"No one did see him. He wasn't there. You were hallucinating," said Maggie, her voice shrill.

"I don't do drugs. Except antibiotics. And they don't cause hallucinations."

"Fever does. Sometimes. You had a fever. I think Shirley is right—you do sleepwalk. You could have moved your razor. And your watch. And the box of—" Maggie stopped abruptly. Discussing condoms with Nick, even though she had told Shirley the story, did not seem like a good idea.

"I haven't had a fever for a week. And I sure didn't

sleepwalk in here with my cell phone last night. The doors were locked."

"Were the shop doors locked this morning, Maggie?" asked Shirley.

"Yes." She always locked up at night. But last night, Jaye had whisked her out and up the stairs so fast, maybe she had forgotten. "Maybe. I might have left the side door unlocked. I don't think I did, but I could have. I must have," said Maggie.

"There. You see, Nick? You must have brought your phone down here last night, even if you don't remember doing it," said Shirley.

"Not last night, I didn't," said Nick, scowling at Maggie. "I was otherwise occupied."

Maggie felt her face grow hot. "You might have done it earlier, before we—"

"Before you?" asked Shirley, obviously angling for more juicy details.

"Before we went out," said Maggie.

Nick threw up his hands. "All right, ladies. Explain the coughing alarm clock. It woke me up again this morning."

"That's easy," said Maggie. "Emcee. He coughs sometimes. Was he there?"

"I don't know. I didn't see him."

"He could have followed Maggie up the spiral staircase last night," Shirley pointed out.

Nick shot a disgusted look at Maggie. "You told her about coming up the staircase?"

"Yes, she did." Shirley scowled at Nick. "You ought to be ashamed of yourself. Treating a sweet girl like Maggie the way you did. Maybe whoever coughed was outside, on the street. Acoustics in these old buildings can do strange things."

"Very good. The cat coughs, and I dreamed the guy

in the corner. I moved things around in my sleep, and a ventriloquist on Royal Street managed to throw a few sneezes into my bedroom. The apartment is not haunted. Not by a ghost, anyway."

"What is that supposed to mean?" asked Maggie. "Are you accusing us of—"

Shirley held up a hand. "Wait. Nick, tell me about the man in the corner. What did he look like?"

Nick frowned, but he answered her. "Medium height, medium build. Looked to be in his thirties. Dark hair. Sideburns, mustache. Old-fashioned clothes."

"Why did you call him fuzzy?" asked Shirley.

"Because he was blurry. Around the edges."

"Have you seen him since that first night?"

"You ought to know, Madame Fortunata. All knowing, all seeing—isn't that your line?"

"There's no need to be rude, Nick. I thought perhaps it was Marcel's image. Marcel Beaulieu, that is. The former owner of the building."

Nick paled. "Did he die in my bedroom?"

"Oh, no. Marcel didn't even sleep in that room. He used the front bedroom, but he did not die there, either. Marcel died at Touro—in the emergency room. We were all with him," said Maggie.

"Plus Marcel was in his eighties, not his thirties. And he did not have a mustache or sideburns," Shirley said. "He couldn't have been the man in the corner."

"Of course not. You two, maybe all four of you, are playing tricks on me. You, and your friend in the ghost suit."

"We are *not* playing tricks on you!" said Maggie, stung. "Why would we?"

"You tell me. For some reason you want me to leave

this place. Well, you won. I'm leaving. Today, if possible." Nick coughed.

"Now look what you've done." Shirley made a clucking noise. "Gotten yourself all worked up over nothing, and you're coughing again. Go rest, Nick. Later, we'll put our heads together and figure out what's going on."

"I know what's going on. I'm leaving." Nick walked out the side door.

They heard the door to Royal Street open and close.

"He's going out in the rain. Idiot." Shirley turned to Maggie. "What happened last night, sweet pea? A lovers' quarrel? Is that why you're sad and Nick's mad?"

"We did not have a lovers' quarrel. We are not lovers. Things did not progress that far."

"Because of the missing condoms?"

"Because Nick decided we hid the—" Someone knocked on the storefront door. Maggie looked at the door. "Oh, shit. Now my day is really perfect."

Corinne Ellis stood outside the door. She had a man with her. He was a large man, florid-faced, wearing a western-cut suit and a cowboy hat.

Shirley walked to the door and unlocked it. "Hello, Corinne. What brings you out on such a miserable day?"

Corinne and her companion entered the shop. The man wore tan boots decorated with elaborately hand tooled turquoise peacocks. He took off his hat as he entered. "Mornin', ladies."

Corinne said, "I'm showing the building this morning. Are the other tenants up and about? We wouldn't want to disturb anyone."

"Then, why didn't you call and make an appointment?" Maggie snapped.

Corrine's mouth dropped open. Maggie had never complained to her before.

"Now, now, little lady. Don't go blaming Miss Corinne. This is my doing," said the urban cowboy. "I heard about this place over breakfast, and I hightailed it right over to Miss Corrine's office. I didn't give her time to call and warn you folks we were coming. Sorry about that."

"It's not that early. Almost time for you to open up, isn't it?" asked Corrine. "What about the others? Is Mr. Gerard in?"

"Nick is out. He left right before you arrived. Didn't you see him?"

"No."

"I haven't seen Ed or Jaye this morning. They may still be sleeping," said Shirley.

"Well, we'll just take our chances. Mr. Landon, these are two of the current tenants. Shirley Wyclowsky and Magnolia Mayfair."

"Pleased to meet you, ladies." Landon grabbed Shirley's hand and pumped it up and down.

"Mr. Landon," murmured Maggie.

"Call me Joe, honey. Have you lived here long?"

"Three years. Not nearly as long as the other tenants."

Joe leaned across the counter. In a conspiratorial whisper, he asked, "Tell me, honey. Have you seen the ghost?"

"G-ghost? What ghost?"

"I've heard tell this here building is haunted. Some other people looking for Quarter property said the ghost turned them off this particular building. But not me. I purely delight in ghosts."

"Why?" asked Shirley.

"Well, ma'am, it's this way. You've heard of the Myrtles—that plantation house in Saint Francisville?"

Maggie and Shirley nodded.

"And Le Pavillon—the hotel on Poydras?"

"Yes," said Shirley. "I know the hotel you're talking about."

"Haunted, both of them. And very successful because of it. You might not think so, but haunted hotels are good business." Joe straightened up and offered his arm to Corinne. "Lead on, Miss Corinne. I'm looking forward to seeing this ghost."

"This is the commercial space," said Corinne. "It could easily be converted into a lobby, even a small restaurant if you knocked out that wall and used the apartment behind it."

"That's not a bad idea," said Landon, looking around Maggie's shop. "How many guest rooms do you think this place would accommodate?"

"There are five apartments, three have four rooms each, not counting the bathrooms, and two have three rooms plus baths."

"Eighteen rooms, then."

"At least that. More, if you gut the building and minimize the courtyard. Plus, the attic is basically wasted space now."

"Head room? Would we have to raise the roof?"

"I don't think so. Follow me."

Corinne led Mr. Landon out the side door and into the passageway. Her voice carried back to Maggie and Shirley. "Don't worry about the tenants. You can have them out of here a month after closing."

As soon as they were gone, Maggie turned to Shirley. "Oh, my lordy me. Shirley, did you hear that?

Mr. Landon *wants* a haunted house. Now what are we going to do?"

"Nick is leaving today or tomorrow, he said. I know we don't have conclusive proof, but if there's the slightest chance that Nick is Norton Graves, we should ask him to buy the building. Quick, before that Landon fellow makes an offer."

Maggie's heart lurched at the thought of Nick's leaving. She didn't know why. She could not want him to stay, not after everything that had happened. That would make her crazier than he was. "Nick won't buy the building. He isn't Norton Graves."

"What? How do you know that? Did you ask him? Maggie, you can't expect him to tell the truth about something he's kept secret for"—Shirley stopped abruptly—"twenty years. Oh. Why didn't I see that before? Graves has been publishing his books for almost twenty years. Nick is too young to be Graves."

"Right. Jaye figured it out. Just as well. Even if Nick was a zillionaire, he wouldn't buy the building for us. He *hates* us. Me, especially."

"I know he was downright mean to you last night, but I can't believe Nick hates you, Maggie. I would have sworn that the man was smitten. Maybe we judged him too soon. You should ask him about last night."

"I'm never talking to him again."

"Nick must be regretting that he dismissed you so abruptly. You ought to give him a chance to apologize."

"Shirley. Forget about Nick. Nick cannot help us. He is not Norton Graves. He has no money. And even if he did, he wouldn't buy this building. But Mr. Landon may. He sounded really interested." Maggie could feel tears welling in her eyes again.

"Landon is interested only if the building is haunted," said Shirley. "We know it isn't. It's lucky we dismantled the ghost. Landon won't hear moans and groans. He won't feel the cold spot."

"But what if he talks to Nick?" asked Maggie. "Nick will tell him about the man in the corner, the mysterious movement of razors and other things. Landon will think there is a ghost, after all."

"Don't forget that Nick will also claim that we're responsible for the ghost. At least in his present mood, he will."

"We should be able to keep Nick away from Landon today. Then he'll be g-gone." Maggie swallowed the lump in her throat. She walked to the storefront window and stared out at the rain dripping from the balcony. "Maybe we should go ahead and tell Corrine that we were the ones doing the haunting—in case they don't talk to Nick."

"Confess? I don't think so. This could be a ploy, to get us to admit we've been trying to stop the sale of the building." Shirley joined Maggie at the window and put her arm around her shoulders. "Corinne would like nothing better than to evict the lot of us."

"Oh, Shirley. We created a ghost to scare buyers away. Now a buyer wants a ghost, and we can't chance confessing that we did it."

Shirley smiled grimly. "Ironic, isn't it?"

Eleven

Outside the shop, Nick hesitated. The rain was coming down hard. He should have listened to Maggie and Shirley and gone back to his apartment for an umbrella and a coat. He almost turned back, but remembered that he didn't have his key to the passageway door. That meant he would have to face the two women again.

Nick snorted. He was a grown man, not a little kid needing a mommy to tell him what to do. Getting wet wouldn't hurt him. He wasn't sugar. He wouldn't melt. And he wouldn't have a relapse, either. Rain did not cause pneumonia; a virus did. Any virus messing with him this morning would be in big trouble.

Heading toward Canal, Nick turned left at Ursuline. By staying under the balconies, he managed to keep reasonably dry until he reached his destination. Once he was seated at a table at Molly's in the Market, he ordered an Irish coffee. While he waited for his drink, he took out his cell phone and dialed Renaissance, Inc.

"Renaissance, Inc. How may I help you?"

"Hildy. It's me."

"Nick. What's wrong? You sound disgruntled."

"Disgruntled? I'm mad as hell."

"What's got your hackles up? Did you find proof? Are the tenants really haunting your building?"

"At the moment they're haunting me."

There was a lengthy pause before Hildy spoke again. "And you don't like it."

"No. I don't. I thought they liked me." Nick winced at the whiny tone in his voice.

"I'm sure they do," Hildy said soothingly. "You can be very charming when you put your mind to it. Do they know who you are?"

"I don't think so."

"Then, why are they haunting you?"

"To get rid of me, of course. I'm interfering with their juvenile plot to scare off buyers."

"How?"

"By being here. I'm in the way. Apparently, they rigged their ghostly tricks in my grandfather's old apartment."

"The moaning and the cold spot that Ms. Ellis mentioned? Those kinds of ghostly tricks? Have you actually heard the ghost moaning?" Hildy sounded excited, not disgusted.

"No groans. They're being more subtle now. Things disappear, then reappear somewhere else. My razor was in my suitcase, and then it was on the balcony. My watch moved off the bedside table and back again. The cell phone turned up in Maggie's mask shop. Hildy, have you ever known me to forget where I put things?"

"No, I've never known you to be absent-minded. Single-minded is more your style. But, Nick. Everyone misplaces things from time to time."

"Not every day. And I sure as hell wouldn't have moved the—"

"The?"

"—other things. It's not only objects that appear and disappear. I've seen the ghost once."

"You did not!" Hildy screeched. "What did it look like?"

Nick gritted his teeth. "A ghost."

Hildy sniffed. "There's no need to be sarcastic. Is that what made you so mad today? Actually seeing the ghost?"

"No. I saw their phony ghost the first night I was here. He hasn't put in a visible appearance since. Last night—" Nick stopped himself again. He was not going to tell Hildy about the missing condoms. She showed too much interest in his love life—or lack thereof—as it was. "Never mind about last night. The point is, the tenants are haunting me. Me. Who never did anything to them." He was whining again.

"Except try to sell their homes out from under them," Hildy pointed out.

"They don't know that. They think I'm a tenant just like them." Nick snorted. "I take that back. They think I'm the nuisance who's in their way."

"Are you sure that's what they think? What's Miss Mayfair like? She sounded nice, but she didn't sound southern."

"She's not. Maggie is from Minnesota. St. Paul. She has parents, two sisters, two brothers-in-law, nephews, nieces. Probably a full complement of grandparents, too. She makes turkey gumbo and sews. But you're wrong about her. Magnolia Mayfair is not nice. She's evil."

"Evil? I thought she took care of you while you were sick. For that matter, didn't all of your tenants take care of you? How can you think they're playing tricks on you?"

"Because there is no other explanation. Emcee did not move the con—the cell phone."

"Who is Emcee? One of the other tenants?"

"No. He's my grandfather's cat. Shirley told me the cat was moving things around, but that's a cover-up. That's another thing—they all lie like pros. They say they're helping me with my research, showing me the town. But that was part of their plot, too. Probably thought the sooner I'd soaked up the atmosphere, the sooner I'd leave."

"Well," huffed Hildy. "They misjudged you, didn't they? You aren't leaving until you get good and ready. Nick Gerard never walks away from a job before it's finished."

It was Nick's turn to pause. "Uh. As a matter of fact, Hildy—"

She cut him off. "You'll stay right there. In their way. Until you catch them in the act. Imagine the gall of those tenants, thinking they could scare you away." Hildy made a clucking sound. "Who do they think they're dealing with? A man who turns tail and runs at the first sign of trouble? You'll show them, won't you?"

Nick didn't answer. He was picturing himself slinking away, leaving his building in the hands of the tenants from hell.

"Nick? Are you still there?"

"I'm here, all right. And you are absolutely right. I'm staying put until the job is done."

"Of course you are. Now, about the reason I got in touch with you. Benjamin Ward called."

"Ben? What did he want?"

"Seems as if he turned the business over to his son a couple of years ago, and the son has taken the business straight downhill."

Ben had been Renaissance, Inc.'s, first customer. Nick's success in turning around Ben's microchip business, along with Ben's enthusiastic recommendations, had a lot to do with Nick's success. "That changes things, Hildy. I had intended to stay and deal with my tenants. But if Ben needs me . . . I'll give him a call and let him know I'm on the way."

"Oh, Mr. Ward doesn't need you this soon. He said he would need a couple of weeks at least, to prepare his son for your arrival. It won't take you longer than a week or two to finish up there, will it?"

"No. A week or two is all I'll need." Nick ended the call to Hildy and put the cell phone in his pocket. He had no reason to call the airline now. He wasn't going back to New York. Not yet.

Nick had a niggling feeling Hildy had manipulated him into staying. She had gone out of her way to make him feel like a yellow-bellied coward for even considering an early departure. But she would have had no reason to do that—he hadn't told her he was planning on leaving.

Whether he wanted one or not, he now had a reason to stay in New Orleans, thanks to Hildy. A real man did not run away from danger.

Or phoney ghosts.

Or fake sex kittens.

Nick finished his coffee and walked back to eleven-thirteen Royal Street. He looked in the storefront window. Shirley had her arm around Maggie. They both looked upset. Maggie swiped a hand over her cheek. Had she been crying?

Of course not. What would Maggie have to cry about? As far as she knew, her plan was working. They both had to think that he would be packing his bags and leaving before the day was out. He might have done just that—cut his losses and gone back to New York—if Hildy hadn't reminded him that Nick Gerard was not a quitter.

He had come to New Orleans to expose the tenants' plot to sabotage the sale of his building. He would not leave until he had done just that. And that was not the only thing he intended to do.

No more Mr. Nice Guy.

He would lure Maggie back into his bed, and he would keep her there until he had made sure he would never dream about her again. No need to worry about breaking her heart. Any woman who would stoop to seducing a man just to get him out of the way did not have a heart.

He would give Maggie exactly what she had asked for—meaningless sex.

That meant he had to apologize to her.

Nick's lips curled into a scornful smile. He hated to apologize, but he had brought it on himself. If he had been using his brain to think with last night, instead of another part of his body, he would not have sent Maggie away until they had used up the whole box of condoms.

But when he had tripped over the condom box, he had reacted without thinking. Nick had felt betrayed and hurt. Familiar feelings for an abandoned child, but emotions he thought he had outgrown long ago. Nick ground his teeth together, angry at himself for almost falling for Maggie's line about casual sex. He ought to have seen through it. Fulfilling his fantasy had been nothing but another trick to get him out of the apartment. He supposed he should thank her for wanting to send him away happy.

Nick snorted. Maggie could probably fake an orgasm—if she had been forced to go that far. Plastering a contrite expression on his face, Nick pushed open the door to Mayfair Masks.

Maggie jerked her head up. Her cheeks were wet. "What do you want?"

"Nick, maybe you should come back later," said Shirley. She had a protective arm around Maggie's shoulders.

"This can't wait. I came to apologize. Shirley. Maggie. I'm sorry for what I said this morning. And last night. I never should have accused you of intentionally moving the con—things, or my cell phone. Why would you do that? Maggie, please don't cry."

She sniffled, and two more tears slid down her face. "I'm not crying over you."

Why was she crying? She ought to be gloating. As far as she knew, he was on his way out of town. "I knew that. What's wrong?"

"We've just had a terrible shock, Nick." Shirley dropped her arm from around Maggie's shoulders.

"What? Did someone die? Recently?"

"Recently?" asked Maggie, her green eyes flashing fire. "What are you implying?"

"I'm not implying anything. Will one of you please tell me what's going on?"

Shirley answered. "Corinne Ellis came by with a prospect right after you left. Joseph Landon. It seems Joe wants to buy a haunted building."

"What? Why would anyone want a building that's haunted?" asked Nick.

"Mr. Landon plans to convert the building into a bed and breakfast," said Maggie, wiping tears from her cheeks. "He said haunted hotels do very well."

"What makes him think this building is haunted?" asked Nick.

Maggie and Shirley exchanged guilty looks.

"Well," said Shirley. "We may have had something to do with that. You see, Nick, we were trying to keep the building from selling, so we came up with various schemes to make the place unattractive to buyers. Termites. Bad plumbing. That kind of thing."

Maggie took a tissue from a box on the counter and blew her nose. "But the owner kept repairing things. We had to find something he couldn't fix with money."

"So we manufactured a ghost."

"A ghost?" said Nick, swiping his hand across his mouth to hide his smirk. This was almost too easy. They had admitted what they had been doing. Now all he had to do was get them to tell him exactly how they had done it. "That was clever of you."

"We thought so," said Shirley. "Until today. Now someone wants to buy the building because he heard about our ghost. What are we going to do, Nick?"

"Why are you asking him, Shirley? If the building sells, it won't affect him. He's leaving." Maggie turned her back on him.

"No, I'm not. I changed my mind. I'm staying. As for this potential buyer, it's obvious. All we have to do is prove to Landon that there is no ghost at eleven-thirteen Royal Street."

"How are we going to do that?" asked Shirley.

"Easy. Show him how you rigged your fake ghost." Nick shoved his hands in his pockets to keep from rubbing them together in glee.

"We can't do that," said Maggie, shaking her head. "Corinne will use the information to evict all of us, even without a sale."

"No, Maggie. Nick's suggestion is a good one. We won't have to tell Corinne. We'll go directly to Landon, before he makes an offer. We'll ask him to keep our activities a secret. Landon won't have any reason to tell Corinne—he won't want to let people know he fell for a fake ghost."

"That might work," said Maggie. "I suppose. And if it doesn't, we're no worse off than we were before. Corinne suspected we were behind the ghostly moans and the cold spot, anyway. We can point that out to Landon—the real estate agent withheld vital information from him." She glanced at Nick, meeting his gaze for the first time since he had entered the shop. "Why aren't you leaving?"

"I have unfinished business here. Maggie. Shirley. I live here, too. I want to help explain things to Landon. But to do that, I'll need to know how you did everything. Tell me how you made things move around."

Shirley shook her head. "Nick. Our ghost moaned when someone entered the second-floor apartment. That was a voice-activated tape recorder. There was a cold spot in the kitchen. A chiller hidden in the air-conditioning vent produced that. Our ghost did not move things. It didn't cough, either."

"I can see you wouldn't have rigged that sort of thing for prospective buyers. They wouldn't have been around long enough for those effects. But when I moved in, you had to come up with new tricks, right? To get rid of me?"

"Wrong," said Maggie, glaring at him. "Shirley, he still believes we were haunting him."

Nick held up his hands, palms out. "No, I don't. I told you I was sorry for making those accusations."

"You just made them again." Maggie curled a lip at him.

"I'm sorry. I guess I don't want to believe I hear things, or that I walk in my sleep. Or that I forget where I put things." Nick couldn't understand why they would admit to some tricks, but not others. They must not trust him. "It's unsettling."

"That's understandable," said Shirley. "I feel the same way about my occasional senior moments. But, Nick, don't beat yourself up. Don't forget, you've only just recovered from a serious illness."

Nick couldn't believe it. They were still trying to blame their childish tricks on his illness. Clamping down on his anger, he managed another contrite look. "Does that mean you forgive me? For thinking you were out to get me?"

Shirley nodded. "Of course."

Nick turned to Maggie. "Maggie? How about it? Will you accept my apology?"

"Why should I?" Maggie lifted her chin and sniffed.

"Maggie. Nick said he's sorry. Give the man a break. From what he told us, he's been under a lot of stress. Starting a new career, on top of being sick, could make anyone see things." Shirley glanced out the storefront window. "Time for me to get to work. There are customers lined up outside Oracles. You two kiss and make up." Shirley took a step toward the door.

"Kiss and make up. Good idea," said Nick, advancing on Maggie.

Shirley, her hand on the doorknob, turned and watched.

Maggie scurried behind the counter. "No, it isn't. I'm not kissing you. I am certainly not ever going to climb those stairs again."

"Why not? I said I was sorry."

"You're not sorry." She eyed him suspiciously. "You're up to something."

"What could I be up to?" Nick halted his advance

on Maggie. Maybe he ought to rethink his plan to seduce her. The tenants had admitted their sabotage, there was a buyer about to make an offer on the building, and a client in New York needed his services. He had no reason to stay in New Orleans. None at all.

Except Maggie.

And that fantasy-inducing spiral staircase. Nick took another step in her direction. He might as well admit it. He couldn't leave. He had to stay in New Orleans until Magnolia Mayfair came up those stairs one more time. They needed to finish what they had started. "What would I be up to, Maggie?"

"I don't know. How could I? I'm sane. You're crazy. A ghost who coughs and sneezes? How could you think we would use something like coughing and sneezing to scare people away?"

"I don't think that. Not any longer. You're right. I must have been hearing and seeing things that weren't there. I guess I'm not completely recovered from my illness." Nick faked a weak cough.

"See there? You're coughing again. I knew you shouldn't go out in the rain without a coat." Maggie walked around the counter and stood in front of him. "Shirley, why don't you take him to Oracles and give him a cup of tea."

"I'll do better than that. I'll brew him a cup of Alcira's tisane."

"It's not me coughing. Or sneezing," Nick protested.

"You just coughed," Shirley pointed out, taking him by the arm and steering him out the door. "Come on, Nick. Alcira's potion will put an end to your coughing and sneezing once and for all."

* * *

Someone sneezed.

Maggie woke up instantly, heart pounding, certain someone else was in her bedroom. She could hear someone breathing. It wasn't her. She hadn't taken a breath since she opened her eyes. In a panic, Maggie leaped out of bed and raced up the spiral staircase, her feet barely touching the wrought-iron treads. At the top she lifted her fist to pound on the trap door in the ceiling.

The trap door was open.

Quickly, Maggie climbed the last few steps and entered Nick's bedroom. Kneeling by his bed, she shook him awake.

"Maggie? What are you doing here?" He sat up, pushing the quilt aside.

Maggie threw herself at him.

Nick's arms closed around her, and he held her tight. "Does this mean you've decided to forgive me after all?" He whispered the words with his lips against her forehead.

"Th-there's someone in my b-bedroom." Her teeth were chattering.

Nick let go of her and got out of bed. Grabbing a pair of jeans off the bedpost, he pulled them on and headed for the staircase.

"Wait!" Maggie did not want to be alone.

"Stay here. I'll be right back."

Maggie sat on the bed, pulling the quilt around her shoulders. She was aware of lights being turned on, and she could hear Nick opening and shutting doors. A few minutes later, his head and shoulders appeared in the trap door opening. "No one is there." He emerged from the staircase and walked to the door. He flicked on the light switch. "You must have had a nightmare."

Blinking, Maggie looked at him. She had been dreaming. About Nick. The old animal-trainer-sex-kitten dream. She was not about to tell him that. Maggie shook her head. "No. It was not a dream."

"An hallucination, maybe?"

"I heard something. I didn't see anything. It was dark." She remembered something else. "Why was the trap door open?"

"Don't ask me. It latches on your side. You must have opened it."

"I didn't. It was already unlatched and open when I climbed the stairs. I might have forgotten to latch it last night—I left in something of a hurry. But you closed the trap door behind me. You slammed it shut, remember?"

"Yeah. I remember. Why did you think someone was in your bedroom? What did you hear?"

"Something woke me . . . a sneeze. Someone sneezed right by my bed."

"Emcee."

"No. It was not a cat. It was a man. I heard him breathing."

"Or a ghost." He was sneering. Nick did not believe that she had heard anyone.

"Never mind." She didn't need his help. Now that Maggie was fully awake, the numbing fear she had felt was fading fast. "You're right. It must have been a dream. I'm sorry I woke you up for nothing." Maggie started down the wobbly spiral staircase.

Nick followed. "Wait a minute," he said. "I want to talk to you."

"No. Go away. I don't want to talk to you."

Halfway down the stairs, she froze. Something was on the staircase with her, something cold and terrifying.

Right behind her, Nick muttered, "Damn, it's cold on these stairs."

"You feel it, too?" whispered Maggie.

"Of course I feel it. I'm turning blue. There must be a draft coming from somewhere."

"I d-don't think it's a draft." Maggie flung herself the rest of the way down the stairs.

"What else could it be?"

Standing next to her bed, Maggie wrapped her arms around her middle. "A ghost. A real ghost."

Nick came down the last few steps, stopping in front of her. "Cut the act, Maggie. You could have fallen."

"Act? You think I made this up?" She couldn't stop shaking. Maggie stared at Nick. "The sneeze. That cold. You do think I made it up. You still think I'm playing tricks on you."

"Not playing tricks, no. You were joking, right? You tried to make me see how silly I was to think someone was scaring me with coughs and sneezes."

"I was not joking. Someone did sneeze, right next to my ear. It was terrifying. But not as terrifying as that cold on the stairs. That felt like the cold of a grave. Nick, I saw my breath."

"Maybe your cold spot slipped. I'll bet all the tricks you rigged, the cold spot, the ghostly noises, somehow shifted from the second floor to the first. You were scared by your own creation, Maggie."

"N-no. Our ghost moaned. It didn't sneeze. And we didn't just turn off the tape recorder and the chiller. We took them out of the apartment. Jaye has them hidden in the attic. I didn't scare myself, Nick. Why would I?"

He raised a brow. "So I wouldn't suspect you?"

"Suspect me? Oh, I see. If a ghost scares me, I can't be the ghost. You're calling me a liar, aren't you?

Never mind answering. You don't believe me. Go away, Nick."

With a shrug, Nick put his bare foot on the bottom step. Maggie looked up the spiral staircase.

A man was standing on the seventh wrought-iron tread, a man wearing a swallowtail coat, narrow pants, and knee-high leather boots. He had sideburns and a mustache. His hair was black as night, and his eyes glowed silver.

The tiny hairs on the back of Maggie's neck stiffened and stood up, and goose bumps popped out on her arms. "N-Nick?" Her voice quavered. "There's a man on the stairs."

Nick had stopped. "I see him. You see him, too?"

"Uh huh. So d-does Emcee."

The black cat was at the foot of the staircase, his back arched, his tail puffed out to twice its normal size. The cat hissed.

The figure slowly wound his way up the spiral staircase, getting fainter and fainter the higher he climbed. By the time he reached the top of the stairs, he had faded to nothing more than a faint glimmer of light against the dark of the room above. The trap door closed with a loud bang, making Maggie jump.

She jumped straight into Nick's arms.

Maggie was clinging to him. Or maybe he was clinging to her. Somehow they had ended up in each other's arms. Maggie's head was tucked under his chin, her cheek resting on his shoulder. She was shaking. Shaking so hard that it took him a minute to realize that Maggie had stopped breathing. He loosened his hold on her and used one finger to tilt up her chin. Maggie's eyes were squeezed shut, and her lips were turning blue.

"Maggie! Breathe!" he ordered, giving her a shake.

Maggie's eyes popped open at the same time she took a deep, shuddering breath. She pushed out of his arms and dove for the bed, pulling the comforter over her head.

Nick decided his rubbery knees—nothing prurient—made it a good idea to join her. He crawled onto the narrow bed, on top of the covers, crowding Maggie against the wall. After his heartbeat slowed to a more or less normal rhythm, Nick turned onto his side, propping his head up with one hand. Maggie was completely under the covers. He gave the comforter a tug, exposing her eyes. They were wide open, staring at him.

"Are you all right?" he asked. "Can you breathe?" He pulled the comforter away from her nose and mouth.

She nodded.

"Hey. Maggie, darling. Talk to me."

"Hey," she whispered, her voice quavering. Emcee chose that moment to jump onto the bed. The cat wriggled between him and Maggie and began purring rustily.

"Emcee," said Maggie. She pulled one hand from beneath the covers and began stroking the black cat. "You saw what we saw." She looked at him. "Nick, we saw a . . . a g-ghost."

Nick rolled onto his back and stared at the ceiling, avoiding looking at the top of the staircase. "No, we didn't. I don't believe in ghosts."

"I don't think it—he—cares. You didn't see that . . . thing on the stairs? It looked like a man, but he was transparent. I could see right through him. He got fainter and fainter, and then he just—poof—went away." She lifted a hand and waved it in a circle. "Poof. You didn't see that?"

"I saw it," Nick admitted. "But it was not a ghost."

"What else—oh, I see." She sat up and leaned over him. "You think that was another trick. Get off of my bed, Nicholas Gerard. I don't want you here."

"That is the point, isn't it? To get rid—" Nick stopped. That couldn't be right. The timing was wrong. Landon wanted a ghost. The tenants would have no reason to play their most spectacular trick now. On him. He tried to sit up.

Maggie more or less fell on top of him, clinging again. "What are you doing? Don't you dare leave me alone!"

Wrapping his arms around her, Nick said, "I won't leave you, Maggie. No way. I'm not climbing those stairs. The ghost is up there." And Maggie was here, in his arms, her body sprawled on top of him. His heart rate speeded up again.

"I thought you didn't believe in ghosts."

Nick groaned and rolled over, tucking her beneath him and almost squashing Emcee, who protested loudly before wriggling free and jumping onto the windowsill. "I do now. You couldn't have done that. No one could. That thing was real." Maggie wriggled, too. She wasn't trying to escape, was she? Nick couldn't let her go. Not now. He *needed* her. "Maggie, hold me. I'm scared."

She gave a ladylike snort. "You are not. You're just trying to get into my bed."

"I'm in your bed. Move over a little, will you?"

"You're on my bed, not in it." The comforter was between them. "But you're on me, and you're heavy. This bed isn't big enough for both of us." Her arms were around him again, and she did not seem inclined to let him go.

"It's big enough." Nick raised up a little, resting on

his elbows so he wouldn't crush Maggie. "But you can go upstairs if you want to. There's a nice, big bed up there."

"Not me. I really am scared." She wound her arms around his neck and pulled him closer.

Nick dropped a kiss on her forehead. "So am I. I know it's not manly to admit it. But I saw a ghost. A real ghost. You know what that means. I've been living with a ghost since the day I arrived. He's the one who moved my razor." He gave an exaggerated shudder. "Maggie, kiss me."

She gave him a peck on the lips. "Your watch, too. And the cell phone. Nick, the ghost sneezed in my ear." Maggie trembled. "Oh, Nick. Hold me."

"I am holding you. But the comforter has to go." He reared back and stripped the comforter off the bed. While he was at it, he stood and shucked off his jeans and briefs.

"Oh," she said, her gaze on his erection. "I guess you really do intend to stay."

"Damn right, I'm staying. Move over." She moved, holding the sheets aside and inviting him to join her. Nick's heart swelled with an unfamiliar emotion as he looked at her. For the first time, he noticed what she was wearing. Not much. Some silky blue shorts and a matching top with narrow straps. "Aren't you a little overdressed?"

"Compared to you, I am. You're stark naked. Aren't you cold?"

"No. You won't be, either. It's going to get hot in here. Very hot. Very soon." He lay down beside her and slid one silky strap off a silkier shoulder. "You ought to wear silk all the time." Nick kissed her bare shoulder. "Silk, or nothing at all."

"I vote for nothing at all." Maggie sat up, pulled the

camisole over her head, and tossed it onto the floor. It landed on Emcee, who yowled a protest. "Sorry, Emcee."

The cat freed himself from the camisole and stalked out of the bedroom, tail stiff with feline outrage.

"I think we're embarrassing him," said Nick. "Maybe I should turn off the lights."

"No!"

"Scared of the dark, hmm? Good. I want to see you, every inch of you." Nick pushed the sheets away and looked at her.

"Your eyes are silver," Maggie whispered, reaching for him.

"Not yet. You're still overdressed." Carefully, Nick removed her last silky garment. He took his time, letting his hands slide from her waist down her thighs, past her knees to her ankles. Maggie kicked the garment off.

"Are you cold?"

"A little. Not where you touched me. Your hands warmed me." She arched her back. "But my chest is chilly."

Grinning, Nick put his hands on her breasts. She moaned.

"You like that, don't you?"

"Yes. More. Please."

Lowering his head, Nick took one taut nipple into his mouth. Maggie's arms came around his shoulders. She shuddered. "I'm not cold. I shivered because I—"

Nick's mouth moved to her other breast, giving it equal attention. When he raised his head, Maggie's eyes were tightly closed, her lips parted in invitation.

He accepted, crushing her mouth with his.

Maggie felt the thrust of Nick's tongue, and stiffened. She turned her head, abruptly ending the kiss. "Nick. Stop."

"Stop?" He kissed her again, at the same time he used his hands to stroke her breasts.

Maggie whimpered. She didn't want him to stop. But they had to. "The condoms. We can't do this."

"Sure we can." He pushed himself between her legs. Maggie could feel his arousal on her belly.

"No, we can't," she gasped. "Condoms. Upstairs. Go. Get. Them."

Nick's caresses slowed, then stopped. He took a deep breath. "You go. The ghost won't hurt you. You're a girl."

"What difference does that make? Besides, he never hurt you. All he did was scare you. And me. Go on. Hurry."

With a groan, Nick got out of bed. The moment his feet hit the floor, the trap door opened, and a shower of silver packets fell down the staircase. The door slammed shut again.

Nick roared with laughter. "A ghost after my own heart. Look at this." He held up a foil-wrapped condom.

"I don't understand. Why did he hide them the other night?"

"Maybe he didn't know what they were then."

"They had condoms in the nineteenth century."

"Yeah. But they didn't have foil." Sliding onto the bed, Nick handed her the condom.

Maggie took the packet and opened it. "I've always wanted to do this," she said, as she knelt beside him and sheathed him. Once she was done, she smiled at him. "Now. Where were we?"

"Right about here," said Nick, his eyes molten silver.

He took her mouth again at the same time he entered her, filling her completely with one powerful thrust.

He moved inside her, his strokes maddeningly slow at first. Maggie felt her body clenching around him tighter and tighter with each thrust. She thought she would never get enough of him.

"Maggie!" Nick shouted her name as his climax hit him. She screamed his name at the same time.

Satiated, Nick let himself drift into sleep. His last thought was that this was where he belonged. In this silly single bed, on Royal Street in the French Quarter, with rain dripping from the balconies, with his motley group of tenants and a ghost upstairs. This was where he wanted to be. With Maggie.

Forever.

Twelve

Maggie woke up early Sunday morning. Nick didn't stir. Not that he would be able to move, with her sprawled on top of him. She carefully inched her way off of him, rolling onto her side and pressing herself against the wall underneath the window. Maggie stared at the stuccoed brick wall only centimeters from her nose and thought.

Something momentous had happened last night.

Not the ghost.

Not even the sex.

She had fallen in love.

How could that have happened? She had been there, done that. It was *not* supposed to happen again. Not like this. Not with a man who would be leaving New Orleans any day now. Not with a man who did not believe in marriage. The last thing Nick wanted was a wu-wu-wife. Tears welled in her eyes. She blinked them away. She couldn't tell him she loved him. He would think she had lied to him. All that talk about casual affairs and meaningless sex. And her insistence that marriage was the farthest thing from her mind. Nick would think she had used sex to trap him into marriage.

She hadn't. She couldn't. Even if she confessed how she felt, he wouldn't propose. What was she supposed to do now? After a few moments of contemplation, Maggie made her decision. She and Nick could have a few more days together, happy days. She would hold off being sad until after he was gone. She would not waste those few precious days weeping and wailing. There would be plenty of time for that later.

Maggie felt a tickling breath on the back of her neck.

"Why are you way over there?" asked Nick, his voice husky with sleep.

Maggie looked over her shoulder. Nick was grinning at her, a self-satisfied, very masculine grin. "You snore. I was trying to get away from the noise."

"I do not snore. And you didn't get very far away, did you?"

"No. I ran into a brick wall and I had to stop."

"Good. Now. Come back here, where you belong." Nick wrapped his arms around her and rolled onto his back. Maggie sprawled on top of him.

"I'm glad you recognize where I belong. On top."

Nick rolled again, pinning Maggie to the mattress. "Close. You belong close to me."

Much later, Nick said, "I guess we should talk about it—about what we saw last night."

Maggie shuddered. "We saw a ghost, Nick."

"You're not scared anymore, are you?"

She thought about it. "No. I don't think the ghost means us any harm."

"Neither do I. But I haven't had any experience with the supernatural before. Have you?"

"Only Shirley's tarot card readings. And I never believed in those until recently. Nick, we have to tell the others."

"No, we don't. They'll think we're crazy."

"They will not. What if our pretend haunting upset

a real ghost? This is our fault—theirs and mine—not
yours. We have to fix it."

"Maggie. How do you fix a ghost?"

"You exorcise it, of course." Shirley answered Nick's
question when he repeated it at the hastily called tenants' meeting later Sunday morning. "As it happens,
that is exactly what we must do. Get rid of the ghost
before Mr. Landon makes a final decision about buying the building."

"Who is Landon? What are you talking about?"
asked Ed, taking his usual seat in one of the wing
chairs facing the sofa.

"Corinne brought him by yesterday to show him the
property," said Maggie, sinking onto the sofa. "Mr.
Landon wants a haunted building. Didn't you tell
them, Shirley?"

"Didn't have a chance. Nick knows about our ghost,
by the way. Maggie and I told him about it after
Corinne and Landon left."

"Why would anyone want a ghost?" asked Jaye.

"Landon is looking to open a bed and breakfast. A
haunted bed and breakfast. He said ghosts are good
for business." Shirley began pacing.

"I can see that," said Jaye. "Look at the Myrtles. And
several of the hotels here in New Orleans claim to be
haunted."

Nick sat on the sofa next to Maggie and took her
hand in his.

Shirley noticed, and raised a brow. "That's what
Landon said. He heard about eleven-thirteen from
some of the buyers we scared off. I guess we were a little too good at haunting."

Ed rapped on the table with his Tulane ring. "Our

ghost comes under the heading of old business. Let's get back to the business at hand—this new ghostly phenomena. How do we proceed with this exorcism, Shirley?"

"We have to find out who the ghost is and what he wants."

"How do we find that out? Ask him?" In the light of day, Nick was having a hard time accepting that he and Maggie had seen what they had seen. Or that he had spent the night in her bed. He had made love with a woman meant to marry. Nick couldn't bring himself to regret what he had done, but he didn't feel like a hero, either. Maggie deserved better than what he could offer.

"There is no need for sarcasm, Nick. We're trying to help."

Nick almost shouted, "I don't need help," but he bit down and kept his mouth shut. They were trying to help. The least he could do was listen. "Sorry. I guess I'm still a little unsettled."

"Tell us about the ghost, Nick," asked Ed. "Exactly what has he done?"

Nick listed the ghostly occurrences one by one, ending with him and Maggie watching the ghost climb the spiral staircase. No one blinked an eye, although Ed's cheeks reddened and Maggie squirmed when Nick told the story of the missing condoms. When he finished, everyone remained silent.

Nick eyed them skeptically. He told them there was a ghost, and they were going to accept it?

Jaye found his voice first. "I don't believe in ghosts," he said. He sounded apologetic.

"I'm sure all of us find it hard to believe in things we have not experienced," said Ed. "But we have the evidence of Nick and Maggie. We cannot ignore what they saw, felt, and heard. I find it interesting that a specter can move things, even things as heavy as a wooden trap door. How do you suppose he accomplishes that?"

"It's called psychokinesis," said Shirley, who had stopped pacing and was standing behind Ed's chair. "Moving objects with psychic power. Or supernatural power, in this case."

"I didn't mean to imply that they're lying or anything," said Jaye. "Only that there must be some other explanation. Maybe someone is playing tricks."

"Who?" Ed directed his question to Jaye.

"I don't know," said Jaye.

"Nick thought we were doing it," said Maggie, tugging her hand free.

"What else would he think? If I had experienced what Nick experienced, I would have thought the same thing. I certainly would not have thought a ghostly presence was the cause," Ed said.

"*Thought* being the operative word. I did suspect you—all of you—were behind it. I don't think so now," muttered Nick, as three pairs of eyes looked at him. "Maggie and I saw the ghost together. And it was like nothing I've ever seen before. I don't think anyone—anyone alive—could create a vision like that."

"This is your area of expertise, Shirley," said Ed. As an aside to Nick, he added, "Shirley once worked as a magician's assistant. How could these things Nick experienced be accomplished?"

"By a live human being, you mean? The coughing and sneezing Nick heard could have been done the same way we made our ghost moan and groan, I suppose."

"I looked for a tape recorder," said Nick. "There

wasn't one. And the ghost sneezed in Maggie's bedroom, too, remember?"

Shirley nodded. "As for how someone could move things around without being seen, I have no idea. If a human hand did that, there would have been wires, magnets, something."

"Well, if these occurrences are not normal, then we have no choice but to consider the paranormal," said Ed. "Shirley, how does one go about exorcizing a ghost?"

Looking pleased that the professor was deferring to her for once, Shirley sat in the wing chair next to Ed's. "First, we have to find out exactly who is haunting this place."

"Then you'll know how to get rid of him?" asked Nick.

"Then we'll be one step closer to putting the spirit to rest. Once we know who we're dealing with, we'll have to find out what is keeping him on this plane of existence," said Shirley.

"Why now, do you suppose?" mused Ed. "I've lived here over twenty years. I never knew the place to be haunted. Not until we created our ghost."

Shirley said, "Maybe it—the real ghost—has been here all the time. Marcel could have kept the knowledge to himself."

Ed nodded. "That's true. Marcel seldom gave one the time of day. He was not the kind of man to share something as personal as being haunted."

"But why did the ghost suddenly sneeze in Maggie's bedroom?" asked Nick. "After spending most of his time in my apartment?"

"That is a puzzle. Another clue, but one we can't decipher without more data." Ed squared his shoulders and looked at them. "All right. Data we need, and data we'll get. Jaye, look in the attic. When we found the dishes and linens, we located several boxes filled with papers. Marcel may have made some kind of notes about the ghost. See if you can find anything that mentions the specter."

Jaye saluted. "I'll get on it right away."

"On the assumption that the ghost was once a resident of this house, I will check the parish property records to see who resided here before Marcel. Of course, I can't do that until tomorrow, but I'll go first thing. I always meant to look up the history of this house. Never got around to it when I was teaching. But I have time now." Ed rubbed his hands together.

"I'll consult the cards," said Shirley. "And the Ouija board, too, if necessary. Unless you had something else in mind for me, Ed?"

"No. We would be foolish not to take advantage of your talents."

"Oh? Talents? I thought you were of the opinion that I was a fraud."

Ed's cheeks turned pink. "Harrumph. Well. That was before credible witnesses saw a phantom in this very building. I apologize, Shirley, if any of my remarks offended you."

"Why, Ed. Thank you. I wasn't offended, though. I merely considered the source." She grinned at him.

"What about me?" Maggie asked. "What can I do to help?"

"And me?" Nick was feeling left out again. A niggling thought worried him. Would the professor's investigation reveal that he owned the building? He ought to tell them he was their landlord.

And he would. As soon as he was absolutely sure Maggie and the others were not behind the latest ghostly apparition. Nick's rational mind could not quite give up that last grain of doubt. And he wasn't ready to find out how they—especially Maggie—would react once they knew he had lied to them.

"I haven't forgotten you two. Maggie, you and Nick go on the ghost tours. See if anyone resembling our ghost is mentioned."

"When and where?" asked Nick. Ghost tours seemed an unlikely source of information, but who was he to complain? At least he would be with Maggie.

"There are several ghost tours," said Shirley. "Some of them include vampires, thanks to Anne Rice. I have brochures at Oracles. If I remember right, some of the tours start around two in the afternoon."

"Good," said Nick. "We'll get on this right away."

"We? I can't go with you until this evening, Nick," said Maggie. "I have to open my shop. You could check out a few of the tours before it gets dark."

"Okay. But we'll go together tonight."

"That's right," said Ed. "You go with Nick, Maggie. I don't want you wandering the streets at night by yourself. Let's plan on meeting back here tomorrow night. We should have more information to share by then."

"Nick, stop by Oracles and I'll give you the ghost tour brochures. I'm pretty sure I've got all of them." Shirley rearranged her turban and stood. "Are we done here for now?"

They all nodded.

Ed knocked on the table with his knuckles. "Meeting adjourned."

Everyone exited Shirley's apartment at the same time. Jaye and Ed headed up the stairs to the attic. Nick and Shirley walked across the courtyard with

Maggie. To Shirley's obvious enjoyment, Nick kissed Maggie soundly before escorting Shirley down the passageway and out the street door to Oracles.

Lips tingling, Maggie entered her apartment. Mayfair Masks opened at noon on Sundays, and it was almost that but she needed some time alone to think. How had she gotten herself into this predicament? Oh, yes. Her experiment with lust. Nick should have been the perfect candidate for a brief affair—attractive, available, and temporary—but Maggie's heart had done it again. She had gone and fallen in love.

At least she had learned she wasn't cut out for affairs. Man after man after man no longer had any appeal. Just as well. Becoming a serial sex kitten was not her style.

One man, one woman. Forever.

She had believed that once, but Maggie had thought she had gotten over such romantic nonsense after Robert. She had tried very hard to convince herself that after her horrible mistake with Robert, she would never have another Mr. Right.

She had told herself for years that Robert had been her Mr. Right. "I have amazing powers of self-delusion," she told Emcee as the cat strolled into her bedroom.

Seeing her destroyed bed, Maggie blushed. "I'm good in bed, too." Her cheeks got hotter, thinking about what she and Nick had done in that bed. She tucked in the sheets and smoothed the covers, picking up the pillow where Nick's head had lain. She buried her face in the pillow, inhaling the smell of him.

A squeak brought her out of her reverie. "Emcee. Stop rocking the rocker. You'll rock on your tail again."

Grinning, she lowered the pillow. The cat was on the bed.

But the rocker was rocking. Gently, but steadily. As if a person were sitting in it.

"Oh, my lordy me. You're here, aren't you?"

The rocker rocked vigorously.

"Who are you? What do you want? Ohmigod. I'm talking to a chair. And I thought Nick was crazy because he kept losing things. I'm losing my mind." Knees wobbling, Maggie sank onto the bed.

The chair gently rocked.

After a few moments, Maggie's heart rate slowed, and her breathing became regular. She felt calm. The rocker's gentle movements were soothing, comforting. The ghost wasn't going to hurt her. She eyed the chair.

"You might be able to help. I need someone to talk to. I know you can't talk—at least I don't think you can talk—but you can listen, can't you?"

The chair stilled momentarily, then started rocking again.

"Was that a yes?"

For the second time, the chair stopped rocking, then began again.

"That was a yes. Okay. Well, sir. I'm an ostrich. Head in the sand. That's me. I've been hiding from the truth for years and years. I made up this whole fantasy about Mr. Right and Mr. Wrong. Do you know about Robert? If you've been here for long, you must have heard me talk about him."

The rocker paused.

"I thought so. Well, I sold myself this bill of goods about Robert being my one and only Mr. Right. Robert will never be any woman's Mr. Right. He's a cad. A jerk. A rat. I was stupid to fall in love with a man like that. Worse than stupid. Gullible. Naive."

The rocker paused.

"You agree. Well. That's not the worst of it. I let Robert—a grade A, number one, top drawer rat—make me think for years that I didn't want what I have always wanted ever since I was six years old and got my first baby doll. Nick saw right through me. He knew from the beginning that I am the marrying kind, and he was right. I want to get married. I want to cook and sew and have babies.

"All that fancy folderol about hormones and experiments with lust—rationalization. That's what it was. A silly, stupid way to protect my heart from another Robert. As if I would have ever met another Robert. No one could be that unlucky." Maggie swallowed a sob. "I'll never meet another Nick, either.

"And Nick could be the right man for me. Oh, he has that thing about marriage. Because of his family. But you know what I think? I think Nick is using his awful family the same way that I used Robert. To keep his heart safe.

"Safe seems good. I certainly went through all kinds of mental gyrations to keep my heart whole. But safe isn't good, not if it means never taking a chance on love."

The rocker stopped rocking for a full minute.

"But if I had made it clear from the very beginning that I was exactly what Nick thought I was—wu-wu-wife material—what would have happened? He would have run away from me as fast as he could. You know that's true."

No rocking for a millisecond.

"Now what? I can't change horses in midstream. I

told him I was only interested in a brief affair. What am I going to do?"

The chair stilled.

Maggie waited, but nothing happened. After a few minutes, she realized that the air in her apartment felt different. Emptier. The ghost had gone.

"Well. He was no help. I'm going to work, Emcee."

Nick was waiting in the passageway, a handful of colorful brochures in one hand and an Oracles bag in the other. "Shirley sent coffee and scones."

Maggie opened the door to her shop and let Nick enter ahead of her. "That was nice of her. I didn't get breakfast this morning. Or lunch, for that matter."

"I know. I was there, remember?" Nick leaned down and kissed her. "Some things are more important than food."

"Yes." Maggie unlocked the Royal Street door and returned to the counter. Nick had set the pastries and coffee cups on a corner of the counter. Then he took Maggie in his arms and kissed her again.

"My. What was that for?"

"It feels good. How do you feel?"

"A little strange, if you want to know the truth. I just had a long conversation with our friend the ghost."

"What? He talked to you?"

"No. I did most of the talking. All of the talking, actually. He was in my rocking chair, rocking. He stopped rocking when he wanted to say yes. I think."

"In the rocking chair? I wonder if he was there last night."

From the way her face felt, Maggie knew she had to be red as a boiled mud bug. "Watching us? You think he was watching us?" she shrieked.

Nick gave her a smoldering look. "Maybe. Does that turn you on? Knowing we were not alone when we—"

"No! Yes. A little. Maybe." She was turned on, but Maggie was pretty sure it was the look Nick was giving her that was doing the trick, not a voyeuristic phantom. "Nick, I have to go to work."

The bell over the door tinkled, and her first customer of the day entered.

While she waited on customers, Nick sat on her stool, sipping coffee and thumbing through the brochures. During a lull, he held up one of the brochures. "Here's the one Shirley mentioned. Lafitte's Blacksmith Shop. One tour begins at six, the next at eight. Which one do you want to take?"

"Eight. I don't close up until six. Unless you want to go at six without me."

"We're in this together, Maggie. I'll wait and go with you at eight. Are you sure you can't close up early?"

"How early?"

"Now."

"Now? Customers are waiting. And the first tour isn't until this afternoon. What would we do until— oh. Tempting, but I really need to sell as many masks as I can. I just know that Mr. Landon is going to make an offer on the building."

"As long as you're tempted. Don't worry about Landon. Once the building is ghost-free, he won't want it. See you at six. We'll go to dinner first. We'll need fuel for ghost hunting, don't you think? And for later?"

Maggie blushed for the eleventh time that morning.

Sunday night, after dinner at Bacco's, Maggie and Nick walked hand in hand to Lafitte's Blacksmith Shop.

The tour guide was dressed in black. Black shirt,

black jeans, black boots. He also wore a black cape, lined in red silk, and a battered top hat. He carried a black cane, topped with a silver wolf's head. A small group of people had gathered on the sidewalk, waiting for the tour to begin.

As they milled around, a man bumped into Maggie, pushing her against Nick's chest. His arms closed around her waist. "Steady," he said.

"I'm all right. You can let me go," Maggie whispered.

Nick tightened his hold on her. He hadn't let her go earlier, either. Not until he had kissed her silly. Once he had had her sagging against him, weak-kneed and breathless, he had left her to go on an afternoon ghost and vampire tour.

He had been touching her ever since they started on their assignment. Taking her by the arm, steering her with a hand at the small of her back. Now he was holding her against him as if he would never let her go. She ought to have stuck to her guns and gone on a separate tour. Nick was trying very hard to be irresistible. And lovable.

She would resist telling him she loved him. She had to. It was a matter of self-preservation.

Maggie looked around at the people gathered on the sidewalk. She wondered how many of them believed in ghosts. Not many, she would guess. Maybe she and Nick were the only ones. She could understand now why Nick had persisted in believing that she and the other tenants had been responsible for the ghostly goings-on at eleven-thirteen. No rational person would think a real ghost was behind the strange happenings in Nick's apartment. It took a lot to make a person a believer.

Seeing was believing.

The sneeze alone hadn't been enough to make her

a believer. She had thought a live burglar had wakened her, not a ghost. That had been enough to send her flying up the spiral staircase, something she had sworn never to do again.

But she had gone up those stairs. True, she had been terrified at the time, which would excuse her inability to think clearly. Making allowances for her terror, Maggie could just as easily have gone out the French doors in her bedroom and across the courtyard to Shirley's. Her instincts had taken her to Nick.

Her instincts, not her hormones. Maggie knew for sure that love, not lust, had sent her flying up the spiral staircase a second time.

Nick nibbled on her ear, interrupting her thoughts. Maggie gasped. "What are you doing?"

"Nibbling. You taste good." His breath tickled her temple. Maggie sighed. She would have one affair. With Nick. And then retire to the cavern of celibacy and emulate Aunt Maureen. That would give her memories to go along with her cats.

Leaning against Nick's chest, feeling his arms around her waist, she felt as if she were right where she belonged. But for how long?

Maggie shivered.

Nick held her closer. "Are you cold? You know, Maggie, Jaye and the others are right. You ought to buy a coat."

Maggie was wearing a white silk blouse topped with a heavy wool sweater. She had on cuffed wool slacks pleated at the waist, the same shade of blue as the sweater. "I'm not cold. The tour guide is scary looking."

"Is he supposed to be a vampire or a werewolf?" Nick whispered, his mouth close to Maggie's ear.

His breath tickled her neck. "I'm not sure," Maggie

said, moving a step away from Nick. Touching him made her quiver with longing. "Somehow, I don't think we're going to learn anything useful on this trip."

"It's not a total waste of time. I get to hold hands with you." Matching action to speech, Nick took her hand in his. "If you get scared, feel free to throw yourself into my arms again."

"I did not throw myself at you. That man pushed me."

"I was talking about last night. You threw yourself at me when you saw the ghost last night."

"That doesn't mean anything. I would have thrown myself at anyone handy." Maggie tried tugging her hand loose, but ended her small struggle when the tour guide spoke. She did not intend to allow Nick to distract her from their purpose, to learn about the ghost at eleven-thirteen Royal Street. Not until she was ready to distract him right back, anyway.

"Is everyone ready to meet a ghost or two?"

Several people murmured affirmative responses. "Good. My name is Victor. I will be your guide tonight. Follow me, and stay close. Stragglers have been known to disappear." He laughed evilly.

The tour began. Victor carried a lantern, battery-operated, but designed to look like an old kerosine lamp. He held it beneath his chin when he spoke, the light making shadows on his face that turned his otherwise unremarkable features into something evil.

"Not bad theatrics," whispered Nick, taking Maggie's hand in his. "He has a good voice, too. Deep and sinister." Nick put his mouth close to her ear. "Boo."

Maggie jumped. "Stop it, Nick. We're supposed to be doing research here." She smiled to herself. Nick seemed relaxed, as though he was really enjoying himself. Strange that coming face-to-face with a ghost would have that effect on him. Slanting a glance at him, she asked, "Why are you so happy?"

"Happy?" He looked surprised at the idea. "I don't know. Mind-blowing sex might have something to do with it, I suppose."

Pleased, Maggie squeezed his hand. "Oh. I thought it might be Victor."

"I don't think Victor's goal is to make people happy."

"No, I guess not."

Victor proved he was out to terrify at the next stop. At the corner of Royal and Governor Nicholls, the guide stopped underneath a lamppost. "This is eleven-forty Royal Street, otherwise known as the LaLaurie House."

Maggie squeezed Nick's hand. She whispered, "I don't like this story. Madame LaLaurie was a wicked, wicked person."

"You've heard of it?"

"Many times. It's so close to eleven-thirteen Royal that everyone thinks I should hear the story. But I've never heard the screams."

"Screams? Who screams? Besides you when you—"

"Nick! I was talking about the ghosts, of course. Hush. Listen to what Victor is saying."

"Madame Delphine LaLaurie had the house built in 1832. Delphine was a very rich woman, so rich that she could afford to keep numerous slaves, slaves who disappeared with sinister regularity.

"On one occasion, neighbors witnessed Madame LaLaurie chase a young girl up to the roof-top. The girl screamed for help, but before anyone could rescue her, she jumped from the roof. As a result of the young girl's death, city officials forced Delphine to sell her slaves.

"The poor slaves must have thought they were finally free of their cruel mistress, but friends of Delphine bought the slaves and gave them back to her.

"A few weeks later, a cook set fire to the kitchen. When the fire brigade arrived, she told them she had set the fire so that they would come and see the evil in the house. She directed them to the attic." Victor paused and pointed to the third floor of the building. "Up there, the fireman found a torture chamber. Slaves were chained to the walls. Some were barely alive. Some were dead, rotting in their chains."

Maggie moved closer to Nick. "I don't like this," she whispered, not able to suppress a shudder. "I'm going to have nightmares."

"I think he's almost finished," said Nick. He put his arm around her shoulders and fitted her to his side. "Don't worry about things that go bump in the night, Maggie. I'll stay with you again."

Victor continued the grisly story. "After word spread of LaLaurie's torture chamber, even her friends turned against her. Madame LaLaurie escaped minutes before a mob arrived at her house, determined to drag her from the house and make her pay for her crimes. She was never seen again. Alive, that is."

"Is she the one who haunts the house?" asked one of the tourists.

"Among others. The slaves are seen, too, from time to time. And many people swear they have heard their screams."

When Victor finished the gruesome tale of torture

and murder, Nick asked, "Have you ever heard of a ghost at eleven-thirteen Royal Street?"

Victor scratched his chin. "No. Can't say that I have. But there are ghosts in every French Quarter house. New Orleans is an old city, and the French Quarter is filled with old souls. Many people have died here. Many remain here after death. Now, on to Toulouse Street and the soldier ghost of Maison de Ville."

"Spooky. Ghosts everywhere." Nick took Maggie by the arm and followed the crowd.

After a few more ghost stories, each gorier than the last, Nick stopped. "Maggie. Let's go home and see if the ghost has moved the condoms again."

"Nick! Hush. They'll hear you."

"No, they won't. They're a block away. Home?"

"Home."

When they arrived at eleven-thirteen, Nick pulled Maggie down the passageway and through the court-yard to her apartment. "Home?" asked Maggie. "You think of my apartment as home?"

He nodded, and Maggie's heart cracked. But it didn't break. That would come later.

Thirteen

Nick and Maggie were the last to arrive at the Monday evening meeting of the Beaulieu Building Tenants' Association. They had taken one last ghost tour before the meeting. A few brows were raised as they entered Shirley's living room arm in arm. Maggie, apparently embarrassed, moved away from Nick and sat down on the sofa next to Jaye.

"How were the ghost tours?" asked Jaye, lounging on the sofa.

"Spooky," said Nick. "But not very useful. Apparently every house in the French Quarter is haunted except this one. How about you? Did you find out anything useful?"

Ed, seated in the wing-back chair, tapped on the table with his knuckles. "Let's have order here. Nick, make your formal report, please."

"Maggie and I have been on every ghost tour offered. We went on the ghost and vampire tour."

"Not to be confused with the ghost and voodoo tour," said Maggie, with a grin. "We also went on the ghost and witch tour. Did you know that there are no less than three covens currently practicing in the Quarter?"

"No wonder I keep meeting so many witchy people," Jaye muttered.

"Don't forget the ghost and zombie tour. I'm afraid all our research was in vain, however. Not one tour guide mentioned a ghost at eleven-thirteen Royal Street." Nick squeezed onto the sofa with Maggie and Jaye. Jaye grinned at him over Maggie's head.

"If the ghost tours are anything like the so-called history tours, I am not surprised. Entertainment, not education, seems to be the guiding principle behind these tours for tourists," said Ed, looking dismayed. "Be that as it may. Using a scholarly approach and impeccable sources, I was able to locate some useful information. I'll go next." Ed opened a folder and took out a sheaf of papers.

"Good grief. The professor has written another book," Shirley murmured.

Ed ignored her. "I discovered that this building has always been owned by the same family. The original owner was Antoine Emile Pardu, Marcel's grandfather. Pardu's wife and son died in a steamboat accident in 1889. The boat exploded and burned while tied up at the Governor Nicholls wharf. I copied the newspaper articles about the tragedy. Pardu's obituary, too." Leaning across the table, Ed passed the copies to Jaye.

"Yeah," said Jaye, scanning the obituary. "Says here he got sick after he jumped into the Mississippi."

"A futile attempt to save his wife and son," said Ed. "Pardu had gone to the wharf to see them off. Instead, he witnessed the explosion and fire."

Nudging Nick, Jaye passed him the articles. Nick barely glanced at them. Christ. Antoine Pardu was his ancestor. Even dead, his family wouldn't leave him alone.

Maggie took the copies from him and scanned the article about the steamboat accident. "Oh, my. Pardu saw the boat on fire, knowing that his wife and son were on board. That must have been a horrible experience."

"Yes, I'm sure it was. Nick, are you all right?" asked Shirley. "You look a little green around the gills."

"I'm all right," said Nick. "It all happened over a hundred years ago. No reason to let it bother me."

"It bothers me," said Maggie. "Imagine watching your family die, and not being able to do anything to help them."

Ed cleared his throat. "That wasn't the end of the tragedy. According to the obituary, Pardu himself died a few weeks later of inflammation of the lungs. He was only thirty-five."

"Inflammation of the lungs—isn't that what they used to call pneumonia? That explains the coughing and sneezing. If this Antoine Pardu is our ghost, that is," said Shirley.

"Hold on," said Jaye. "We're missing something here. If Pardu's son died, who inherited this house when Antoine passed? I thought you said the building had been in the same family for generations."

Ed took his papers back from Maggie and replaced them carefully in the folder. "His daughter inherited. She had married a Beaulieu in 1888."

"Any idea what Pardu looked like?" asked Nick, although he was pretty sure he knew. He had seen him. Twice.

"I tried to find a photograph of him, without success," Ed answered.

Jaye reached in the box he had placed on the floor next to the couch. "I found a few old photographs in here." He took them out and handed them to Maggie. "Recognize anyone?"

Maggie looked through the old photos. She

handed one of them to Nick. "Isn't this the man we saw?"

Nick looked at the daguerreotype. "Yes. That's him." He turned the photograph over. "There's no name."

"It must be Antoine. It looks just like the man on the stairs. Besides, I don't think Marcel would have kept the photograph of someone he wasn't related to." Maggie handed the picture to Shirley, who examined it before passing it on to Ed.

"Good," said Ed, with an approving nod. "If this photo is one of Marcel's grandfather, as we must surmise, then Nick and Maggie saw the ghost of Antoine Pardu.

"As I said, Pardu's daughter married Hector Beaulieu, Marcel's father. As we know, Marcel left only one heir, his daughter Angelique. This property passed out of the Beaulieu family's ownership when Marcel died."

"When Angelique sold it to Renaissance, Inc.," said Maggie with a nod.

"So we assume," said Ed. "I did not verify that fact. Perhaps I should check the more recent property records at the Recorders' Office."

"No need for that," said Nick, knowing exactly what the property records would reveal—that he had inherited the building, not his mother. "The ghost has to be the original owner of the building. He's the right age. And he died of pneumonia."

"Nick's right," said Jaye. "You don't need to look at the property records to verify that Angelique sold the building. We know she did."

Nick breathed a sigh of relief. He ought to take the opportunity to confess, but he wasn't ready to do that yet. He had a plan, a plan that needed time to develop. Telling them he was their landlord now would spoil his surprise. In the end, a few more days of keeping them in the dark wouldn't matter.

"But if Antoine is who Nick and Maggie saw, why hasn't he manifested before?" asked Shirley, her brows knitted in a frown. "I've been in this building for almost twenty years and never had an inkling that there was a spirit on the premises."

"Perhaps he only showed himself to Marcel," said Ed.

Jaye looked dubious. "Marcel never said anything about a ghost."

"Marcel never said anything much about anything," Shirley pointed out. "He was a recluse."

"We need to find out more about Antoine," said Maggie. "To figure out why he's still here."

"Let's see what the others have to report," said Ed. "What did you discover, Jaye?" Ed asked. "Besides the photographs?"

"Not much that's helpful. I found the family Bible—the last entry is Angelique's birth—and the photos. There was also a diary of sorts."

"Marcel kept a diary?" asked Shirley.

"More of a record book. It includes information about the building—repairs, changes, that sort of thing. I read it from cover to cover. No mention of a ghost."

"Anything else of interest, Jaye?" asked Ed.

"A letter from Marcel's wife, postmarked Greenwich, Connecticut. She had left New Orleans to take care of her elderly parents. In the letter, she pleaded with Marcel to join her. I guess he didn't want to go. The next document was a copy of their divorce decree."

"Marcel wouldn't leave his business." Shirley shook her head. "Poor man. He never understood the importance of family. It was all work, work, work to him."

Nick started. He had never thought of his work ethic as being genetically programed—his father and mother avoided work at all costs. "He couldn't up and leave his business," he blurted, feeling obligated to defend his grandfather's choice.

"What was his business?" Maggie asked, leaning forward. "I thought Mr. Beaulieu lived off the rents from this building."

"Oh, no, sweet pea. Marcel had an antique store on the corner of Royal and St. Ann. A very prestigious store, inherited from his father. Marcel sold it and retired a few years before you arrived."

"I never knew that," said Maggie. She sank back against the sofa cushions.

The professor turned to Shirley. "Madame Fortunata. Anything to report?"

"The cards shed some light," offered Shirley. "Nick is the catalyst."

Nick gave another guilty start. "Me? I don't think so. Maybe it was your fake ghost that stirred him up. He didn't like the competition."

Shirley gave her head a violent shake, unseating her turban. "No. The cards clearly named you as the immediate cause, Nick. Why that should be, the cards did not reveal. But one change often begets other changes. Think of ripples in a pool."

"Let's think about this," mused Maggie. "What did change? Marcel died. The building passed out of the family's ownership for the first time."

Nick clenched his teeth to keep from blurting out that the building was still owned by the Beaulieu family, and that it was his ancestor who haunted eleven-thirteen Royal Street.

"Nick arrived," said Maggie, patting him on the knee.

Nick looked at Maggie. She smiled at him. She wouldn't be smiling if she knew he was her landlord. Maggie wouldn't like the fact that he had lied to her. But once his plan came to fruition, she would forgive him for concealing his identity. At least, he hoped she would.

"With pneumonia. The same illness that killed Marcel's ancestor," said Shirley. "Maybe that's the connection. Sharing a disease provided some sort of sympathetic link between Antoine and Nick."

"That seems a rather tenuous connection," said Ed, eyeing Nick speculatively.

Good hunch, Professor, thought Nick. More than a common disease connected him to Pardu—they shared the same blood. "What does he—Antoine—want?"

"Maybe the old boy doesn't want the building to sell," said Jaye. He snickered. "Y'all. Have you thought about this? We were haunting a haunted apartment. How silly was that?"

"I'm sure Antoine was amused by our puny efforts," said Ed. "I am assuming, of course, that spirits have emotions, an assumption completely without scholarly support."

"Oh, spirits feel," said Shirley. "I'm sure of that."

"They must feel sadness, wouldn't you think?" asked Maggie. "Being so alone and forgotten."

Nick took her hand in his and squeezed it. Maggie slanted a curious look at him, but she didn't withdraw her hand.

"Well. If Antoine didn't want the building to sell, he showed himself too late," said Jaye.

"That's true," said Maggie. "Why didn't we see him before Angelique sold the building to Renaissance, Inc.?"

"No one was in the apartment then. The ghost must need a live-in witness," contributed Shirley.

"Is that a rule?" asked Ed, sounding skeptical.

"Who makes up rules for ghosts?" asked Nick, bemused. He didn't know much about ghosts, but it was logical for Antoine to have appeared to a relative first. Nick swallowed a groan. Logic and ghosts did not belong in the same thought. If the others hadn't been taking the whole haunting thing so seriously, Nick would have been convinced he was losing his mind.

"I suppose they make up their own rules," Maggie answered.

"No. There are rules," insisted Shirley. "Everything has rules."

"What are they?" persisted Ed.

Shirley threw up her hands. "I don't know, you old coot. No one knows. But it makes sense that a ghost wouldn't haunt an empty apartment. What would be the point?"

"The ghost isn't tied to Marcel's apartment. Antoine haunted me, too, remember?" asked Maggie. "He came right down that spiral staircase. Why didn't he do that sooner?"

Nick said, "The trap door was closed until—"

Maggie hit him in the ribs with her elbow.

"Until?" asked Ed. "You opened the trap door?"

"Not me," said Nick. "Maggie did. When she ran up the stairs after hearing the ghost sneeze."

"No, I didn't open it, not last night," said Maggie. "The trap door was already opened when I got to the top of the stairs. The ghost must have done that."

"Why would he bother? Ghosts can walk through walls, even seep through key holes." Jaye laughed evilly.

"We're getting off track here. Settle down, now, all

of you." Ed used his most professorial tone. "Does anyone have a serious contribution to this discussion?"

"I think the ghost haunted Maggie because Nick
didn't believe in him. Nick thought we were haunting
him." Shirley shifted her gaze from Nick to Maggie.
"The ghost needed you to corroborate his existence."

"Well. I can do that," said Maggie. "He scared me
to—uh, right up that staircase."

"We need to find out more about Antoine," said
Jaye. "But how? Ed's covered the historical angle, and
Shirley's explored the psychic plane. The ghost tours
were a bust, and Marcel didn't leave any clues. We've
done all that we can do, haven't we?"

Shirley stood up. "No, we haven't. Ed's scientific approach has given us the probable identity of the
ghost, but science has reached a dead end. There is
only one course of action left to us. We must go right
to the source. We need to contact Antoine Pardu."

"Superstitious nonsense," muttered Ed.

"A closed mind is a terrible thing," Shirley shot
back. "I thought you had agreed to keep an open
mind. Remember, Ed, two people in this house have
seen Antoine. His spirit is here. A séance may allow us
to speak with him, if Antoine is willing. However, a
séance will not work unless all who participate are
true believers."

"I believe Nick and Maggie saw a ghost," said Ed.
"But I have doubts about the efficacy of a séance. I'm
not sure I could suppress those doubts."

"A séance?" said Maggie. "You want us to try to
make contact with the ghost? Oh, my lordy me."

"That sounds intriguing," said Jaye.

Ed spoke up again. "Before we make a final decision, I would like to point out that there is one
remaining source of information you overlooked,

Shirley. Marcel's daughter. We should try to find Angelique Beaulieu."

"Why would you want to do that?" Nick tugged on his collar. All he needed was for his mother to get involved. If she found out he had seen a ghost, she would have him committed in a New York minute. And have herself appointed his financial guardian. "How could she help?"

"I see Ed's point," said Jaye. "Angelique must have lived here when she was a girl. Maybe she knows about the ghost. After all, it is her great, great, etcetera, grandfather."

Shirley snorted. "Waste of time. We tried to find her when Marcel died, remember? We couldn't locate her then. And no wonder. Angelique left years before Marcel turned the building into apartments. That would have been twenty or thirty years ago."

"More like thirty or forty years," said the professor. "Angelique left Louisiana with her mother—Antoinette was her name—after Marcel and Antoinette divorced."

"Oh, right," said Jaye. "You told us that before."

Closer to forty years ago, Nick figured. She had left New Orleans when she was sixteen—that would have been in 1961. Too long ago for the tenants to be able to trace her. Angelique had changed names almost as often as she had changed addresses. "How do you know when Angelique left town?" he asked Ed.

"Marcel told me. He was less of a recluse when I first moved in—I was his first tenant, by the way. That was in the fall of 1978. I think Marcel was lonely. No, I know he was lonely. He told me he converted the building into apartments because he was tired of rattling around in the big house all by himself."

Nineteen seventy-eight. That would have been a

year after he had visited his grandfather. Nick winced inwardly. What had happened during that last visit that made his grandfather so sure he would never see his daughter and grandson again?

"Angelique never visited him?" asked Maggie.

"Not that I know of." Ed rubbed his chin. "The only thing Marcel told me about his daughter was that she had moved back east with her mother sometime in the sixties. Difficult to trace a person after that many years—especially a woman. Women change their names when they marry. You may be right, Shirley. We could search for weeks and not find Angelique."

Ed was gracious in defeat, thought Nick, admitting that it would be difficult if not impossible to find Angelique. That may have been the reason Marcel had left the building to him, now that he thought about it. His grandfather must have lost track of Angelique's name and address over the years. But he had known his grandson's name. And somehow, Marcel had tracked down his address and the name of his company. Knowing that his grandfather had kept up with him over the years made Nick wonder. If Marcel had gone to that much trouble, why hadn't he tried to make contact before he died?

"We didn't find Angelique. But Marcel's lawyer did find her. He must have. It wouldn't take long to ask him where she is." Shirley smiled at Ed.

Nick swallowed a groan. Why weren't Ed and Shirley fighting tooth and nail like usual? They had picked a fine time to become cooperative.

"He might not tell us," said Jaye. "Lawyers are so picky about client confidentiality."

"Why do you want to find her?" asked Nick. The last thing he wanted was for the tenants to talk to his mother. "If she hasn't been around for thirty or forty years, what kind of help could she be?"

"Angelique may know something about the ghost. She did live in this house, after all. What was Marcel's lawyer's name? I can't remember. Do any of you?" Shirley posed the question to the rest of the group.

Jaye answered with a question of his own. "Did we ever know who he was? It seems to me Corinne told us about the new owner before we had a chance to do much more than look in Marcel's address book for Angelique's address."

"You're right, Jaye," said Maggie. "We had only talked about contacting the lawyer. We never did it, not after Corinne told us where to send the rent checks."

"Now, there's a thought," said Jaye. "We could ask Corinne if she knows who Marcel's lawyer was. She might. Ellis Realty managed the building for years before Marcel died."

"That's right. Marcel must have had a lawyer draft our leases," said Maggie. "But do we want to talk to Corinne just now? When she's got Mr. Landon on the hook? All it would take to reel him in would be for her to find out we've really got a ghost here."

"We wouldn't tell her that, Maggie. We'd just ask for Marcel's attorney's name." Jaye patted Maggie on the head.

"And Corinne would want to know why. You know how she is."

"And we'd tell her we were trying to find Angelique," said Jaye.

"And Corinne would want to know why," repeated Maggie. "What would we tell her? That we needed to ask Angelique if she'd ever been scared by a ghost on the premises?"

Jaye shot a disgusted look Maggie's way. "Of course not. We could tell Corinne that we'd found some family documents—the Bible, for instance—and that we wanted to return them to Marcel's only living relative."

"This is getting too complicated," said Ed. "We can't be sure that Corinne knows who Marcel's lawyer was. As to the leases, Ellis Reality probably has a lawyer on retainer to take care of that sort of thing."

"Well, then," said Shirley. "We're back to my idea. Let's go directly to the source."

"Are you still promoting your séance idea?" asked Ed.

"Séances are a proven method of contacting those who have passed over."

"Proven? Where's the proof? Do you have references to scientific journals, Shirley? Or are you relying on your usual psychic mumbo jumbo?" Ed leaned back in his chair and looked up at her.

"Mumbo jumbo? There's no need to be rude, Professor. I thought we were in this together." Shirley straightened her turban and glared at the professor.

"We are," said Maggie. "And I, for one, do not see the harm in trying a séance."

"Might as well," agreed Jaye. "What could go wrong?"

"I think it will prove to be a waste of time, but if you all are for it, then I will participate," said Ed grudgingly. "However, I cannot guarantee that my skepticism will not come through."

"When do you want to do this?" asked Maggie, looking excited at the prospect of speaking with Antoine.

"Why not now?" asked Jaye.

"No can do," said Shirley. "A séance requires preparation. Tomorrow. Tuesday. At midnight."

"Midnight? Isn't that a bit over the top?" Ed asked.

"No, it's not, Ed." Shirley adjusted her turban. "We'll start the séance at midnight, the traditional time for spirits to walk the earth. Be here at eleven-thirty tomorrow night for instructions. Jaye, can you be here before midnight?"

Jaye nodded. "Yeah, no problem. I've got the early show tomorrow night."

"Well, are we finished for now?" asked Ed.

Everyone nodded.

"Then, this meeting is adjourned," said the professor.

Nick picked up the box of photographs. Maggie held the door for him, then walked with him across the courtyard. "Are you all right?" she asked. "You look pale. I hope all this running around in the damp night air doesn't make you sick again."

"I'm not sickly. If I'm pale, it's because we've all decided there is in fact a ghost haunting this place. Don't you find that . . . disturbing?"

"Not particularly. I'm getting used to the idea, I guess. Antoine hasn't hurt anyone. And he's a very good listener." Maggie stopped in front of her door. "Do you want to come in?"

Nodding, Nick followed her into her apartment. He refrained from mentioning the missing condoms. If their interrupted lovemaking the first night hadn't left Maggie in pain, he wasn't going to talk about how he had felt. "He almost made you fall down the stairs—when you walked through him the other night."

"But I didn't fall. I don't think he wants to hurt us. I think he wants us to help him. Just put the box on the coffee table. Would you like coffee?"

Nick put the box down and sat on Maggie's plump sofa. "Help him what? He's dead." He patted the cushion next to him. "Have a seat."

Maggie curled up next to him, resting her head on his shoulder. "Antoine is not at rest. Once we find out what he wants, we can help him rest in peace."

"Is that another Rule for Ghosts?"

"Weren't you listening to any of the people on the ghost tours? They all agreed that ghosts remain behind after they die because something holds them on this plane—guilt, or a desire for revenge—something they need to come to terms with."

"I heard them. I just didn't believe them. Ghosts, if there are ghosts, are some kind of cosmic mistake. They ought not exist."

"But they do. We've both experienced the ghost."

"Have we? Maybe I *am* crazy, and all of you are just being polite."

"You're not crazy. I'm not, either. We saw a ghost, and now we're pretty sure we know who we saw. We're making progress. All we have to do now is figure out what Antoine wants and give it to him. The séance may tell us everything we need to know." Maggie slanted a curious glance his way. "You didn't say if you believed in séances."

"I didn't believe in ghosts until a day or two ago. I'm keeping an open mind. But maybe Antoine doesn't want anything. Who says ghosts have to want something?"

"Conventional wisdom has it that a spirit who remains in this world after death has unfinished business."

"Business which he—or she—must complete before proceeding on the final journey to . . ."

"Heaven?"

"Hell would seem to be a more likely possibility. My money's still on some kind of group hallucination. We're all dreaming the same dream. Maybe a side effect of something we've eaten. Or the water. The professor told me that New Orleans gets its drinking water from the Mississippi River."

"Perhaps. But it won't hurt to do a little more detective work. If nothing else, you can use it in a book. How's the writing going, by the way?" asked Maggie, snuggling closer.

"Slow. Very slow." Nick winced. He was not a wannabe author. As Maggie snuggled against him, Nick was tempted to go ahead and tell her he owned the building. And he would, as soon as he talked to Corinne and got his plan moving. Then, in a few days, he would be able to show Maggie and the others how much he appreciated all they had done for him.

Nick still had trouble understanding why a group of strangers had been so kind to him. He had been ill, and they had nursed him back to health. He had told them he was in New Orleans to research the setting for his novel, and they had acted as guides. He had seen a ghost, and they had believed the unbelievable for him. Not only believed, but come up with a plan to help him exorcise the phantom.

And there was a phantom. Nick had no doubts about that any longer. He had seen it more than once, and Maggie had seen it, too. She had been genuinely afraid when Antoine had awakened her with a sneeze. And when she had been scared, she had turned to him.

Maggie had trusted him to protect her. Giving her home and shop to her was the least he could do for her.

It occurred to Nick that he had finally experienced what it was like to be part of a functional family, a family whose members trusted each other, helped each other. A family who stood together against adversity.

Like someone trying to sell their homes out from under them.

"So. The writing is going slowly."

"Yeah. I keep getting distracted. Want to come upstairs and distract me some more?" He wiggled his eyebrows at her. "Or would you rather go out somewhere for dinner?"

Maggie wrinkled her brow. "Dinner? Sex? Sex? Dinner? That's a hard choice. Why can't I have both?"

"That's what I like about you, Maggie. You're greedy. Both it is. Dinner first?"

"Yes. I'm sure you need to keep up your strength."

"Is that a complaint?"

"Not at all. I have nothing to complain about. I am very impressed with your stamina. I just don't want to wear you out."

"No chance of that. I'll see you in what? Half an hour?"

"Better make it an hour. I've got a few things to do. Between ghost tours and other activities, I neglected my Monday chores."

Nick left Maggie and walked up the outside staircase to his apartment. He had important calls to make. Once he was inside, he found his cell phone and dialed the number of Ellis Realty. Corinne advised him of Landon's offer, and he told her to turn it down. In response to his questions, Corinne told him that it would not be possible to convert the apartments at eleven-thirteen to condominiums, at least not at the present time. The Vieux Carre Commission, the governing board for all French Quarter property, had imposed a moratorium on conversions. Nick had anticipated red tape, but was disappointed that his brilliant plan had been thwarted so soon. Nick asked Corinne to see if there was another way for him to transfer ownership to individual apartment owners and hung up.

Next, he had to find out about Antoine Pardu, and he had to do it fast. Nick dialed his mother's number.

"Nick, what's wrong? Something must be wrong. It's almost a year until Christmas."

"I know that, Mother. Nothing is wrong. I need some information, that's all. Did Grandfather ever say anything to you about ghosts?"

"Ghosts? Nick, have you been drinking?"

"No. Did he?"

"Where are you?"

"I'm in New Orleans, trying to sell Grandfather's building."

"It still hasn't sold? That's surprising. French Quarter property usually sells fast. You must be asking too much. How much are you asking? I always wondered why Father left the building to you. By rights, it should have come to me."

"Mother. Ghosts. Did Grandfather ever mention ghosts?"

"Ghosts? What about ghosts?"

"I'm doing a little research on Grandfather's building. Apparently the building is not selling because people think it's haunted."

"That's ridiculous. There are no ghosts in that building. Father never said one thing about ghosts. Neither did Mother. I certainly never saw anything that smacked of the paranormal when I lived there," said Angelique. After a short pause, she added, "Father did tell me about a family curse once."

"Curse?" Nick felt a chill run down his spine.

"Yes. Let me think, now. What was it all about? Oh, I remember. Your grandfather's grandfather, a man named Pardu, I think, was the cause of the curse. His mother-in-law cursed him." Angelique sighed. "Everyone always blames the mother-in-law. You wouldn't believe the things my daughter-in-law says about me, Nick."

He probably would believe, thought Nick. "Mother, back to the curse. What did Antoine do that pissed off his wife's mother?"

"The wife died. She blamed Pardu. She put a curse on him."

"Why did she blame him?"

"I don't know. I think the wife was running away from Pardu, and she died while making her escape."

"She died in a steamboat accident."

"Really? I'm not sure I ever knew that. Why the sudden interest in our family history? Are you mellowing?"

"No. What was the curse?"

"Father said the curse was that no descendant of Pardu would ever have a happy marriage. Come to think of it, he told me about the curse around the time Mother left him. I thought he made it up."

"Why would he make something like that up?"

"So he'd have something or someone but himself to blame for driving Mother and me away. A curse makes a convenient excuse, don't you think?"

"That's it? All Pardu's descendants are doomed to have bad marriages? That's our family curse?"

"That's what dear old Dad said. Which is a crock. I'm very happy with Terrence."

"Terrence is your third husband, Mother."

"Fourth. But who's counting? Is that all you wanted, dear? I've really got to run. I'm late for lunch with Gloria and Jo Ann."

"One more question. Did Marcel say anything about how the curse could be ended?"

"Not that I remember. Curses must last forever, don't you think? Otherwise, what would be the point?"

"I don't know, Mother. Well, thanks." For some reason, he hesitated before breaking the connection.

"Nicholas? Are you still there?"

"Yeah. What?" That was what he had been waiting for—for her to ask for something.

"You know, Nick, you never asked me for anything before, not even for information. You've always been so damned self-sufficient. This was nice. Thank you." Her voice sounded rusty. She cleared her throat. "And now, I really must go. The girls are waiting for me. Ta ta."

"Uh huh." Nick, his own throat threatening to clog, ended the connection and put his cell phone back in his pocket.

Cursed. He was cursed.

It figured.

Fourteen

Juggling two cardboard coffee cups and a box of
pastries, Nick let himself into Maggie's apartment.
After another night in Maggie's bed, Nick decided
there were worse things than being cursed. And, if
Maggie ever decided she wanted more than a brief affair, he would have the perfect out. *I can't marry you,
my dear. I am cursed.*

Nick scowled. He shouldn't be making jokes about
Maggie's feelings. Not even to himself. Must be some
kind of perverse method of guilt suppression, he decided.

And he did feel guilty.

He had seduced a marrying kind of woman. Never
mind that Maggie had participated enthusiastically in
her seduction. Or that she had told him over and over
that all she wanted was his body, not his heart. Nick
was torn between taking Maggie at her word, which
made him a sex object, or not believing a word she
said, which made him a heel.

"Coffee," Maggie called out, as Nick let the French
door close behind him. "Is that coffee I smell?"

"Yes, ma'am. As commanded, your obedient ser-
vant brings you breakfast in bed. You are still in bed,
aren't you?" he asked, pushing open the door to her
bedroom with his hip.

Nick watched appreciatively as Maggie sat up and stretched. "You took long enough," Maggie grumbled. "I missed you."

Nick leaned down and planted a kiss on her mouth. "Not my fault. Shirley had to read my palm—she wanted to read my cards, too, but I told her I had a breakfast date." Nick handed Maggie one of the cups and sat on the bed next to her.

Maggie opened the box and took out the oval coffee cake. The cake had purple, green, and yellow icing, but Maggie did not look at it in horror. On the contrary, she seemed pleased. "Oh, a king cake. Yummy." She broke off a piece and handed the box to him. "Watch out for the baby."

Nick choked on his coffee. "Baby? What baby? You're not pregnant. You couldn't be. We used protection."

"Good lord, Nick. Don't get your boxers in a twist. I was referring to the baby in the king cake. Don't you know about king cakes?"

"No. Is this some kind of Louisiana aphrodisiac, like oysters?"

"No, silly. King cakes are sold from Epiphany until Ash Wednesday. They have a little plastic baby baked inside. Whoever gets the baby has to buy the next king cake. What did Shirley see in your palm?" Maggie asked around a mouthful of king cake.

Nick took a big bite of his piece before answering. "King cake, huh? Tastes like a cinnamon roll to me. Shirley said I would have a long and happy life, complete with a w-w-wife and three children. Not going to happen. I'm never going to get married. I told you that, right?"

"Yes, you told me. I would have known you hadn't

had a change of heart, anyway. You're still saying wu-wu-wife. I thought maybe——"

"Maybe what?"

She lowered her lashes, hiding her expressive eyes. "Never mind."

"Tell me."

"Well. You said we were treating you like family. I thought it might be possible that you had decided families aren't so bad after all."

"You'd have to know my family. But hearing about Antoine Pardu taught me one thing. There are worse things than having a family."

"Like what?"

"Losing them."

"Oh, Nick. You do feel a connection with Antoine, don't you? That must be why he's haunting you."

"It's my apartment he's haunting. Not me." Nick's denial rang false in his ears. He knew his connection to Antoine, but that wasn't something he was ready to share.

"But he never haunted anyone before. Except Marcel, maybe. You are the one he's appeared to most often. You know, it could be that he's trying to tell you something."

"Me? Specifically? Like what?"

"I don't know. Maybe we're wrong about the ghost wanting us to help him. Maybe he wants to help us. You, in particular."

"Help me what? I don't need any help."

"Everyone needs help now and then."

"Not me. I have it on the best authority—my mother—that I am very self-sufficient."

"Oh. Well. You're probably right. Antoine needs us to do something for him. And we have to help him—

otherwise, he'll end up a tourist attraction, haunting Landon's bed and breakfast."

"I don't think you have to worry about that," said Nick. "I've got a feeling—a very strong feeling—that Landon is not going to buy this building."

"Is that a premonition?"

Nick shrugged. "Could be. Maybe after being around Shirley and Antoine, I'm developing psychic abilities."

"Well. I hope your prognostication turns out to be true. I don't want to move. I love this place."

"But you'll move someday, won't you? When you get married. This apartment is too small for a family."

Her lashes lowered again. "Oh, I'm not going to get married. Not ever. That's one prediction you can count on." She raised her lashes and gazed at him, her eyes sparkling. "So. We're going to have a séance tonight. Are you excited?"

"Not particularly." He was relieved. He might have his doubts, but at least Maggie still believed she would never marry. "Neither is the professor. Ed is still trying to get Shirley to show him documented proof that seances actually work."

"Ed was at Shirley's place? He never goes there. What was he doing?"

"Drinking tea and eating an eclair. He wants to set up a tour business, operating out of Oracles. He took me along to soften her up."

"Well, did you? Is Shirley going to let him do that?"

"She was, for a percentage of his take. That was before he started grilling her about the science of séances. She was getting madder by the minute, so she may change her mind. What are you doing later?"

"How much later?"

He looked at his watch. "Now?"

"What did you have in mind?"

"Want to act out a fantasy? You said something once about an animal trainer and a sex kitten. I don't have a whip, but we could improvise."

Maggie eyed the staircase. "Or we could try your fantasy again. I could climb the stairs."

"No. It's your turn. You made my dream come true. Let me do the same for you."

"I dreamed about you before I met you, did I ever tell you that?"

"No. How did you manage that?"

"Shirley predicted that a man with silver eyes would come and sweep me off my feet. Of course, she also said he would have coal black hair. She got that part wrong."

"She got it all wrong. My eyes aren't silver. They're gray."

"Sometimes they're silver."

"What times?"

"When the light hits them just right. When you're angry. When you're aroused. They're silver right now." Maggie's eyes widened. "You're not angry, are you?"

"No."

"Are you aroused?"

"Oh, yeah." He pushed her down and leaned over her. "How about going upstairs? We'll need more room if I'm going to try and tame a sex kitten."

Maggie turned pink. She looked up the spiral staircase. "I don't know. What if he's up there?"

"Our ghost is not a voyeur. He left us alone the other night. He slammed the trap door shut after he rained condoms on us."

"He could have peeked."

"Antoine wouldn't do that. Not to his—" Nick bit

his tongue. He had almost said, not to his relative. "Not when we're his only hope for redemption."

"I suppose not. He seems like a polite sort of phantom. He's a good listener."

"You never told me what you talked about with him."

"Oh, this and that. Nothing important." Maggie's gaze was fixed on a spot behind his left ear. Nick had the feeling whatever she had shared with Antoine, it hadn't been unimportant. He would have to ask her about it again. Later. Now he had a more urgent agenda.

"Let's go upstairs. I just thought of a new fantasy."

She met his gaze. Her eyes widened. "Really? What?"

"It involves me undressing you. And vice versa."

"That sounds . . . doable."

Nick followed Maggie up the spiral staircase, stopping on every other tread to pick up one of the condoms the ghost had flung down the stairs.

Maggie stopped at the top of the stairs. "You were right. He's not here."

"How can you tell?"

"Something about the way the air feels. I noticed it when we had our little talk earlier. We're alone." She took the final step that brought her into Nick's bedroom.

Nick followed, standing behind her. He put his hands on her waist and pulled her against him. "Good. Although, I wouldn't mind if he were here. Poor guy. He hasn't had sex in over a century. I wouldn't blame him if he wanted to watch."

"Nick! Ghosts can't have sex."

"That's my point. Watching might be all he can do." Nick unbuttoned the top button on Maggie's blouse.

"This blouse is silk, isn't it?" Nick released another button.

"Ummm. Yes, from the forties or fifties—before polyester." She looked around the room again. "Antoine is not watching."

"I knew sex kittens wore silk."

"Sex kitten? I thought you'd forgotten about that."

"I haven't forgotten anything about you." He would never forget her. He *would* forget about the small voice reminding him that no matter what Maggie said, she was the marrying kind. Forget his scruples about seducing a woman who had majored in home economics. Forget about everything but the way she looked at him, eyes all wide with wonder, then lids drooping as she became aroused. But he would never forget Magnolia Mayfair. He shuddered.

"Are you cold?" Maggie asked.

"No. Hot. I'm hot."

Maggie puffed out a breath. "No wonder. You've got all your clothes on. Why is that?"

"Someone hasn't been doing her job."

"Which is?"

"I'm undressing you. You're supposed to return the favor."

"Oh. Well. Never let it be said that I'm a slacker."

Maggie shoved Nick's jacket off his shoulders and began unbuttoning his shirt. "I probably shouldn't tell you this, but the sight of your bare chest makes my toes curl. That first night you were here, the quilt kept slipping down, exposing all that yummy maleness." She ran her hands over his shirt-covered chest and sighed. "And I had to cover you up."

"To keep me warm?"

"Nope. To cool me down."

"I don't want you cool tonight."

"Don't worry. Even a cold spot couldn't put out the fire inside me now."

Nick got her blouse unbuttoned and slid it off her shoulders. His mouth found her breast. Maggie's back arched as soon as his lips closed around her nipple. "If you keep that up, I'll never get your shirt unbuttoned."

Nick raised his head. "You could be right about that. Change of plan. Forget the disrobing fantasy. Let's have some healthy competition here. I'll bet I can get naked before you." Ignoring the buttons, Nick ripped his shirt open. Buttons flew everywhere. His hands went to his belt. "Well? Are you in this race or not?"

Maggie was frozen, apparently mesmerized by the sight of his naked chest. Nick flexed his muscles just to see her eyes cloud with desire.

She blinked. "What? Oh, yes." She unhooked her bra and tossed it over her shoulder, then unzipped her slacks.

Nick took his hands away from his belt and reached for her. She slapped his hands away. "No more touching 'til you're naked."

His hands closed on her bare breasts. "This is my game. I make the rules."

"Then, I'm going to cheat." Maggie pulled his belt free and unzipped his pants. She shoved them past his hips.

Nick stepped out of his pants and toed off his loafers. His knit briefs stretched tightly over his erection. "Foul play, huh? You have to pay the penalty."

"Which is?"

"You've got to finish stripping while I watch." Nick sat on the bed and pulled off his socks.

"I thought this was a race."

"It is. I'm winning."

Maggie kicked off her shoes and shoved her slacks and panties off in one quick movement. She raised her arms. "Ta da! Done."

"Not quite," said Nick, pointing to her feet. "Socks."

"Briefs," she countered, ogling his crotch.

They each quickly disposed of their remaining garments.

Nick lay back on the bed. "What are you doing way over there?" Maggie was standing in the middle of the room.

"Looking at you. You're very . . . impressive."

"Well, then, come here and be impressed, he invited." "You're trembling. Scared?"

"No. Excited. Aroused." And scared, too. But she was not going to tell Nick that. It was not the ghost that terrified her, not even the thought of being watched by someone who had been dead for a hundred years or more.

She was scared of the way Nick made her feel inside. Hot. Gooey. Like a toasted marshmallow. She might melt away to nothing. That was scary. And while she was melting, she might blurt out that she loved him. She couldn't do that. She wanted every minute she had left with Nick to be a happy one. A person could live forever on happy memories. She was counting on that.

"You're frowning," said Nick, running his hand over her forehead and smoothing out the wrinkles. "Worried about the ghost?"

"What ghost?"

Nick chuckled. "We'll spend all night and all day in bed. We can't let those condoms go to waste. Tuesday is your day off, right?"

"Wrong. Monday. And we spent most of the day in bed yesterday. In between ghost tours."

"Close the shop today, too."

"I can't do that," said Maggie. She wanted to. There couldn't be too many more days like this. Nick's lease would be up soon, and he would be leaving. "Well. Maybe I could open late and close early."

"If that's the best you can do . . . Come here, Magnolia. I want to show you something."

"Oh. My. That's amazing."

"You ain't seen nothing, yet. We're going to use up the rest of the condoms today."

"I don't think that's possible. You'll have to prove it to me."

And he did.

Tuesday night at eleven, Nick had Maggie in his bed again. He had come up with some new fantasies, and she had fulfilled every one of them. "We have to get dressed," he told her, regret in his voice.

"Why? I'm reconsidering the need for clothes."

"It's eleven o'clock. The séance starts in half an hour."

"Oh. Séance. Right." Maggie shoved the quilt aside and got up. "Where are my clothes?"

"Look in the kitchen. That's where we started."

Maggie wandered out of the bedroom, leaving Nick to stare at the ceiling. Nick stirred restlessly, unable to squelch the feeling that something bad was about to happen. Surely the séance wouldn't work. Ed had the right of it. Séances were superstitious nonsense. It wasn't possible for the living to speak with the dead. On the other hand, two weeks ago he hadn't believed it was possible for ghosts to haunt the living. That belief had been turned on its head.

Maggie reappeared in the doorway, dressed. "Well? Are you coming or not?"

Shirley greeted everyone at the door, wearing a deep blue robe and a white turban. "Come into the dining room. I've got everything ready."

"Shouldn't we hold the séance in Nick's apartment?" asked Jaye as they headed for the dining room. "Seeing as how that's where Tony spends most of his time."

"I considered that," said Shirley. "But he also appeared in Maggie's apartment. Pardu owned the entire building when he was alive, and I'm sure he is not restricted to only one apartment. We'll try here first, and if we don't make contact, we can move to Nick's."

Shirley's apartment was L-shaped, and the dining room was in the short leg of the L. As soon as they turned the corner into the room, Nick sniffed. "Incense?"

"Cinnamon for energy, frankincense to expand consciousness, sandalwood to help us focus." Shirley said, moving to the sideboard where she turned on a CD player. New age music filled the air. Shirley's round oak table was covered with a white cloth. Five fat candles, three white and two purple, sat in the middle of the table.

Shirley indicated the five chairs arranged around the table. "Please take a seat."

They sat down. Nick had Maggie on one side, Jaye on the other. Ed was next to Jaye, who sat next to Shirley. "Do we hold hands?" asked Nick.

"Not yet. First we must choose a medium."

"Oh, you've got to be the medium, Shirley," said Jaye. "You're the only one who has done this before."

"Very well." She picked up one of the white candles. "We must charge the candles. Each of you take this candle in turn. When you hold it, close your eyes and visualize its symbolic power. White is for purity and peace." She closed her eyes for a few seconds, then passed it to Maggie and picked up one of the purple candles. "Purple is for spiritual power."

When all five candles had been passed around and returned to the center of the table, Shirley lit the candles. "Jaye, please turn off the music and the lights."

Jaye did as Shirley asked and returned to his seat at the table.

"Now we join hands."

Maggie's hand was cold. Jaye had a sweaty palm.

"Bless this gathering. We mean no harm to you, spirit, and we ask that no harm come to us," Shirley intoned. "Now, all of you, breathe in slowly through your nose, out slowly through your mouth. Five deep breaths. Start now."

"Repeat these words along with me: 'Antoine Pardu, come and move among us.' Continue the chant until Antoine is here."

"How will we know?" whispered Maggie.

"He will give us a sign," said Shirley. "Chant."

Five voices said, "Antoine Pardu, come and move among us."

At the third repetition, the candle flames wavered. The temperature in the room dropped suddenly. Maggie shivered.

"I am with you. Why have you summoned me?"

It was the professor who spoke, but the voice coming from his mouth was not his.

Shirley said, "We want to help you. Tell us why you remain on this plane of existence, in this place."

A moan came from the professor's throat, a sound so mournful that Maggie felt her blood run cold. "I drove my wife and son from me. I refused them my heart, preferring success and wealth to lasting love. I cannot rest until one of my descendants gives his heart to his one true love and remains with her for a lifetime."

"Angelique Beaulieu is your last hope, then?" asked Shirley.

"Not Angelique. She has failed me. Her son."

Maggie gasped. "Angelique has a son?"

"He is here among you," said the spectral voice.

The candles went out, plunging the room into darkness.

Jaye got up and turned on the lights. The others remained seated, not speaking. Ed's head lolled back, his eyes closed. Jaye shook him gently. "Ed. Wake up."

Ed's eyes opened. "Well. When do we start?"

"We're done. Antoine chose you to speak through." Shirley sounded bemused. "You were the medium, Ed."

"I was? Shirley, you jest."

"She's telling the truth," said Maggie, her gaze on Nick. "Antoine used you to speak. But the voice that came out of your mouth did not sound like you. It had a slight French accent."

"Good grief," said Ed, slumping in his chair. "What did Monsieur Pardu have to say?"

Shirley answered. "He said that because he did not value love and family when he was alive, he was doomed to remain on this plane until one of his descendants had a long and happy marriage."

"The most interesting thing he said was that Angelique's son was here with us. You realize what that means, don't you? Nick is Angelique's son." Jaye crossed his arms and looked at Nick, an insincere smile on his face.

Ed stared at Nick. "Angelique's son? Then, you are not Norton Graves?"

"Norton Graves?" Nick repeated stupidly. His brain had ceased functioning when Pardu's voice had come out of Ed's mouth. He shook his head to clear it. "The author? No. I am not Norton Graves. Why would you think that?"

Jaye sat down at the table. "Shirley read an article in the newspaper that said Graves was in Louisiana researching a book. You had the same initials as Graves. And you dressed well—better than an out-of-work, unpublished author would be expected to dress. So. For a while we thought you might be him—until we figured out you weren't old enough."

"Why didn't anyone bother to tell me that?" Ed snapped. "Never mind. Graves isn't important. Nick is. Are you Antoine Pardu's descendant? Did his spirit tell the truth?"

"Ghosts don't lie," said Shirley.

"Pardu told the truth. I am Angelique's son." Nick sat in his chair, unable to move. His ancestor had spoken to him. He couldn't take it in. Seeing a ghost had been weird enough. And even though he had known, hearing Antoine name him as his descendant had been shocking.

Ed's revelation that they had believed he was Norton Graves had been even more shocking.

Nick might have withstood the shock better if his tenants had been what they claimed—his best friends. But they had faked friendship, all of them. They had never liked him, Nicholas Gerard, fledgling author.

All this time, they had been sucking up to Norton Graves, famous novelist. Famous, *rich* novelist. They had plotted to get him to buy the damn building. "So. You thought I was some rich guy. No wonder you treated me so well."

Nick felt sick. Not pneumonia sick. Sick at heart. Sick of once again being hurt by people he thought cared about him. He looked at Maggie. She averted her eyes. She couldn't even look at him.

Jaye and Shirley were staring at him, identical guilty expressions on their faces. The professor looked confused. No reason for that. Everything was perfectly clear.

"Why didn't you tell us who you really were?" asked Maggie. "Why did you pretend to be a writer?"

"Maybe Nick wanted to explore his roots incognito for some reason," offered Shirley.

"I can see why he wouldn't tell us he was Marcel's grandson," said Jaye. "His mother had sold the building. Nick must have thought we'd blame him for that."

Nick laughed harshly. "No. My mother did not sell the building to Renaissance, Inc. Marcel left the building to me."

"You sold the building?" asked Ed. "A building your family had owned for five generations?"

"I don't give a damn about my family, living or dead. And I haven't sold my building. Not yet, thanks to all of you."

"Your building? Renaissance, Inc., is the owner," said Maggie. Her voice shook.

"Renaissance is my company," said Nick.

"Your company?" said Jaye. "You're our landlord?"

"Yes. I am."

There was an awkward silence.

Maggie spoke first. "You lied to us? To me?"

"The cards said you had a secret. They were right." Shirley sounded surprised.

"You lied to us," Maggie repeated. Her voice was barely a whisper. She looked as if she might burst into tears at any moment.

Nick hardened his heart. Let her cry. Let them all weep and wail. Their tears would be crocodile tears. He wouldn't fall for their tricks again; didn't they know that?

"Explain why you lied to Maggie. To all of us." Jaye's tone was firm.

The professor shook his head. "Now, Jaye, let's not assume the worst. Nick must need the money from the sale to support himself until he makes it as a writer. Since he isn't the rich author we took him for."

Jaye snorted. "Don't you get it, Ed? Nick isn't a writer at all. That was a lie, too."

"I prefer to think of it as my cover story," said Nick.

"Whatever. Do you need the money?" asked Jaye.

"No. I have plenty of money."

"Then, you don't need to sell the building for financial reasons?" Jaye continued his interrogation.

"No."

Shirley spoke up. "Why did you put the building on the market in the first place? And why didn't you ever visit your grandfather?"

"I did. Once. When I was nine years old. We didn't hit it off."

"Marcel never mentioned you," said Shirley.

"I'm easy to forget."

"Nonsense," said Ed. "Marcel Beaulieu didn't know how to love. That's why his wife left him, and his daughter. No reason for you to feel guilty for ignoring him."

"I don't feel guilty."

"Are you going to sell the building?" asked Maggie.

"Of course he isn't going to sell the building, Maggie. Now that he knows about Antoine, he'll want to keep the ghost in the family. Won't you, Nick? After all, Antoine is depending on you." Shirley gave him a weak smile.

"Well," said Ed. "This is amazing. And it's worked out just as we planned. Better. We don't have to ask Norton Graves to buy the building for us. Nick isn't Graves, but he already owns the building."

"You really expected me to buy the building for you?" Nick sneered.

"We thought it was a possibility—"

"Christ. You're just like my family. Expecting me to solve your problems with my money. You want to hear the best part? I almost fell for it. I was going to turn the building over to you as soon as Corinne and the lawyers could figure out a way to do it that would get by the Vieux Carré Commission. I guess I should be grateful for red tape—it kept me from making an even bigger fool of myself."

Nick got up and walked out of the dining room.

"Uh oh," murmured Jaye. "I think we goofed. Big time."

"Nick owns the building. He's our landlord." Maggie stood, gripping the edge of the table to keep from sinking back into her chair. Her heart was breaking—not because Nick didn't love her. She had never expected that. But because he hadn't trusted them enough to tell them who he was until he had no choice.

"He was going to give us our apartments," said

Shirley. "This is all my fault. If I hadn't gotten that stupid idea about him being Norton Graves—that's what set him off. He thinks everything we did for him was done to get him to buy the building."

"As to that. Some of it was, Shirley." Ed shook his head in dismay.

"Only a little." Maggie pushed her chair away from the table and stood up. "We've got to go after him. Explain that we only thought he was Norton Graves for a few days. After he was sick and before—" Maggie stopped. Nick thought she had slept with him, made love with him, because of his money.

"Not now, Maggie," said Shirley, grabbing her by the arm. "Nick won't listen now. He's too angry with us. And he's probably in shock, too. Imagine learning that your ancestor is still around, doomed to remain here until one of his descendants learns the true meaning of love. We'll wait for him to calm down, and then—"

"Wait a minute, Shirley." Jaye stood up, too. "I thought Tony said until one of his line stays happily married."

"Same thing," said Shirley. "Nick loves you, Maggie. You and he are going to be the ones to end the curse. I feel it in my bones."

"Are you sure about that?" asked Ed, who had wandered to the French door looking out onto the courtyard. "He's leaving."

"Leaving?" Shirley and Jaye rushed to Ed's side. Maggie followed more slowly.

They all watched as Nick walked down the passageway and disappeared onto Royal Street.

"He left," said Maggie, sinking into the chair again. "He just walked away. I'll never see him again." She burst into tears.

Maggie wasn't the only one crushed by Nick's departure.

As soon as Nick walked out the Royal Street door, all hell broke loose. Shutters opened and slammed shut. The wisteria vine coiled and uncoiled. The fountain in the middle of the courtyard sent up a geyser that rivaled Old Faithful. The balconies shook, dislodging hanging baskets of ferns and sending them crashing to the sidewalk below, barely missing a couple from Ohio who were window shopping at Mayfair Masks.

The strange happenings at eleven-thirteen Royal Street made the evening news that night. The television anchor called the event a poltergeist-type disturbance. A representative of Ellis Realty confirmed that several potential buyers had witnessed other paranormal phenomena, but nothing as dramatic as what had happened today.

The reporter sent to the address reported that the tenants all seemed to be extremely upset, but none of them would agree to be interviewed on camera. The reporter did manage to find a ghost tour director who said his tour would definitely add the ghost at eleven-thirteen Royal Street to his tour's itinerary.

Joe Landon, watching on his hotel room television set, called the TV station and requested a taped copy of the newscast. Every owner of a haunted hotel needed documented proof. Now that Gerard had accepted his offer, Joe had everything he needed for a successful haunted hotel.

Fifteen

Nick went from New Orleans directly to New Hampshire, where he spent almost a month with Ben Ward and Ben's son Jeremy. Long hours and hard work should have made it impossible for him to spend time thinking about New Orleans. But he had thought of Maggie every damn day. He couldn't get her out of his head.

Not only Maggie. He had found himself thinking about Shirley, Ed, and Jay at odd times, too. The truth was, he missed them all.

And he regretted what he had done to them.

Enough that he had tried to buy the building back from Landon. Landon, ecstatic over the news coverage of the ghost at eleven-thirteen Royal Street, refused to sell at any price.

Nick tried assuaging his guilt by reminding himself that his former tenants weren't free from blame—they had tried to use him. But they had also taken care of him. Once his anger had cooled, Nick found it hard to believe that all their kindnesses to him had been motivated solely by greed. They had been desperate to save their homes. And to stay together.

When he had attempted negotiating with Landon, Nick had learned from Corinne that Maggie was having a going-out-of-business sale. Corinne told Nick that she had offered to find her another shop to rent, but Maggie had refused. As to the other tenants, as far as Corinne knew, they were all looking for other apartments.

Every day, Nick thought about calling New Orleans. The one time he had gotten up the nerve to dial Maggie's number, the operator informed him that the number was not in service.

Just as well. Maggie probably would have hung up on him.

Nick might have given up on ever seeing Maggie again, but his subconscious hadn't. It had come up with a new dream. The new fantasy had Maggie appearing on his doorstep pregnant with his child. The funny thing about the dream was that it didn't feel like a nightmare. It felt right. Like destiny.

Maggie had sold every mask in her shop, but one, before Mardi Gras. For some stupidly sentimental reason, she had kept the Sex Kitten mask. As if she needed anything to remind her of her experiment in lust.

After her going-out-of-business sale, Maggie packed her bags, bought a cat carrier from Dr. Hector, and flew home to St. Paul. At least she had learned that the place to be when she was hurting was with her mother and father. She had told them the whole sorry story of her affair with Nicholas Gerard. They had held her when she cried, and they hadn't called her foolish—even though they would have been justified in doing so. Her father had turned red when she had related the condom story, but he'd hugged her after she had finished.

Maggie had intended to leave Antoine out of her

tale of woe—not even loving parents could be expected to believe in ghosts if they had never seen one. However, Antoine took care of that by showing up at dinner the day Maggie arrived home.

Maggie had just finished telling them about Nick's arrival in New Orleans when the gravy boat floated a foot off the table. She had known right away that Antoine was the cause because Emcee had arched his back and hissed.

So her parents knew the whole story, ghost included. Antoine took some getting used to, but they were managing. And they were doing their best to soothe her aching heart.

On a gray February morning, Maggie wandered into her mother's kitchen, heading for the window seat in the bay window. Emcee had gotten there before her, but there was room for both of them. It was snowing. She sighed. "I forgot how long winter lasts in Minnesota. I don't like cold weather."

"I know you don't, darling." Maggie's mother was kneading bread dough on the marble pastry counter. "The Weather Channel showed temperatures in the seventies in New Orleans today."

"That's not unusual for late February. It will probably be even warmer next week when I go back." She gave her mother a wobbly smile. "But I won't stay. This time, I'll remember to come home."

"Are you sure? I thought New Orleans was where you belonged."

"It was, for a while. But there's nothing for me there any longer, Mom. No apartment. No business."

"No young man," her mother added.

"Nick wasn't so young. Definitely old enough to know how to lie."

"Well. To be fair, from what you told me, you weren't exactly truthful with him."

"Mother. I never lied to him."

"Now, Maggie. You know better than that. You told him you were not the marrying kind. That was not the truth. And you lied to him—and yourself—about Robert. How could you have ever thought that Robert Bennett was your Mr. Right?"

"He was. And you only get one." Maggie had reverted to her old beliefs on the theory that if Robert had been her Mr. Right, Nick couldn't have been. She had the idea that she would get over Nick a lot quicker if she thought of him as her first and last Mr. Wrong.

So far, it wasn't working.

"You only get one? Where on earth did you get that idea?"

"From you. And Jasmine and Camillia. You all found your Mr. Right and married him." Maggie swallowed a sniffle. She had shed more than enough tears over Nicholas Gerard.

"Yes. We did. You did not marry Robert, however. With good reason, I might add. You should have told us at the time what that rat did to you."

"I fell in love with Robert. I was going to *marry* him. He must have been my Mr. Right."

"Is that so, Magnolia? You can't make a mistake?" Her mother slapped the ball of dough onto the counter and began viciously pounding on it. "Well, let me tell you something, missy. I did. Your father was not the first love of my life."

Shocked, Maggie shifted her gaze from the snow outside the bay window to her mother. "He wasn't?"

"No. Harry Olsen was my first love. As it turned out, he was something of a cad. Not as bad as Robert, but the kind of man who used women. He broke my heart."

"You loved someone before Father?" Maggie's mouth dropped open.

"I did. Just because you fall in love with someone does not necessarily mean that man is the right man for you. Women make mistakes. So do men. I don't know where you got the idea that you were too smart to fall in love with the wrong man. Love has very little to do with brains."

"So, what are you saying? That I've made two mistakes?"

"Did you ever tell Nicholas that you loved him? That you wanted to be his wife?"

"Of course not. I can just imagine what hearing me say that would have done to him. He would have been terrified, more terrified than the time we saw Antoine on the stairs. Mom, the man cannot say the word wu-wu-wife without stuttering."

"Then, you say it for him. Say, 'Nick, I love you and I want to be your wife.' Where is it written that the man has to be the one to bring up marriage? I thought you modern young women asked men out."

"Mother! Proposing marriage is not the same thing as asking a man on a date. Anyway, I never did that, either." The only bold thing she had ever done was ask a man to have a casual affair with her.

"Well, you've got to do something. You can't sit in that window seat for the rest of your life. And you've got to do something about that . . . thing you brought home with you."

The flour sifter lifted off the counter and floated under her mother's nose.

"Don't you dare sift flour all over my clean kitchen," Maggie's mother shrieked. "Maggie! Make him stop."

"Antoine. Calm down. Mom didn't mean to call you a thing. Remember, she's not used to being haunted. No one in Minnesota gets haunted. It's not like Louisiana."

The sifter settled onto the counter.

Maggie's mother breathed a sigh of relief. "Thank you, Antoine. And I apologize if I hurt your feelings. Oh, my lordy me. I'm apologizing to a ghost. What would the neighbors think?"

"I do not understand why Antoine followed me to Minnesota. Why didn't he stay in New Orleans? Joe Landon would have welcomed him with open arms. He could have gone to New York with Nick. Nick is his last hope, after all. Not me."

"Are you sure? It seems to me a ghost would know where his hope of eternal rest lay. Antoine obviously thinks you're the one who will free him from this earth."

"I don't see how."

"Don't you? Well. I still think you ought to see your Nick one more time. Tell him how you feel about him."

Maggie chewed on her bottom lip. "He's not my Nick, Mother. He hates me. He thinks I did what I did to get him to buy the building."

"Oh, I doubt that he hates you. You hurt him, Maggie. You and the others. I know you didn't mean to do that, but you did. He was hurt and angry when he left New Orleans."

"You really think I should see him and tell him I love him? Mom, do you think Nick is the right man for me?"

"I don't know. But I do know that you need to find out whether he is or not."

"What if he's my Mr. Right, but I'm his Ms. Wrong?"

Her mother smiled. "That won't happen. What makes a man the right man for you is that you're the right woman for him. Sometimes we have to convince them of that fact. Men being how they are."

"Dense?"

"Oblivious."

"What if I can't convince him? Nick has this thing about family. He thinks he doesn't want one."

"Poor boy. From what you've told me about his relatives, his attitude is understandable. But he's never had a *real* family."

Maggie's heart began beating faster. The thought of seeing Nick, of telling him how she felt, was scary. Much scarier than coming face-to-face with a ghost. She had gotten used to Antoine following her around like an invisible puppy.

Maggie met her mother's gaze. Her mother's green eyes were filled with love, warming Maggie's broken heart. Nick should experience that. She owed it to him, and to herself, to try. "So you think I ought to go to New York?"

"You're going to New Orleans for the wedding. You could stop over in New York on your way. And, Maggie? Take Antoine with you."

Having successfully completed turning around Ben's business for the second time, Nick returned to New York. Hildy looked up as he entered the Renaissance, Inc., office. "You have a stack of personal mail on your desk."

Nick groaned. "It's only February. The family usually waits until after the Fourth of July before they decide the Christmas season has begun."

"Oh, the letters aren't from your relatives. They're postmarked New Orleans."

"You checked postmarks? Why didn't you go all the way and open them? Or did you?"

"I never open your personal mail." Hildy narrowed her eyes. "You're not getting sick again, are you? You look like you've lost weight."

Nick frowned. The letters from New Orleans were probably from Corinne Ellis, although why Hildy would think letters with the Ellis Realty return address were personal, he couldn't fathom. "Only the pounds I put on in New Orleans. I feel swell."

Except for the constant pain in his chest. That had been scary enough that he had visited a doctor as soon as he had arrived in New Hampshire. After a complete physical, the medical man had assured him that there was nothing wrong with his heart, or any other part of his anatomy.

"Oh, and your spiral staircase arrived. The workmen are reassembling it in your apartment even as we speak. I still don't understand why you want a staircase in your bedroom. It doesn't go anywhere. And it's going to cost you a pretty penny when all is said and done. They had to reinforce your floor to take the extra weight."

"It has sentimental value," said Nick. "It's all I have left from my grandfather." And the only tangible proof he had that once upon a time, someone had tried to make his dream come true.

"You'd have a whole building to remember your grandfather by if you hadn't sold it."

"Yeah. I know. I shouldn't have done that, but I was pissed at the time. I tried to get it back, but Landon wouldn't sell it back to me. He's convinced the place is haunted." And no wonder. Corinne had sent him

the article in the *Times-Picayune* that described Antoine's antics the day Nick had left New Orleans. That
was also a source of guilt, as if he needed another one.
He had let Antoine down.

"Aren't you going to read your mail?" asked Hildy.
"One of the envelopes looks like a wedding invitation."

"Wedding?" Nick's heart stopped beating. "In New
Orleans?"

"Yep. That one arrived yesterday."

Maggie was getting married. It had to be from her.
Rubbing it in. And why wouldn't she? He had destroyed her home and business, after all. A decent
human being would be happy for her. Maggie had
found a man to marry.

In less than a month? Nick gritted his teeth. Rebound. She couldn't have gotten over him this soon.

He sure as hell hadn't had enough time to get over
her.

Maybe the guy Shirley had predicted had finally
shown up. The guy with silver eyes and coal black hair,
the man Maggie had mistaken him for. Nick's stomach clenched. He did not want Maggie to marry some
joker Shirley had found in a deck of cards.

But he wouldn't let Maggie know that. He would
send his regrets, but he would also send the most expensive wedding present he could find. "Hildy. What
kind of wedding present do you give a bride who majored in home economics?"

Hildy's eyes glazed over. "A Kitchen Aid mixer," she
said dreamily. "With all the attachments."

"I never knew you coveted kitchen appliances."

Hildy blinked, then scowled. "There's a lot you
don't know about me. Go read your mail."

Nick went into his office, shutting the door behind
him. He didn't want Hildy to hear him cursing, or

sobbing, when he found out who Maggie was going to marry. He sat at his desk for several minutes before he got up enough nerve to open the creamy white envelope.

The invitation turned out to be from Shirley and Ed. They were getting married. To each other, wonder of wonders. Nick had a letter from Shirley, full of news about how well Ed's historical tours were doing, and how her tarot card classes were filled to capacity. Jaye had gotten a gig on the Mississippi coast at one of the largest casinos. He was going to be Ed's best man. Shirley confided that Jaye had argued for maid of honor, but Ed wouldn't hear of it. That role was reserved for Maggie.

Shirley also explained that her theory about him being Norton Graves had only lasted for a few days. And that Maggie had never believed it.

Nick had barely finished the letter when Hildy buzzed him on the intercom. "There's a Ms. Mayfair to see you. Shall I tell her to make an appointment?"

"Maggie? Maggie is here?" That couldn't be right. Maggie was in New Orleans, getting ready for Shirley and Ed's wedding. Hildy must have gotten the name wrong.

He heard Hildy ask, "Is your name Maggie, dear?"

"Yes, ma'am. Short for Magnolia. If Mr. Gerard is busy, I could come back later."

Nick scrambled out of his chair and burst through the door to the reception area. Maggie *was* there, standing in front of Hildy's desk. Nick stared at Maggie. "You've got on a coat."

"Yes. It's cold in Minnesota."

"Minnesota? You've been in Minnesota? I thought you were still in New Orleans."

"No. I went home after—a couple of weeks ago.

Nick, I need to talk to you. In private." She smiled at Hildy. "I don't mean to be rude, but—"

Hildy stopped her with a raised hand. "Please."

Nick ushered Maggie into his office. As soon as the door was shut, Nick took her in his arms. "Don't worry, Maggie. Everything will be all right."

"Nick, let me go. You're smothering me."

"Oh, sorry. Here, let me take your coat." Nick's gaze immediately went to Maggie's abdomen. Her flat abdomen. It must be too soon for her to show. Of course it was too soon—it had been less than a month since they had last made love. He escorted her to a chair. "Sit down. Would you like a glass of water? Coffee? Soda? Anything?"

"No. Stop hovering. You're making me nervous."

"Sorry."

"And stop apologizing. Good lord. You're making this very difficult. And I don't have much time. My plane for New Orleans leaves at five o'clock."

"New Orleans. You're going to New Orleans?"

"Yes. I stopped by here on my way to Shirley and Ed's wedding. You did know that they're getting married?"

"I just opened my invitation to the wedding." Nick sat down behind his desk and held up the invitation. "How did this happen? They were always squabbling."

"It's your fault, really. When we got our eviction notices—and let me tell you, Mr. Landon didn't waste any time sending those—they started looking for apartments. One became available in the Oracles building, and they both wanted it. They fought over which one of them would get it, and while they were arguing, they realized they could share it if they were married."

"They're getting married for an apartment?" Nick was appalled. "That's not a good enough reason."

"Of course it isn't. They're getting married because they're in love. But having to move was what made them realize that they loved each other and didn't want to be apart."

"So some good came out of my selling the building?"

"Some. But some bad things happened, too."

"You think it's bad?" Nick's gaze went to Maggie's stomach again. Of course she would think it was bad. Pregnant. Unmarried. Pregnant. "Wait just a minute. You flew from New Orleans to St. Paul, and from St. Paul to New York, and you're going to fly from here to New Orleans? Is that wise? What does your doctor say? Should you be doing so much flying in your condition?"

"My condition?" She stared at him blankly. "What condition would that be?"

"You can tell me, Maggie. I thought this might happen."

"What? You thought that Antoine would follow me to St. Paul?"

"Antoine?" It was Nick's turn to look blank. "What's Antoine got to do with your being pregnant?"

"I'm not pregnant. Where did you get that idea? We used protection."

"You're not pregnant? Then why are you here?"

She scowled at him. "I can't believe you thought I was pregnant. How would that have happened?"

"I thought maybe Antoine had done something to the condoms. Stuck pins in them, or something."

"On the theory that if I got pregnant, you would marry me?"

"Yeah. I would, you know. Are you sure you're not—"

"Yes. I did not come here to get you to marry me because I'm having your baby. I came to give you back your ghost. He's annoying."

"Antoine has been haunting you? Why would he do that?"

"He most certainly has. He followed me home to St. Paul. I don't know why."

"Are you sure? Have you seen him?"

"No. But he's there. Moving things around. Coughing and sneezing. Cold spots don't work too well in Minnesota—everyone thinks it's nothing but a draft. So he's come up with a few new tricks. He rocks in Mother's favorite rocking chair. He does something to Emcee that makes Emcee do his Halloween cat imitation. You know, arching his back, puffing his tail, and hissing? My parents have been very understanding so far, but it is putting a strain on them."

"You told your parents about Antoine?"

"I wasn't going to, but after he started his shenanigans, I had no choice."

"Antoine is in Minnesota." Nick sank into his executive chair.

"He's here now."

Nick looked around his office. "Where? How do you know he's here? Maybe he stayed in St. Paul."

"Oh, he's here. He was on the plane with me. Antoine stole all the peanuts. They didn't turn up until we were getting off the plane—the flight attendants swore they weren't in the galley when they were serving drinks. And then there they were. Right where they were supposed to be. Mom and Dad will be so relieved to have their house to themselves. I can't take him back with me."

"Your parents—they know about Antoine. Do they know about me?"

"Oh, yes. I told my parents everything about you."

"Everything?" Nick tugged on his collar. "They know that we . . . that you and I . . ."

"Yes. Don't worry, though. They know how you feel about marriage and families. You made it very clear that you would never consider marriage under any circumstances."

"I may have overstated my feelings on the subject. Like I said, if you had been pregnant, that would have changed everything."

"Would it? Well, then. Lucky for you. You don't have to change a thing. Except Antoine. You've got to talk him into staying with you. Or going back to New Orleans. Mr. Landon would love to have him. He's going to have a haunted hotel with no ghost." Maggie got up.

He couldn't let her go. "I tried to buy the building back, you know."

"What? When?" She sank back into the chair.

"About a week after I left. Landon wouldn't sell. Not even when I offered him double what he paid."

"Why did you do that?"

"Because. I didn't want to hurt you. Or Shirley. Or Ed, or Jaye."

"What were you going to do with the building? If Joe had sold it back to you? Turn it into condominiums?"

"No. I was going to sell it to you and the others."

"Oh. We couldn't have afforded it."

"Yes. You could have. I was going to sell it to you for a dollar."

"One dollar?"

"Each. Four bucks, total."

"Why would you do that?"

"Because you took care of me when I was sick. You helped me research a book I never intended to write. You believed me when I said I saw a ghost."

"I saw him, too. Until that happened, you thought we made up the ghost."

"I know. I'm sorry. It's just that I haven't had much experience with families. You made me a part of the tenant family. Families do things for family members. Maggie. I think about New Orleans, all the time."

"Is that so? Well, it's not an easy place to forget, especially if you have a souvenir like Antoine. All his coughing and sneezing makes me think about—"

"Me?"

"—things. I don't think about you."

"Never?"

"Hardly ever. Sometimes I dream about—"

"Me?"

"New Orleans. The Quarter. That spiral staircase."

"I've got the staircase."

"What? Where? How?"

"When Landon wouldn't sell me the whole building, I asked him for the staircase. He wasn't going to use it."

"Where is it?"

"In my condominium. It doesn't go anywhere now, but—"

"Why would you buy a staircase?"

"My souvenir. To remember the most exciting night of my life."

"The most exciting—really?" She smiled at him. "I thought it was exciting, too."

"Why did you go back to Minnesota? I thought you hated the cold."

"I do. But I love my family, and they love me. I needed to be with them after—well, just after."

"Did you open a mask shop in St. Paul?"

"No. There's not much demand for masks in Minnesota. Except for ski masks. I'm working for my father temporarily. As a receptionist, secretary, gofer. It's his busy season. I'll look for another job after the fifteenth of April. Something will turn up."

Nick stood up. His conscious had finally caught up with his subconscious. He had dreamed about Maggie being pregnant for a reason. She might not be pregnant now, but she would be soon. He walked around the desk and stood over her. "You have a degree in home economics. I think you should do what you prepared to do in college. Become a wife and mother."

"Nick." Maggie's eyes widened. "You said 'wife' without stuttering."

"I've been practicing." He didn't tell her the practice had been in his sleep.

"Practicing? Why?"

Nick knelt in front of her and took both of her hands in his. "So I could say, 'Magnolia Mayfair, will you be my wife?'"

"Why do you want to marry me? To end the curse? The curse won't end unless we have a happy marriage."

"We will have the happiest marriage in the world. Guaranteed."

"How can you be sure?"

"Because. I love you. And you love me. And Antoine will go away once he knows we're getting married."

"You love me?"

"Of course I love you. I've loved you since the first time I saw you, all sleepy and cuddly in your pink chenille robe."

"You did not. You did?"

"I did. And I'm going to love you until the day I die. Considering my family history, maybe even after I die."

"Don't die for a long, long time, okay?" She took his face in her hands and kissed him.

When the kiss ended, they were both breathing hard. Nick said, once he could talk, "Okay. Now. Are you going to answer me or not? I think Antoine is getting anxious. I know I am. Maggie, will you marry me?"

Maggie threw herself into Nick's waiting arms. "You better believe I will. Not only that, I plan to stay married to you forever. I love you, Nick."

"Well. That should take care of one family curse. Goodbye, Antoine. Rest in peace."

EPILOGUE

Nick walked into the bedroom, skirting the spiral staircase in the corner of the room. Maggie was seated on the bed, painting her toenails. His wife, on his bed, in his apartment. He still had trouble believing his dream had come true. He had a family. A family who loved him. Maggie. Shirley and Ed. And Jaye. He wasn't on the outside looking in any longer. Blinking away the unmanly moisture gathering in his eyes, Nick asked, "Honey, have you seen my razor?"

She looked up and smiled at him. "Isn't in the bathroom?"

"No. I wonder where he put it this time. I do not see why Antoine is still playing his tricks on me. I've done what he wanted. I have a wife. One I intend to keep forever."

"Yes. You certainly do. Poor Antoine. I don't think he likes New York. Probably the weather."

"You don't mind the weather, do you? It's not as warm as New Orleans, but it's not as cold here as in St. Paul."

"I don't mind the weather. I'm never cold these days. I have a husband who keeps me warm."

"Only warm? Not hot?" Nick advanced on her.

"Nick! You'll smear my nail polish."

"Do you mind?"

"No. Antoine? You'd better leave us alone for a while. Nick's eyes are turning silver, and you know what that means."

Nick lay on the bed next to Maggie. "Why Antoine had to move in with us, I do not understand. He should be gone to his just reward. And another thing. Why didn't he ever haunt Mother? He stayed in New Orleans for all four of her marriages."

"He must have known Angelique wouldn't be the one to end the curse. Speaking of your mother—"

"I'd rather not." Nick grinned. "Thinking about Landon and his ghost-free bed and breakfast is almost worth having Antoine here. Serves him right for refusing to sell the building back to me. For twice what he paid for it."

"He did sell you the staircase." Maggie and Nick both looked at the wrought-iron staircase in the corner of the bedroom. "Are you sure the contractor reinforced the floor enough to hold the weight of that thing?"

"Thing? You dare to call our staircase a thing?"

"It doesn't go anywhere."

"It will. I put in an offer on the apartment above us." He waited a beat. "No argument? You said we didn't need the extra room."

"Oh, I guess you can never have enough room." She grinned at him.

Nick eyed her suspiciously. Maggie was hiding something from him. He could tell by the way her green eyes sparkled mischievously. "Hmmm. Getting back to Antoine. The curse is over. Why doesn't he go away?"

"We've **talk**ed about that. He must have to stay around **until** there is absolutely no doubt that this marriage is going to last. Getting back to your mother, I had lunch with her today."

"Why?"

"She invited me."

"Was there an emergency involved?"

"No."

"It's not Christmas, is it?"

"Not for three more months. Angelique told me about your 'no contact except in emergencies or at Christmas' rule."

"I'll bet I know why. She tried to convince you to ask me to rescind the rule."

"Not rescind. Modify. She wanted the rule expanded to cover other holidays. Especially holidays when families traditionally get together. Like Thanksgiving. And the Fourth of July. Birthdays. It seemed a reasonable compromise to me."

"Maggie. She forgot me. From the time I was nine until the day my picture appeared on *Forbes* magazine, my own mother forgot all about me. So did the others. I don't owe them anything."

"No, of course you don't. But they owe you. Why not give them a chance to make it up to you?"

"I don't think I could afford it."

"Oh, well. As to that, I told your mother there wouldn't be any more financial assistance. Except for birthday, Christmas, wedding, and anniversary gifts. I also told her there would be a limit on the cost of the gifts. No more than a hundred dollars each. Was that too much? We can always spend less, of course. It was an upper limit, not a guarantee. Oh, and I made it clear that any expanded contact between you and your family would be strictly for making family memories. Good memories."

"And she went along with that?"

"Uh huh. And she is sure the others will, too. Most of them, anyway. Some of your younger siblings want to get to know you better."

"Let me get this straight. You talked my mother into giving up access to my bank account in exchange for nothing but a hundred-dollar Christmas gift?"

"And birthday gifts. Anniversary gifts were left up in the air." She climbed on top of him. Sprawled on his chest, her chin resting on her folded arms, she grinned that grin again. "There was one more consideration. I think it may have been what tipped the scales."

"What else?"

"I told her she could spend one week with us when the baby is born. After my mother and before Shirley. I'll need some extra help then, and mothers and mothers-in-law are traditionally the ones who—"

"Baby? We're having a baby?"

"Yes. And just think. We have a resident baby-sitter."

"You're not thinking of Hildy, are you? I don't think we should impose on—"

"Not Hildy, Nick. I know you would never ask your administrative assistant to do something personal like baby-sit. I meant Antoine. He's always around. Baby-sitting would give him something useful to do."

"You want a ghost to take care of our baby? I'm not sure—"

Maggie put her fingers on Nick's mouth. "Are you listening, Antoine? If you can move a razor, you can change a diaper."

Nick threw his head back and roared with laughter. "If that doesn't get rid of him, nothing will. But I'll miss him if he goes. He's my good luck charm. Ever since I met Antoine, all my dreams have come true."

ABOUT THE AUTHOR

Dixie Kane used to be a lawyer, but she got over it. She lived in the French Quarter for five years, and she will never get over that. Romantic, sensual—and you would not believe the funny things she saw there. Her next romantic comedy, *Chasing Lily*, will be published in July 2003.

Dixie loves to hear from readers. You may write to her at P.O. Box 8523, Mandeville, Louisiana, 70470.

From Best-selling Author
Fern Michaels

__Wish List	0-8217-7363-1	$7.50US/$9.50CAN
__Yesterday	0-8217-6785-2	$7.50US/$9.50CAN
__The Guest List	0-8217-6657-0	$7.50US/$9.50CAN
__Finders Keepers	0-8217-7364-X	$7.50US/$9.50CAN
__Annie's Rainbow	0-8217-7366-6	$7.50US/$9.50CAN
__Dear Emily	0-8217-7365-8	$7.50US/$9.50CAN
__Sara's Song	0-8217-5856-X	$6.99US/$8.50CAN
__Celebration	0-8217-6452-7	$6.99US/$8.99CAN
__Vegas Heat	0-8217-7207-4	$7.50US/$9.50CAN
__Vegas Rich	0-8217-7206-6	$7.50US/$9.50CAN
__Vegas Sunrise	0-8217-7208-2	$7.50US/$9.50CAN
__What You Wish For	0-8217-6828-X	$7.99US/$9.99CAN
__Charming Lily	0-8217-7019-5	$7.99US/$9.99CAN